MAFIOSA PRINCESS
BEGINNINGS

LIZA MALLOY

CHAPTER 1

ANOTHER DAY, ANOTHER BOARDING SCHOOL

- Giada -

The jade wool of the chair scratched my thighs as I sat. I shifted side to side, then stilled when I caught my mom's eye. She'd told me not to wear shorts, although not because she worried about my comfort. Mom was more concerned with making a good impression at my new boarding school.

But since my parents still hadn't offered any explanation as to why they forced me to leave my old school, I wasn't about to let my mom control any other details of my life. Besides, the shorts were classy. They were Prada, and a bold magenta color perfect for late summer. I'd paired the shorts with a cap-sleeved black blouse and matching embellished Louboutin sandals to ensure the look was perfect.

My mom may have focused on the dean's first impression, but my concern was my classmates. Private school kids were viscous. Boarding school kids were even more so. I'd only get one chance to ensure my new classmates wanted to get to know me.

A click of the door alerted us to the dean's entrance. Mom

jerked to her feet and nodded for me to do the same. I suppressed an eye roll and stood. The man entering looked way too young to be in charge of an entire school. He was tall, thin, and clean-shaven, with neatly cropped hair. The moment he smiled and flashed those bright blue eyes at us, I just knew the girls all joked about fooling around with him.

Honestly, it just didn't seem appropriate for the Dean of a high school to be attractive. *Not* that he was my type. And actually, I wasn't the sort of girl who'd ever flirt with a teacher, but that didn't mean I couldn't recognize the kind of man that other girls my age would hit on.

"Please, take your seats. My apologies for making you wait. I'm Sean Andrews, Dean here. Welcome to campus."

He extended his hand to my mom, then me. His fingers—cold and clammy—made me wonder if he'd been savoring an iced latte while we'd waited.

"I'm Martina Conti and this is my daughter Giada. We're delighted to be here. We just finished the tour and it's a gorgeous campus. Those views, and the buildings…just breathtaking, really."

I cast a gaze at my mom, trying to decide if she was flirting or if her tone was merely part of some elaborate politeness mission to ensure the Dean let me attend the school. Although, it wasn't like we had to beg. I'd already been admitted and registered for classes. And besides, my grades were good and we had money for the tuition. I didn't believe for a minute anything else mattered to these Ivy League prep school types.

The campus was actually beautiful though. I couldn't fathom why my parents had chosen some podunk academy in Rhode Island, but the moment we drove through the foreboding stone-lined gates, I felt like I'd been transported to some Scottish castle on a cliff. Well, maybe not Scottish. But it looked all medieval and the campus sat so close to the ocean that I struggled to sustain my bad attitude.

"We are honored you have chosen our school for your daughter," Dean Andrews replied, shuffling some papers on his desk as we sat. "My secretary informed me that you've already checked into your dorm, finished the campus tour, and received a copy of your schedule. After we're done here, I've arranged for your dorm parent to introduce herself and go over all the school rules with you. Then we'll set you free."

Mr. Andrews flashed me another smile and I mimicked the expression back to him. He and my mom chatted for a few more minutes, and then he walked us back to my dorm. As we strolled, we passed several different groups of students, leading me to draw another important conclusion. Rich Rhode Island boys were hot.

Maybe this school wouldn't be so bad after all.

We met the dorm mom who, no-joke, was actually named Karen, and I zoned out while she reviewed the rules with us. There was scarcely any variation between the rules at one boarding school versus another, and I knew from past experience that there would be a dorm-wide meeting to go over the rules and expectations before classes began anyway. This particular school had a dress code, but no uniform for anything but athletics, which was awesome. The curfew wasn't terrible, either.

I'd been a total rule follower at my last school, but I hadn't yet decided if I planned to stick to that tactic. Now that I was a Sophomore, a little fun was probably in order. I'd already been banished to an out-of-state school, so it wasn't like there was much else my parents could do to me if I got in trouble, anyway.

My mom walked me to my room. While we'd been touring campus and meeting with the Dean and Miss Karen, my aunt Bianca had made my bed and arranged all of my clothes neatly in the closet. When she'd insisted on joining us and completing that task, I'd initially been mortified. But now that she'd finished and all I had left to do was tackle my accessories, toiletries, and desk area, I felt nothing but gratitude. Especially since my roommate was still MIA.

"How's your schedule look?" Bianca asked me.

I shrugged, but pulled the printed version out of my pocket to show her. The school offered breakfast from 7:30-8:15, and my first class was Science, at 8:30. After that, I went to Math, Social Studies, and English. We had an hour-long break for lunch, and then all my fun classes were in the afternoon: Art, World Religion, Interior Design, and then Tennis, to fulfill the physical education credit. I was happy with the electives the school offered. It wasn't ideal to have all my challenging classes back-to-back, but at least I'd have something to look forward to after lunch.

I hugged my mom and aunt, then busied myself organizing my desk.

Once my mom and aunt left, I tried to stay busy so I wouldn't get homesick. Unfortunately, since my aunt had so expertly unpacked my room, there wasn't a ton left for me to do.

My roommate had moved her stuff in earlier, so I scanned her side of the room. Without snooping, I struggled to form any verdicts about my roommate's personality. I didn't see any red flags, like a comforter covered in kittens and rainbows, and she didn't seem like a total slob. So that was all good.

Judging from her clothes, she was trendy, but either couldn't afford the high end designer labels or didn't like them. I didn't know much else about her except that she'd been at the school the year before and her roommate had been an international student who had to return home due to some local political drama or something.

I sunk onto my bed and pulled out my phone to start making a list of the essentials. I needed to find a nail salon, hair salon, coffee shop, and church—all within walking distance of the school or a bus stop. I'd just highlighted two possible hairstylists when the door swung open.

A tall girl with dirty blonde hair froze in the entry, then smiled cautiously. "You must be my new roommate," she said, her eyes scanning the room where all of my belongings had joined hers.

I rose to my feet. "Giada Conti. And you're Elise, right?"

She nodded.

"Nice to meet you."

Elise smiled again, then walked past me to her desk. "When my roommate left last spring, I sort of thought I'd have the room to myself this year," she said.

I couldn't decipher from her tone if that would've been a good thing or a bad one in her mind. I decided to give her the benefit of the doubt.

"Hey, um, I could really use some caffeine before the floor meeting tonight. Are there any good coffee shops we could get to in time? My treat."

Elise turned and gazed at me again as though deep in thought. Her eyes dropped to her fitness watch then back to mine. "Sure. Do you want to see if our suitemates want to come too?"

Relief flooded me. "That would be great. I haven't met anyone yet."

Elise introduced me to Blair and Brinley. They had their own room but shared a bathroom with Elise and me. A long, narrow living area connected our rooms with another identical suite, complete with two more bedrooms and another tiny bathroom. I met Delaney and Harlow, but the remaining two girls weren't in their room at the time. Elise told me their names were Erin and Ansley, and assured me they were all cool. Harlow was apparently new, too, but unlike me, she'd never been to boarding school before.

The six of us walked to a café about fifteen minutes from campus. We barely had time to taste our drinks before we needed to start the walk back to campus for our meeting. Still, I was grateful for the chance to get to know the girls I'd be living with all year. Blair and Delaney shared tons of tips about campus, and Brinley, who had gorgeous blonde hair, graciously texted her hair dresser to see if she was accepting new clients.

I listened to their gossip about the teachers, the other girls, and the guys, trying to absorb as much critical info as I could. We even made some plans for the next couple of days, since classes wouldn't start until Tuesday.

By the time we returned home for the lecture from Karen, I actually felt like the year might not be so bad.

- Luca -

I reached for my water bottle and joined Gavin behind the bleachers. He'd been my roommate since Freshman year, and we always had multiple classes together each term, too. We were less than a week into the new semester, but so far it was shaping up to be our best one yet.

"Any hot ones?" our suitemate Grant asked, sidling up beside us.

I followed Gavin's gaze across the field, where a girls' tennis class was just finishing up.

"Like you'd get the nerve to talk to them anyway," I teased.

Grant was a rule follower, whereas I lived to push boundaries. Gavin balanced us both out. Somehow, we got along and managed to enjoy taunting each other.

"The one by the tree looks good," Gavin said.

I squinted to get a better look, right as Grant spoke up. "That's Erin Fraskin."

"Wow. She grew up this summer," I commented.

"What about the brunette over there?" Grant said, pointing.

Gavin and I both nodded in agreement. From where I sat, I couldn't find any fault.

I peered closer at the girl. Her long, dark brown hair was pulled back into a low ponytail. As she turned, I noted everything about her face was flawless, from the big brown eyes to the full lips that she nervously chewed. And even the stupid regulation-length shorts and tee shirt couldn't hide that she had amazing legs and perky boobs.

The girl stared in our direction for a moment. Gavin quickly looked away, not wanting to get busted, but I let my gaze linger a little longer. Something about the girl was familiar.

I pulled out my cell phone, eliciting a sharp groan from Grant probably over the minor detail that cell phones weren't allowed during athletic time. *Whatever.* It took me less than two minutes to confirm my hunch.

"I know her," I said, pushing off the half wall where we were seated.

I walked across the field, intercepting her right as she left the tennis court. She turned in my direction just as I slowed to a stop.

"Giada Conti, right?"

She stared at me for a moment, then nodded. I didn't think my ego could handle it if she really didn't remember me, so I quickly introduced myself.

"Luca Marino. Come on, our families go way back."

Recognition flitted across her face but was quickly replaced with confusion. "Of course, right. I remember you. I just...didn't know you went here." She paused and gazed past me towards Gavin, who was approaching. "I thought you lived in Italy."

"I do. I mean, when I'm not here."

She nodded. "So are you, um a Senior?"

"Junior." I paused, thinking she didn't look like a Freshman, but she must be since she was new.

"Right. I forgot we're only a year apart."

I cocked my head to the side. "You're not a Freshman?"

She shook her head slowly.

"Just new to boarding school?"

Another shake. "No, just new here. I've been in boarding school since seventh grade."

"Did you get kicked out of your last one?" Gavin asked, butting into the conversation.

"No," Giada replied quickly, not bothering to elaborate.

I introduced them, then added that Gavin was on his way out. He glared, but headed off to join Grant.

"So do you have one roommate and then a bathroom connecting to another room?" Giada asked, her brows furrowing in an adorable fashion.

"Yeah. Then there's the same thing on the other side and all eight of us share a tiny living room. Not the best use of space, but..." I let my voice trail off and gazed to the side, trying to minimize the obviousness of my efforts to check her out.

"The rooms were bigger at my last school, but there was only one big living room per floor. We just used it for dorm meetings. I don't see the purpose of those tiny rooms. Do you study in there?"

I shrugged. "If you're into that sort of thing, yeah. It's also a good place to go if your roommate is...entertaining." I eagerly awaited her response, and she didn't disappoint.

Color rushed to her cheeks as her eyes widened almost imperceptibly.

Not wanting her to think I was intentionally embarrassing her, I switched the subject promptly. "Can I see your schedule?"

Giada peered around before reaching into her bag to retrieve her cellphone. Its bold purple, glittery case seemed to say a lot about her, but then her screen saver was a tame photo of a sunset over an oddly familiar building.

I accepted her phone and looked closer, feeling my lips part in a smile. "Basilica di San Pietro? That's not far from my home."

She nodded shyly as though I'd caught her stalking, and not just enjoying one of the most famous sites in Rome. "I thought your family lived in Sicily."

"Yeah, we have a place in Palermo but also an apartment in Rome. And one in Staten Island."

"That's cool. We just have the one house in boring old Connecticut."

"If my memory serves me, your one boring house is bigger than my three homes combined."

Her eyes narrowed as her brow ticked upward. "But surely size isn't important?"

My heart thudded. Beautiful, sassy, and a little daring? *Oh yes.* This was a girl I could have fun with. "Oh no, size matters. Never trust a man who tells you otherwise."

She blushed again, so I scrolled onto the school's app and clicked to open her schedule.

Her first class was Science. "I had Mr. Dyer last year," I told her. "He acts like a badass, but he'll let you retake tests and do extra credit if you beg. I haven't had Ms. Cushman, but Trigonometry sucks however you slice it. Mr. Kellerman is my fourth period teacher and he seems okay so far."

"I'm surprised I haven't noticed you when I'm leaving class yet if you're in the room right after me," she interrupted.

I bit back a smile. "I don't make a habit of arriving early, but maybe now that I have motivation to get there sooner…"

I waited for her to blush again before dropping my eyes back to the schedule. "Ms. Wyatt, your English teacher, is a crazy woman who thinks everyone wants to spend all day reading lame stuff. Oh, we do have the same lunch, so lucky you."

"Doesn't everyone have the same lunch?"

"No. Some people eat fourth period. Umm, I haven't had Mrs. Libby for art, or Kornman. Wait, is Interior Design seriously a class?"

Giada's laugh was like music to my ears. "Yeah. People study that at college and go into it as a career. I actually think that's what I want to do with my life, so watch your tone before you mock it."

I filed that information away for later then returned to the one class I hadn't yet commented on. She had World Religions at the same time as my study hall. I'd heard the class was an easy A, and my mother would love anything having to do with religion, but I hadn't given it serious consideration before because, well, why would I?

"I actually might be moving into your seventh period class. How's Mr. Cobb?"

She shrugged. "I'm only in the second day, so who knows? What do you have now?"

"Study Hall, but my papà is pitching a fit over that and there was only one other class open that period for me to transfer into."

"I didn't know Study Hall was an option!"

"Only for Upper Classmen."

Giada wrinkled her nose. "Bummer. Well, I should probably go. I'm a little confused on what all the rules are here, but it seems everyone else headed back to the locker room."

I nodded. "I'm a pro at all the rules here now. I'll teach you this weekend, okay?"

"Um, sure?"

I couldn't help but smile. I didn't remember Giada being so unsure of herself, but maybe it wasn't a bad thing.

"It's a date," I said, winking. I sauntered off without waiting for her response, feeling pretty damn cool.

- Giada -

J wasn't normally "that kid" who called home daily, but my mom seemed uneasy about my new school. My dad was clearly the one who abruptly decided to switch schools, and even though my mom purported to support his decision, I wasn't going to punish her just because he was being an ass.

I did wish Mom would clue me in as to why he'd made the sudden change though. I hated not knowing things. This was different from my initial move to boarding school. That decision I'd understood.

Shortly before my dad banished me to my first boarding school, his dad—my grandpa—died. Except he didn't die in his sleep or from cancer or heart disease or any of those things that seemed to wipe out all my other friends' grandparents. No, my grandfather was shot, point blank. During a mugging.

And it was my fault.

Well, I didn't pull the trigger, of course, but I'd insisted on joining him at work that day. If I hadn't distracted him, he would've noticed them coming. He could've saved himself and not just me.

My mom swore I wasn't being banished, that my dad just wanted to keep me safe. But that didn't make sense. They could've protected me at home better than from out-of-state. Besides, the danger was gone. Random muggers weren't going to hunt me down next.

I knew my dad still loved me, and I didn't blame him for not wanting to look at me every single day after what I'd done. He'd been so close to his own dad, after all. They'd lived together—all of us in a big house in suburban Connecticut—and they'd worked together. When my grandpa died, Dad had taken over the family business. Now he worked at the docks every day. At least he had security guards with him to make sure nothing bad happened to him.

My father and I used to be close, before the shooting. I'd always played the role of the stereotypical daddy's little girl, and my father treated me like a princess. We'd never openly discussed him blaming me—or banishing me— but our relationship never recovered. Now, we both kept our interactions cool and minimal.

And he assuaged his guilt over banishing me by spoiling me at every opportunity.

After the funeral, my grandma moved back to Italy. I never knew if she was just sad and lonely in the house after her husband's death, or if she too couldn't stand to see me. I preferred to not think about it.

"Giada?" my mom's familiar face greeted me on my laptop screen, snapping me out of my dismal thoughts. I settled into my desk chair and smiled as Mom gushed over how pretty I looked before asking me how school was going.

"Is it really the best school on the east coast?" she asked before I could answer her first question.

"I don't know. It's only Wednesday. I just got here. The campus is pretty and the classrooms are nice though."

"Are you making lots of new friends? How are your teachers? What's your roommate like?"

I laughed at all of her questions, then gave filtered responses. I told her my roommate was great, but didn't mention that the other girls hadn't really warmed up to me yet. I got it. I was the new girl, and they didn't know yet where I'd fit in. It might be a new boarding school, but the basic rules were all the same. Every girl was the competition, and a possible threat, until she proved herself otherwise.

After what felt like an eternity of talking without pause, my dad appeared behind my mom.

"Marco!" Mom shouted with such intensity that I half expected someone to reply "Polo."

"It's your daughter. Giada," she clarified, even though he had no other daughters and could clearly see me.

I waved and tried to conceal my bitterness. "Hi."

His greeting to me was similarly awkward.

My mom filled the silence with more of her overly enthusiastic questions, but then, I remembered I did have some news that actually might interest both of them.

"Hey, you wouldn't believe who I ran into on campus," I began. "Luca Marino. Do you still work with his dad? Did you know Luca was a student here?"

My dad's mouth twitched into a slight hint of a smile but then his face went blank as my mother turned and glared at him. She didn't say anything, but she didn't have to. She clearly had no idea Luca was at my school, and she wasn't happy about it.

I filed that information away for another time.

"Knock, knock," a trill voice said right as I ended the video chat with my parents.

"Come in," I called.

Elise popped her head around as though expecting a dog to jump out. She looked disappointed when none did.

"I thought I heard a boy's voice in here," she said.

I grimaced. "I was video chatting with my parents. You probably heard my dad."

Elise sighed and planted herself in front of her closet, flipping through outfit after outfit. "I have nothing to wear," she groaned.

I wasn't sure why she needed to change for dinner in the school cafeteria, but I saw my opening. So far, Elise and I had gotten along okay. We weren't best friends yet, but we also weren't tattling on each other. I thought we both saw the potential for friendship and were both simply too nervous to take the first step.

"You're welcome to borrow any of my stuff," I said. "Not that my clothes are any better, but maybe just some variety would be nice. We're probably the same size," I added, even though we weren't. Elise was more of what I'd call an athletic build. She definitely didn't have my curves.

Elise smiled. "Really? That's super nice of you. If there's anything you want to borrow from my closet, you totally can. I mean, if you ask first."

"Of course!" I said, as if I couldn't dream of such an atrocity.

She settled for borrowing one of my wrap tops and then we walked to the dining hall together.

"Hey, so do you know Luca Marino?" I asked, curious what his reputation was at the school. "He's a Junior."

Her eyes widened and she turned to me. "Uh yeah. Don't tell me he's already hit on you!"

I laughed, unsure how to interpret that. "We actually know each other. I mean, our dads are friends or something, and we used to hang out some as kids. I didn't realize he went here until I ran into him by the soccer fields."

She appeared both surprised and impressed by this, but said nothing, so I pressed onward, opting for the blunt approach.

"So what kind of reputation does he have here?"

Elise giggled. "Well, he's pretty popular. I mean, in case you didn't notice, he's hot. So, all the girls want to date him and all the guys want to be him."

"Really?" I wasn't surprised at all about the girls. Luca was tall, with dark brownish-black hair, an olive complexion, and an athletic build. His striking eyes were an intriguing mixture of chocolate brown and golden flecks, and his eyelashes were thick enough for most girls to envy. He had straight, white teeth and a smile that was just the slightest bit lopsided and somehow created even more charm.

But the Luca I remembered didn't play well with other boys. At least not my brothers. He was arrogant and indignant and never seemed to care what others thought of him. Maybe he'd matured.

Elise nodded. "And I think he gets into trouble a lot, so he might not be the best influence if you're determined to make the Dean's List."

My phone buzzed against my hip as she spoke. I slid it out of my pocket and stopped dead in my tracks when I saw who it was from.

"Speak of the devil," I said, wondering how Luca had gotten

my contact information—or entered himself into my phone—without me noticing.

I shifted my phone so Elise could read the message, as he'd invited me and my suitemates to some coed football game, then off campus for frozen yogurt Friday evening.

"So is he such a bad influence that we should say no and keep our distance?" I asked her.

Elise shook her head, eyes wide. "Hell no. This sounds fun, and usually only upperclassmen go to the powderpuff games. We should totally go."

I grinned back at her and told Luca we'd see him there.

CHAPTER 2

THE PERPETUAL FLIRT

- Giada -

I saw Luca at breakfast Thursday. He sauntered in for the last five minutes, stole food off a handful of different people's plates, then gave me a nondescript nod before taking just as the bell rang. Then, I spotted him again Friday as I was leaving Social Studies. I'd stuck around to ask the teacher a question about the assignment, mostly just to see if I'd run into Luca.

When I actually did, it took serious effort not to smile too obviously.

Mr. Perpetually Cool did his same nod, so I offered a demure wave. Then, he swiveled to follow me.

"Hey, why doesn't Matteo go here?"

I gritted my teeth together, having asked myself the same question many times. Matteo was a Senior at a private day school near our home. He'd been there since he was a Freshman, just like our older brother Angelo. I was the only child in the family to be banished to boarding school.

"Guess my parents like having him around more."

Luca frowned. "Anyone who'd choose his company over yours is insane. You sure you weren't just too much of a handful?"

"I am angelic," I insisted, heading off to my next class. I hoped Luca would assume I was being ironic. But in reality, I was a rule-follower. Or I had been, so far. My grades were decent, I went to church every Sunday, and I considered myself to be a good person.

But now that my parents had preemptively punished me for some unknown crime by switching me to a new school, I had nothing to lose. I loved dancing, parties, and friends. I might as well enjoy all three.

I was just finishing up lunch when I next saw Luca. He swooped into the seat beside me, reaching for my fries.

"You gonna eat these?"

I shook my head, nose wrinkled. Still, I expected Luca to stay and chat, but instead, he simply grabbed the fries, thanked me, then left.

I watched as Luca made his way across the cafeteria, joking with a few other guys and then whispering something to a girl that made her laugh uproariously. He lingered by her just long enough to make me wonder if she was his girlfriend…not that it mattered. If I was going to date, it absolutely would not be someone my dad liked. If he was going to banish me, I was going to date whatever boy he'd hate the most.

Later, right as World Religions began, Luca barged into the room. After a brief discussion, the teacher pointed Luca to a seat. With fifteen minutes of class remaining, Mr. Cobb told us to meet with a partner to discuss the pros and cons of organized religion.

I turned to the girl next to me, as we'd paired up for all of the earlier assignments, but before I could speak, a chair dropped in front of me. Luca swung a leg over to straddle the chair backwards, a bent spiral notebook in his hand and a pencil behind his ear.

"Hey, Partner," he said, smiling cockily.

"I was going to…" I started, but by that point, Jacquelyn was already working with someone else.

Luca followed my gaze towards Jacquelyn then turned back to me with a shrug. He leaned into my hair and inhaled loudly. "You smell amazing. What is that?"

My mouth fell open, but it took me a moment to piece together any words. "Strawberry shampoo."

Luca appeared intrigued by that, but instead of simply moving on to the assignment, he reached for my hand and sniffed my bare arm, leaving a trail of goosebumps in his wake. "More shampoo?"

"Lotion. Vanilla cupcake."

"Do you want someone to eat you?" he asked, his expression completely serious.

"Can we just do the assignment?"

Luca grinned. "We could, but we both know that you already have an idea so why don't you just write that down and then when he asks us all to brainstorm as a group, you can raise your hand?"

Luca knew me surprisingly well for someone who hadn't seen me in over a year.

"So you're bringing your roommate to the game tonight?" he asked, apparently content that I agreed with his plan of ignoring the assignment.

I nodded. "Elise."

"Yeah, I know who she is. Small school."

"Is that alright?"

"Sure. The more the merrier."

"Are you playing in the game?"

He laughed. "No, only girls play."

"Oh, I thought it was co-ed."

"Girls play, boys coach. Football-playing boys. American football."

I nodded, then suddenly felt brave. "Is your girlfriend playing?"

Luca's eyes locked on me as he shook his head.

Mr. Cobb called us back to attention. I silently swore. Was Luca confirming that he had a girlfriend, but she wasn't playing, or was he saying no, he didn't have a girlfriend? I'd never get the nerve to ask again, and I already hated the fact that I cared so much.

As Luca had predicted, I raised my hand to contribute to the discussion, but it was more to distract myself than anything else. The moment the bell rang, I shot out of my seat ready to get as far away from him as possible. But just as I reached the freedom of the hallway, I felt a presence right behind me.

"Six o'clock, okay?" Luca said, his deep voice so close to my ear that his breath tickled me.

"Sounds good," I said, ready to bolt.

"Giada," he continued, sending shivers up my spine with the way his tongue curled around the vowels in my name. "There's no girlfriend."

Then he winked before sauntering off.

My stomach flip-flopped.

That night, I brought a chef salad from the dining hall back to my room to eat so I could maximize my time to get ready for the game. I styled my hair into loose waves, shimmied into my shortest denim cutoffs and a flimsy white top with short sleeves that split over the shoulders.

The outside temperature was scorching, so I wanted to dress appropriately. Sure it would cool off once the sun set, but I was banking on having someone by my side to keep me warm by then.

When Elise and I arrived at the game, we didn't spot Luca. But as we made our way to the bleachers, I noticed a guy who looked a lot like Luca. His hand gripped some girl's shoulder and his head tilted down like he was about to kiss her.

I wrinkled my nose, then quickly turned away. It did not matter if Luca was messing around with some girl. I'd already decided I would never go out with some boy my dad loved. Luca's flirting was a moot point.

"Hey is that…" Elise said, pointing at Luca.

"Probably. God, he's such a man whore."

Elise offered a polite chuckle as she turned to me. "Are you okay? I thought you guys like had plans to meet up tonight?"

I shook my head. "No, it's not like that. We are just friends."

She shrugged, content with my explanation, and I managed to convince myself it was the truth, too. We found a spot near the top of the bleachers, and before the game started, a few boys from our other classes came to sit by us.

"I'm Greg," said the guy who sat beside me. "We're in the same science class."

"And English, right?" I said, shaking his hand. "I'm Giada."

Greg had a great smile and the kind of wavy blond hair that made him look like he should shoot ads for some surfing company. He was cute and he seemed interested…unlike a certain other boy that I was not thinking about.

Greg and I went through the basics, which always seemed to revolve around everyone's confusion about why I transferred to a new school sophomore year if I hadn't been in trouble at my last one.

With two minutes left on the clock for the first half, I excused myself, turning to Elise. "I'm going to grab a drink before the concession stand lines pick up. Want anything?"

"I'm good," she said, looking happy as a clam, surrounded by the boys.

Smiling, I weaved my way down the bleachers then across the field. It perplexed me how an event such as this could take place on school property and use the school concession stand, but not count as an official school event. As far as I could tell, the school didn't even encourage this sort of thing, but it sure didn't seem like anyone in administration minded.

I smiled politely at the girl working the concession booth. She appeared to be a student, but I didn't recognize her. "Can I get a diet soda please?" I asked.

"And a popcorn, some M&Ms and a bottled water," someone shouted, jumping beside me. It was Luca, of course.

I rolled my eyes but nodded at the girl, so she rang up our order. Luca tossed money on the counter. "My treat," he said.

I thanked Luca and walked back towards the bleachers, fully aware he was right behind me.

"You enjoying the game so far?" he asked, pausing off to the side where it was less crowded.

"Yeah, I'm having a great time."

"You sure know a lot of guys," he said, gesturing to where I'd been sitting.

I laughed. "You sure know a lot of girls," I said, sipping my drink then letting the straw linger between my lips while I awaited his reaction.

Luca shrugged. "You like surfer boy?"

"I might," I replied. "Wait, is he really a surfer?"

"I don't think so. But that hair…"

I giggled. "Yeah."

Luca held out the popcorn, so I helped myself to a handful, acutely aware of the way he watched my lips as I chewed.

"I should get back to Elise and…Greg," I said.

"Yeah, the halftime show is not to be missed."

"Thanks again," I said, holding up my soda.

Luca grinned, and off I went.

- Luca -

*M*y papà called and woke me up way too early Saturday morning. He always did shit like that. With all his travel between Italy and the U.S., you'd think he'd learn the time difference. Although, something told me he was aware and just did it to mess with me. *Whatever.*

The night before, I'd returned to my dorm before curfew. I'd gone for fro-yo with the group, but this girl, Ashley, had gotten clingy. I liked hanging out with her and loved making out in the quad, but the second she tried to hold my hand, I was done. Hand holding meant something completely different to girls, and I wasn't down for that. Yeah, I liked Ashley, but I also liked Courtney and Leila. And Giada.

Crap. I couldn't keep my mind off of Giada lately. She was hot and she was new to the school, which generally meant I'd be interested. But it seemed to me that the fact that I already knew her should make me *less* intrigued, not more. Something about Giada just kept pulling me in. It didn't help that she played the game so well. She pretended to be all sweet and innocent, but the way she dressed and the way she twirled her hair around…Giada Conti knew exactly what she was doing.

"Luca!" my papà's sharp tone brought me back to reality.

"Sorry. I was asleep. It's only nine-fifteen. This is literally one of the only days I can sleep in at this prison you sent me to," I whined.

My papà mumbled a quip in Italian then punctuated it with a loud sigh to let me know I was still an epic disappointment.

"I'd like you to go on some errands with Lodovico today. He'll pick you up at noon and you'll be back to campus well before curfew."

I groaned silently. "Why?"

"Because I said so, Luca. It's past time for you to start learning the family business. Lodovico has work to do in the area today, so you will help him. If you want to complain, I can take back that car and stop paying your credit card bill."

"Fine," I grumbled.

My papà must have anticipated more protest from me, because he quieted for a moment before asking about my classes.

"It's only been a week," I reminded him. "Oh, but I did drop the study hall like you asked. I'm now in World Religion, so I guess Mom will be happy too. Funniest thing though, Giada Conti is in that class."

"Marco's daughter?"

I could practically hear the smile in his voice as he asked.

"Yep. Anyway, she seems nice."

He chuckled. "Marco mentioned he might transfer her there, but I didn't realize it was official. How does la principessa like the school so far?"

"She seems happy enough."

"Good. Happy princess, happy rulers."

I rubbed my forehead, trying to make sense of that. "Why do you call her the princess?"

"Because that is what she is, my boy. Her father, with his business, well, he rules he land in Connecticut, and she is his princess. Just like you, my boy, are the prince. Only you will have to take over for me some day, and the Conti girl simply has to look pretty and stay out of trouble. Her brothers aren't at school with you are they?"

"No. Giada said Matteo is a senior back in Connecticut. Angelo is out of school. Maybe college? I don't know."

"You be nice to la principessa. And don't make Lodovico wait. He doesn't like that."

Papà disconnected the call before I could agree. I shoved my phone under my pillow and went back to sleep.

By the time I ate, showered, and full caffeinated myself, Lodovico was already standing in front of his Land Rover. I glanced down at my watch and shook my head.

"I'm not late and I brought coffee."

He scowled at the coffee, then opened the back door of the car.

"I don't even get to ride in the front?" I protested as I climbed in, careful not to spill either coffee. Then I spotted the other guy in the car, the driver. He looked familiar, but I wasn't sure if I'd ever been formally introduced to him.

"Luca, this is Iacopo," Lodovico said, nodding for the driver to take off.

"Can I call you Jake for short?" I asked. Iacopo was actually a ridiculously common name in Italy, but you didn't hear it much state-side. Either way, the guy didn't answer. "Not a morning person, huh? That's alright, man. Me neither."

"He doesn't speak English," Lodovico said.

I figured he was lying, but there was an easy way to find out. "So he won't be offended if I talk shit about his funky bald spot?"

The car slammed to a stop, causing me to spill my coffee all over my jeans and the back of the seat in front of me.

"Fucker," I mumbled, realizing the driver had done that on purpose. In a flash he had swiveled to face me and a massive silver pistol was pressed against my chest.

Lodovico sighed and slowly pressed downward on the barrel of the gun till Iacopo no longer had it aimed at me. "Boss's kid, Iacopo. Boss's kid. You hurt him, you die. Capisci?" He didn't wait for Iacopo to answer before turning to me. "And you, Luca. We aren't babysitting. Stop acting like a culo and we'll stop treating you like one."

I rolled my eyes but busied myself sopping up the coffee with a towel from the side door. *Fucking Saturdays.*

For the next two hours, Iacopo drove us around town. Every so often, Lodovico and I would hop out and head into a store or restaurant, collect money, then return to the car. Mid-afternoon, we grabbed drinks and fries from a diner, then we went on to a warehouse I vaguely recognized.

"What's on the agenda now?" I asked, not bothering to conceal my boredom.

"We wait for a shipment."

"Fun. So is this what you guys do every day? Just drive around?"

"Your dad said the Conti girl goes to school with you," Lodovico said, ignoring my question. "What's she like?"

"Hot," I said, proud to finally have elicited a grin out of both men.

"Her mom's not so bad on the eyes," Iacopo said.

"Eww." Realizing they might tell me more than my papà had, I pressed further. "Why does everyone call her la principessa? I know it's because of her dad's business, but he's hardly royalty."

Iacopo laughed again, shaking his head. Lodovico swiveled to face me. "Your papà may be a bigger deal internationally, but hers heads up one of the biggest families on the East Coast."

I squinted, trying to piece together his words. Marco only had the three kids, so Lodovico wasn't talking about a biological family. But I'd also never heard him—or anyone—speak so liberally about a mob family.

"But I don't get what that has to do with Giada. She's fifteen. She couldn't be involved in some crime family."

"Who said anything about her being involved?" Iacopo asked. "If Marco has it his way, his princess will bury her head in the sand till the end of time."

"She's not that dumb," I said.

Both men chuckled and exchanged glances that suggested they believed otherwise.

"So that's why she's at boarding school, so she doesn't figure it out?"

"And to keep her safe," Lodovico said.

"She's in danger?"

"No. No one is dumb enough to go after the princess," Iacopo said, gazing out his window with increased interest.

"Is she..." Lodovico started to talk, then stopped as Iacopo swatted his leg. Both men sat up straighter and turned to the left, where a beat-up black sedan was quickly approaching.

Iacopo swore under his breath.

"Sal said he didn't anticipate any trouble today," Lodovico said. "Maybe..."

I stared at the car, unsure why both men seemed tense, when suddenly Iacopo rolled down his window and blasted off two shots. One of them hit the car near the tire, causing it to spin.

"What the—" I began, but Lodovico flew out of the car before I could say anything else.

Iacopo swung his hand into the back seat towards my head, shouting, "Get down!"

There was a flurry of explosions.

I didn't remember moving, but as the SUV roared to life, swerving wildly, I realized I was crouched on the ground between my seat and the one in front of me. The noise was deafening, and between that and the rocking of the SUV, I felt nauseous.

The car stopped abruptly, and I heard Iacopo make a phone call. I couldn't hear the other side of the call, but his instructions translated clearly to "abort the shipment."

The passenger door opened then closed, and I peered up, seeing Lodovico hop back in. "You alright Luca?" he asked.

"I...um...yes?"

"Let's go," he said, and Iacopo took off.

For once in my life, I kept quiet. We drove for a good fifteen minutes. Lodovico fielded a couple of phone calls, but nothing from his side of the conversation told me any more than what I'd ascertained already. Someone apparently came for the same shipment we were awaiting. And there was some shooting.

Lodovico hung up, looked around, then frowned. "This isn't the way back to campus."

"The kid got shot at. I figured we'd take him to the club for a drink first," Iacopo explained.

Lodovico turned to stare at me. "You ok?"

"Yes," I said, aware that I was shaking my head in contrast to my words.

"Well, maybe it's for the best. Your papà wants you to learn the ins and outs of the family business. You simply got more of a lesson today than he bargained for."

"Who were they?" I asked.

Lodovico pulled out his cell phone and read two names from what appeared to be drivers' licenses. "You recognize either of those?"

"No. Why did you photograph their ID?"

"Now we know who they were and where they lived. I got the license plate too."

I swallowed the lump in my throat as I realized he spoke in past tense.

"You wear gloves if you're checking someone's wallet. Or touching anything that the cops might come near ever. But you don't want to take anything you don't have to," he continued, apparently teaching me a lesson in forensic coverups.

"They're dead," I said, having meant it as a question.

"You don't shoot at a Marino and live to tell about it," Iacopo replied, slowing to a stop in front of a building.

A shady looking guy positioned in front of the solid metallic door nodded at us, and Lodovico climbed out and held my door.

"This is my papà's club?" I asked, not remembering it. A small inscription on the door read 4th and Main, which sounded vaguely familiar, but I couldn't recall ever having been there. Not that my papà regularly brought me to any of his clubs.

"One of them," he replied.

The shady guy opened the next door for us and we were greeted with an overpowering bass beat and the stale smell of tobacco smoke. Lodovico escorted me down a private hallway, past several guys, then unlocked a door. "That's your father's private bathroom. Use it and get cleaned up, then we'll have a drink."

I stumbled into the room still in a daze. I washed my face and hands then stared into the mirror for several minutes. I looked the same, but somehow, I knew I was different. Something had changed today, and I would never be the same person I was that morning.

Afraid to be alone with my thoughts any longer, I left the bathroom and made my way back down the hall. Iacopo and Lodovico were both seated at the solid wood bar. Iacopo slid a maple colored drink with an orange slice garnish towards me. I sniffed it, confirming it was not soda.

"What is this?"

"Negroni," he said. "Vermouth, Campari, Gin. It's an Italian man's drink."

Gin typically repulsed me, but now, I didn't mind. I poured a large swig into my mouth, swallowing without tasting. The second sip was smoother, and as I was about to go for the third, I heard a woman's voice.

"I heard *il principe* was here," she said.

I turned, wondering what woman possibly had the gull to call me *the prince* after what I'd been through. I came face to face with a massive set of tits.

Iacopo and Lodovico both laughed, probably from my expression.

"You guys are so mean. Did you even give him food?" she said.

"Luca, this is Anaya. Are you hungry?" Lodovico asked.

Food was the last thing on my mind, but I mumbled "sure."

Anaya grabbed two drinks from the bartender then and walked off to deliver them to a table without another word. I watched her walk off, finally taking in my surroundings more fully.

"Holy shit," I said, not sure whether to stare at the half naked woman on stage, wrapping herself around a pole, or the topless waitresses.

Iacopo laughed again. "I think we know how to cheer him up."

Lodovico swatted my arm. "Hey, Luca, you want a burger or what?"

"Uh sure," I said, keeping my eyes on the ladies.

He sighed and pressed a cold metal object into my hand. "Alright. You got twenty minutes. The key opens that door."

I turned to see him point to a door marked Private.

"I'll send Anaya in."

My pulse skyrocketed but I didn't want to jump to conclusions. "For…what?"

"Whatever you want," Iacopo said with a laugh.

"My treat," Lodovico said. "Go. Your food will be ready when you come back."

I did as I was told.

- Giada -

On Saturday, I took the school shuttle bus into town to shop for the perfect gift for my dad's upcoming birthday. Almost immediately, I found a charming shop with etched glass barware- and they'd be able to personalize it in time. I'd simply make sure my driver swung by the shop with me on our way back home for my father's birthday party.

Just thinking about the festivities made me homesick. Not long had passed since I'd seen my immediate family, but for a big event like my dad's birthday, I would see the entire extended family. Between the aunts and uncles and cousins, there could easily be fifty or more people gathered at my family's home. We'd have the most amazing Italian food and we'd all just relax and catch up outside. If I were home the whole weekend, I could stop off at my home parish too.

I daydreamed until I reached my second stop for the day—the local Catholic church. The school offered services on Sundays, but I preferred to attend a true mass inside a church if possible. Something about the physical confines of a sanctuary had always relaxed me, and I didn't get the full benefit from a service in my school's multi-purpose chapel.

I was a little surprised that I hadn't heard from Luca the rest of the weekend, but didn't think much of it until he also missed class Monday. I looked for him again at the end of the day after my tennis clinic, but instead, I just saw his roommate, Grant.

"Hi. Where's Luca? He missed class earlier."

"Oh uh, he had some family stuff. He left campus Saturday and just came back a little bit ago. Want me to tell him you were looking for him?"

"Sure, but I'm heading to the chapel so he doesn't need to call or anything," I said, glad to actually have plans.

As it turned out, one of the priests from the local church performed the shortened mass at school. So after the full mass Saturday, I'd stayed to chat with him and then volunteered to help him organize some of the charity projects for the semester at school. Back home, I'd helped with some of the church's programs for poor local kids, organizing school supply drives at the end of summer, collecting coats and hats in the fall, and chairing the holiday angel program where we bought Christmas gifts for needy kids.

At school, the priest wanted to focus all of our efforts on a local children's hospital. First, we were going to make cards for the patients. If I drummed up enough involvement on campus with that though, he promised to let me organize a toy drive for the holidays. I had typed up some fliers for other students, and had just gotten the priest's approval to send them out to my classmates.

I started out of the chapel, whistling happily. I barely made it through the door before I noticed a familiar figure lounging against a tree across the sidewalk.

I stopped and waved.

"Grant said you were at the chapel and I couldn't believe it," Luca said, walking to me. "What kind of a teen spends her free time at a chapel?"

"One who doesn't want to rot in hell?" I suggested.

"Seriously, what crimes are you repenting for?"

"Nothing! I was just…"

"Goodnight Giada," Father Harris said, exiting the chapel behind me. He smiled politely at Luca then went to his car.

Luca's eyes widened. "Are you sleeping with the priest?"

I slapped him before I even realized what I was doing. Then I clasped both hands over my mouth. "Oh my gosh. I'm sorry. I never hit anyone. I just…" I shook my head, realizing I should be mad at him, not myself. "You should show some respect! He is a priest. Nothing inappropriate is going on. Nothing!"

"Okay, so you're just hanging out, perfectly platonically, in an empty chapel?"

"Yes. He's letting me organize a card drive for the children's hospital."

Luca stared blankly for several moments. "Are you being serious?"

I nodded. "And I'd appreciate you not making any more corrupt priest jokes."

"Yeah, noted," he said, rubbing his cheek where I'd hit him. Honestly, though there wasn't even a mark.

"I went to check out the church in town Saturday. I like spending time at church."

Luca bit back a laugh.

"What?"

He shook his head. "Nothing. You just, well, you come across as this cliché popular girl who's obsessed with jewelry and clothes and stuff and you just told me you spent your Saturday at church. Just surprising is all."

I rolled my eyes. "And I suppose you had super cool plans Saturday? Let me guess—drag racing cars then bar hopping with your besties?"

His smile faded, and as I goaded him again to tell me what he did Saturday, his face went ashen.

"Nevermind," he said.

I couldn't pinpoint the cause in his sudden mood change, but I didn't press it. We both started walking back towards the dorms.

"You picked a great day to ditch World Religions," I said. "We watched some old movie on the history of Christianity. The DVD was so staticky that you couldn't hear half of it."

His mouth relaxed into a smile. "I dunno. I would've loved a nap. Did you sleep through it?"

"I would never sleep through a class."

"Santarellina," he said, grinning before translating. "Goody two shoes."

"It sounds prettier in Italian," I admitted, not taking offense.

"Most things do. You gonna learn the language some day?"

I shrugged. "My old school had a teacher that did some private lessons in it, but I didn't pick up much, honestly. Maybe in college?"

Luca grinned again, turning to face me. He began to speak in his native language, and even though I'd heard dozens of guys speak Italian over the years, it had never before made my heart beat quite that fast. When Luca finally paused, I was dying for him to translate. Instead, he simply winked.

"Wait, what did you say? You have to tell me."

"If you want to know so badly, you should probably learn the language," he said.

I sighed, certain he really wasn't going to tell me. "Well, I'm starving. I should get to the dining hall before it closes."

Luca grimaced at his watch. "Pretty sure you're too late already."

Crap. How had I lost track of time? "Oh. Well, I have some snacks in my room. I'm not that hungry anyway."

"You just said you were starving."

I had no response for that. I couldn't think straight when I was hungry.

Luca grabbed my arm and tugged me towards the dining hall. "Come on. I have an idea."

I followed Luca around to the back entrance of the dining hall where he knocked on a door labelled "Staff Only."

"Luca, seriously, I'll be fine. It's not worth getting in trouble over," I said, glancing around furtively as though about to get busted on security camera doing a B&E.

"No one's getting in trouble," he promised, just as the door swung open.

An annoyed looking cafeteria lady glared at us.

"Sally!" Luca greeted her like they were old friends. "How's my favorite Yankees fan?"

Her expression lightened as she shook her head. "Don't even start with me about that last game. They were cheated and you know it. The umpire was blind." She turned to walk away, and Luca started in the door, pulling me with him.

"You here for your secret stash?"

"Yes, ma'am. Is an oven still on?"

"Mmm hmm."

"You want some? I've got plenty," he said to her.

She swiveled back to face us. "Boy, I don't care how charming you are with those stupid dimples, I'm still not tasting your momma's lasagna."

Luca laughed and lead me across the kitchen to a large freezer. "We got ziti, mostaccioli, or lasagna. Pick your poison," he said, gesturing to a cardboard box labelled LM Special Diet.

"You have a special diet?"

"No, but that's the only way you can store food here."

"He's supposed to only come get it during meal hours, but that one's a rule breaker," Sally called over her shoulder.

"Mostaccioli," I said, chewing my lip to avoid drooling.

He retrieved an aluminum loaf pan and carried it over to Sally, who stuck it into an oven.

"Miss Sally, this is Giada Conti. She's new here," Luca said.

I waved shyly. She smiled warmly at me then turned to Luca with a scowl.

"Aren't you too old for Freshmen?" she asked him.

"I'm not a—" I began, but Luca cut me off.

"It's not like that Sally. She's an old friend. We're practically family."

She rolled her eyes and leaned closer to me. "You watch out for that one. First he's feeding you, next thing you know he'll be batting those pretty boy eyelashes and you'll get knocked up before graduation."

Luca cleared his throat loudly, sparing me the trouble of coming up with a response to that statement. He walked over to a giant shelf and pulled down one of the racks. I watched in confusion as he began sorting dishes onto the rack.

"Are you loading the dishwasher?" I asked, in awe.

Luca chuckled. "Yep. That's sort of the deal me and Sally here have. She'll let me in after hours if I earn my keep."

"Okay," I said, scooting beside him and helping loading.

By the time the pasta was done cooking, the kitchen looked clean. Luca thanked Sally then snagged two forks and an oven mitt for our food. He carried the entire thing out to the steps behind the staff entrance, then motioned for me to sit.

The sun was setting, leaving cool and refreshing evening air.

"That smells amazing," I said. "Does your mom cook a lot?"

"No, my aunt made this. But it's easier to just tell people it's my mom. Americans don't tend to understand the big Italian family way of doing things."

I chuckled at that. "My family is the same way." I told Luca about my dad's upcoming birthday while we took turns stabbing various cheesy noodle bites with our forks. "Maybe your dad will be there," I said, realizing there usually were a few business associates.

"He hasn't mentioned it, not that we talk much. But he will be in town soon."

We both fell quiet as we ate. I hadn't realized how ravenous I was until the tantalizing aroma of the mostaccioli had reached my nostrils. "This is so good. I mean, the food here isn't terrible, but it isn't—"

"Italian?" he supplied.

I nodded. I didn't know the language, but I sure did appreciate the food.

I caught him eying me while I ate and suddenly felt self-conscious.

"Thank you," I said. "This was really nice of you."

He shrugged. "I needed to eat, too, and this is too much for one person."

"This is too much for two people."

He laughed. "I'll take whatever we don't finish back to the suite. The guys will eat the rest."

I took a few more bites, relishing the warmth in my belly and the overall comfort from a familiar food. Then, I started to think about what Grant had said, how Luca had some family thing this weekend.

"Your roommate said you had some family drama this past weekend, but you said your father was in Italy till this weekend. Were you with your mom?"

I winced as he frowned at me, not having realized how much my words resembled an interrogation until I heard them aloud.

"Sorry, I was just curious," I said.

"I was with my uncle," he said. "Well, except he's not actually my uncle, in the blood relative sort of way."

"I have some of those," I jumped in. Luca was probably the first person outside of my family who could actually relate. I guessed because it was an Italian thing. His expression hardened for a moment, and I could've sworn there was a flicker of sadness.

"Right, well, I guess he's technically my guardian. He's the guy that can check me out of school and shit. He also oversees a lot of my papà's business when he's in Italy. Anyway, we were supposed to just be out for the day, but nothing went according to plan. It was actually complete shit, as far as weekends go. So Lodovico didn't bring me back until this afternoon."

"Lodovico," I repeated, sounding way less cool than Luca had. "I like that name. Very Italian."

He nodded, frowning. "Can I ask you something? Why do you do so much volunteer stuff with the church?"

I shrugged, not having expected us to return to that topic. "Why not? I have the time and the means, and we're supposed to help others."

Luca twirled his fork around a clump of cheese in the past. "So you're not like trying to make amends for something?"

"No. I'm no angel, but I don't think I've done anything *that* bad yet."

"And you're not trying to right the wrongs of someone else?"

Now I had no idea what he was getting at. "I just don't want to live in a society where people don't look out for each other." I paused, dropping my fork in the pan and leaning back. "And I'm stuffed."

Luca grinned.

CHAPTER 3

GOOD GIRLS LIKE BAD BOYS

- Luca -

After ditching classes Monday, homework filled my time the rest of the week. For once, I was happy about that. As long as I kept busy, my mind didn't wander back to the weekend. There was no point in dwelling on it. What had happened had happened.

I hadn't done anything wrong, anyway. And if I was being honest, I didn't think Lodovico or Iacopo had, either. Those guys came at us. *They* were the instigators.

"Hey, Earth to Luca," my roommate called.

I gazed up, wondering how many times he'd already said my name before I heard him.

"You're going to the party at Sullivan's Farm, aren't you?"

I considered that. Sullivan's Farm was a mile or two from campus. At night, they rented out their empty land for events. Their target customer was scout troops wanting a bonfire site or locals wanting to rent a barn for a Sweet Sixteen birthday, but us school kids gave them a lot of business. Their prices were cheap and the cops never showed up to the parties. In contrast, whenever we tried to hang out on the beach, the cops shut us down before the kegs even arrived.

I wasn't in the mood for a party, but I couldn't sit in the dorm alone. I'd have nothing left to do but think, and that was not an option. Besides, I had a reputation to protect.

"You could see if Gia is going," he said.

"Giada," I corrected. "And no way."

"I thought you two were maybe starting something."

I pushed away from my desk. "We are friends. I could never date her because she's…a good girl."

Gavin laughed. "Good girls love bad boys."

He wasn't wrong. And that was exactly why I needed to keep my distance. "It doesn't matter anyway. She would never go to a party like this. She's probably at church or something. What time are we leaving?"

We grabbed a pizza, then we headed out. Our other suitemate, Marcus, had a car too, so he and I both drove, leaving us all options if we didn't want to come home at the same time.

We'd only been at the party for a few minutes when Gavin nudged my arm with his elbow.

"Looks like tonight is your lucky night," he said.

I followed his gaze to the firepit, where a girl who looked an awful lot like Giada was twirling around, drink in her hand.

She was mesmerizing. She spun around and around, her dark hair splayed behind her, her arms spread wide and her head tilted towards the sky. The light from the fire reflected off of her dangling gold earrings and cast an eerie glow on her face. She almost appeared to be shimmering.

"Looks like your good girl has gone wild," Gavin chuckled, handing me a drink.

"She's not mine," I said, ignoring the way my chest tightened at the thought. I raised my cup to my lips, eying the identical cup in Giada's hand. I wouldn't have pegged Giada for a drinker.

Maybe, she wasn't. I hadn't seen her take a sip, so maybe she just held the cup for posterity.

I licked my lips as Giada's mouth curved into a broad smile. She continued dancing, but began singing along with the song, too. Whether or not Giada was drinking, she sure was happy. Another girl—one of her suitemates, I thought—approached her and now the girls were holding hands and singing. Giada tossed her cup on the ground to free up both hands, then continued her carefree shimmy with her friend.

"You have to admit she's hot," Gavin said.

I focused my glare on him right as he brought his cup to his mouth. "Stop checking her out."

He chugged his drink and laughed. "You literally just said she's not yours. That makes her fair game."

My jaw tightened as I continued to stare at Gavin.

"Fine," he relented. "I'll stay away but if you don't make a move, someone else will. You can't look like that and not get attention."

Gavin sauntered off, leaving me gawking. He was right, of course. There was nothing particularly provocative about Giada's outfit—a simple sundress that was fitted up top and flowy on the bottom. And her dancing reminded me more of some gypsy rain-dance than a sexy or seductive routine. But she still looked hot. Breathtaking, really.

The rest of the party was filled with girls who were trying to impress the guys, and Giada clearly couldn't care less. She was dancing how *she* wanted, and I suspected she was completely oblivious to the growing number of guys creepily eying her from the edges of the ring encircling the firepit.

As the song ended, Giada and her friend toppled to the ground in a heap, both of them giggling uproariously. I watched with annoyance as some other guy brought her another drink and helped her to her feet. Giada flashed him that gorgeous, sparkling smile of hers, then slipped out of her shoes and turned back to her friend. The guy hung close for a full minute before taking the hint and stumbling off, rejected.

I waited a moment, then walked forward. Right as I reached her, Giada twirled around and stumbled, pitching forward into my arms. "Whoa," I cautioned, steadying her with my free hand.

She giggled and licked her lips before gazing up through thick, dark lashes. "Luca!"

Any doubt I'd had about whether she'd actually been drinking was erased. Her red-rimmed, brown eyes twinkled brighter than the stars, but didn't seem to be able to focus on a single point. Giada swayed in my arms, then pushed against my chest to right herself.

"All that dizzy makes a girl dance," Giada said. She giggled again, shaking her head. "I mean, all that dancing makes a girl dizzy."

"Yeah. How much have you had to drink?" I asked, prying the cup from her hand.

"What? It's just fruit punch," she said with a mischievous gleam in her eye that told me she was fully aware of its alcohol content.

Someone cranked up the music then and Giada's roommate grabbed her hand and tugged her away.

"The dance floor calls," Giada said by way of apology, scampering off with her friend.

I took a couple sips of Giada's drink before dumping the rest on the patchy grass and doing the same with my own. I wasn't in the mood to drink. I considered heading back to the dorm, but felt oddly unsettled about leaving Giada unsupervised. I didn't know why. Giada was not my responsibility. And she was just as capable of getting herself back to the dorms safely as any of the other drunk girls.

Except something about that didn't seem accurate.

Somehow, Giada seemed more naïve. More innocent. Maybe

I only thought that because of what Iacopo and Lodovico had told me, but maybe not.

So instead of leaving, I chatted with the guys. When I looked for Giada a while later, she was no longer dancing. I decided maybe she'd headed home.

But just as I felt relief from that idea, I spotted Giada's roommate. Surely, Giada wouldn't have taken off without her roommate.

I scanned the group again and finally spotted another person, off in the distance, under the shadow of the tree. Thanks to the darkened night sky, I couldn't be sure it was Giada, but I started off in that direction anyway. As soon as I got close, I heard a deep voice, then Giada's distinct laugh.

It was definitely Giada, and she was not alone. I briefly considered that she might be with some guy she actually liked, but after a beat, I decided I didn't care. Giada was too drunk to be alone with a guy. Besides, it was past curfew for Sophomores.

As I drew closer, I was glad I hadn't backed off. The guy was fiddling with the strap of Giada's dress, nowhere near as subtle in his attempts to slip the strap down her arm as he likely thought. And a very drunken Giada was blathering away about needing to find her roommate.

I cleared my throat, and the guy slowly turned. It was Jack, from my English class. He was an ass.

"Hey man, we're kinda busy here," he said, sounding every bit as drunk as Giada.

I ignored him. "Giada, it's time for you to go home."

I braced myself for a protest from Jack, but he simply shrugged and walked off, saving himself a black eye.

Giada crossed her arms in front of her chest and pouted.

"Lemme get this straight. You steal my drink and then you scare off my...friend," she said, stumbling over the last word. "I already have two big brothers that think they can control me. I don't need another."

"I don't see your brothers here now, so maybe you do need someone to look after you."

She rubbed her hands over her arms, shivering. The air felt ten to fifteen degrees colder this far from the firepit, so I shrugged out of my jacket and draped it over her shoulders.

"I heard you tell Miss Sally that I'm like a sister to you."

That wasn't exactly what I'd said, but it also wasn't the point. "You can't just get drunk in the middle of nowhere on a school night."

"Oh and you can?"

"Not the same and you know it." I took a step forward to offer her my hand.

Giada glared at me and dropped to the ground. Awkwardly, she thrust her arms into the sleeves of the jacket I'd offered her.

I groaned. "Sei testardo."

"Excuse me?"

I frowned, taking in the look of indignance on her face. Then, I remembered. "You don't speak any Italian."

"No. I speak English. So whatever insults you're—"

"Stubborn. I called you stubborn, which you are. Where are your shoes?"

Giada gazed down, frowning when she saw her feet were bare. She glanced around the field, then I spotted her shoes near the fire. I helped Giada into her shoes then motioned for her to follow me.

She took a couple steps, then stumbled. I blew out a sigh, wrapped my arm around her, and guided her to my car.

"You have a car?" she said, dropping awkwardly into the seat.

"Si. Buckle your seatbelt."

Sharing such a small, enclosed space with Giada was torture. I could hear her breathing, and could smell her delicious scent. And the way she'd sat down, her skirt had ridden up, exposing the majority of her thigh. It took all my self-control to keep my eyes on the road and not on that smooth, creamy flesh.

I thought about making small talk while we drove, but silence was easier. Giada was so quiet I almost wondered if she'd passed out. When we parked at the school, I walked around to Giada's side of the car. I offered her a hand, and she swatted it away, standing awkwardly.

"I can get out of a car on my own, thanks," Giada said. Then her expression soured. She clapped both hands over her mouth and her eyes filled with panic.

I groaned inwardly, knowing that look all too well. Giada rushed to the side of the lot, dropped to all fours, and puked all over the bushes. I figured her roommate would've held back her hair or some shit like that, but I kept my distance. I grabbed a bottle of water from my car and simply waited until she finished. Then I approached slowly, handing her the bottle as she rocked back onto her knees.

Giada mumbled her gratitude, then struggled to open the bottle, proving she was even drunker than I'd assumed. I opened it for her, raising it to her lips. She made a face as she drank, but at least she swallowed.

"Can you stand?" I asked, offering my arm for support.

She tried on her own—stubbornly—then accepted my hand.

"I might have drank too much," she said.

"Yeah. You're gonna feel it tomorrow."

"It's my dad's fault," she said, tripping over some invisible obstacle and nearly faceplanting before I could ask what she meant.

I caught her, but realized she'd never be able to tackle the stairs to her room on her own. "Do you have your key?" I asked. I didn't see her student ID lanyard on her, but the dorms were old and the doors still opened via small metallic keys too.

Giada looked down, confused, then smiled. She reached into her dress, seemingly under her boobs, then retrieved the key.

"I don't even want to know where that was," I mumbled, but

of course I did. My entire body tingled at the thought of actually seeing where she'd hidden that damn key.

We walked around to the side door, the one that kids always propped open for returns past curfew. Ideally, we'd avoid the front door, since it was on a timer. Giada's key would unlock it and let her inside, but would also alert the dorm mom that someone was coming in after curfew.

Unfortunately, the side door was firmly shut.

"Shit," Giada said.

"It's fine. We'll go in and jog straight to your room. We'll be out of sight before anyone makes it down to check who came in. If we hear anything sooner, we can duck into that broom closet next to the stairwell."

Giada raised an eyebrow. "You sure know your way around the girls' dorms well."

I shrugged. It was the truth.

"Let me unlock it," I said, certain I'd be quicker than someone who could barely stand unassisted.

She relented, and I swung open the door, ushering her inside and onto the stairs before the security cameras could get a good view of us.

"Head down," I said, sure she hadn't snuck out—or in— enough to know there were also cameras on the stairs.

Her hair covered most of her face, and the way her arm was looped around my neck, I was able to half carry her up the stairs. We made it to her room and I quietly shut the door behind me.

"Now you're stuck," she said, giggling.

I raised a finger to my lips, shushing her, but she was right. If I left now, the dorm mom would surely see me, unless of course she'd ignored the alarm altogether. I paced to the window, but quickly confirmed we were too high up for me to climb down.

"Do you mind if I brush my teeth?" she asked.

I shook my head, chuckling. Giada went into the adjoining bathroom shared with the other two suitemates, so I took the opportunity to check out her room. When she came back, she wore a fluffy pink bathrobe. I couldn't tell if she'd put it on over her sundress or if that was the only thing she was wearing, and the possibility drove me crazy.

"You should keep drinking water," I told her.

Surprisingly, she complied.

"I thought you didn't drink," I said.

Her face soured. "I don't. I mean, I haven't before. And I never will again."

Somehow, I doubted that last part, especially since she already seemed to be sobering up. "What did your father do?"

"What? How did you know about that?" she asked, as awestruck as if I'd predicted the future. Maybe she was still drunker than I thought.

"You told me it was your father's fault you were drinking."

"Oh. He's just being a jerk. He was supposed to have this big birthday party—I mean—he always does. And now he says he isn't having one this year. But like, it's his fiftieth birthday. That's a big one, right? He should still celebrate."

"If it's his birthday, shouldn't he get to decide how he wants to celebrate?"

"Well, yes, but he's not actually canceling his party. It's still happening, just without me. I've been looking forward to seeing the whole family since he first told me he was banishing me to this dumb school, and now..." she sighed and flung herself backwards against her plush unicorn pillow.

"Why would he have a party and not invite you?"

"He hates me."

"Why would he hate you? Because you're a girl?"

"No! And I don't want to get into it. Something happened a few years back and he blames me. Well, I blame me, too, but..." she blew out a sigh. "Whatever. I'm just mad and I thought I would get back at him by going out and doing everything he doesn't want me to do."

"Pretty sure you didn't do *everything* yet," I said with a wink. Giada took way too long to figure out what I was insinuating, but when she did, she chucked a pillow at me. I tucked it behind my back.

We made small talk for a few minutes, but between Giada's drunkenness and my distraction by her near-nakedness, the conversation didn't flow.

"I'm sure the coast is clear now," I said, feeling anything but sure. If I stayed in that room alone with Giada for another minute though, I was certain I'd do something stupid.

I peered out the peephole, and when I didn't see anyone in the hall, I snuck out. I made it down each flight of stairs, then headed for the side door, prepared to prop it open for the next rule-breaker to arrive home.

"Stop!" called a loud voice.

I picked up the pace without checking who had spoken or how close they were, focused solely on getting out that door.

I made it out, and as the cool night air hit my face, I had just enough time to smile before I ran smack dab into the night security guard.

- Giada -

I awoke to an intense throbbing in my head. I squeezed my eyes shut, willing the pain to disappear, then slowly rolled out of bed. I shook open the bottle of pills on my desk and popped two into my mouth, washing them down with half a bottle of water. Pressing my fingers against my temples, I decided to be grateful I only had a headache and wasn't still nauseous.

I tried to remember how much I'd drank, or why I'd thought it was a good idea to drink in the first place. The last half of the night was fuzzy, but I had distinct memories of drinking, dancing, and… Luca.

Oh God.

I spotted Luca's jacket at the foot of my bed and suddenly recalled nearly barfing in his car. If there was something more mortifying than emptying my stomach contents in front of the hot upperclassman who wanted nothing to do with me, it would probably be having to return his jacket.

Crap.

My gut told me to get it over with. Whenever I next saw Luca, it would be mortifying.

I found my phone and tapped out a quick text. "Forgot to return your jacket. Should I drop it by your dorm today?"

I sent the message before I could second guess myself.

Elise returned right around the time my hangover was starting to fade. She still wore her clothes from the night before and seemed perplexingly well-rested for someone who'd been out all night.

"Ahh, I'm so glad you made it home last night. I was worried!" she said.

I smiled, although she hadn't been worried enough to actually call. Or to avoid ditching me at a party with a bunch of people I barely knew. "I left shortly after you did."

"That's good. Did Amber give you a ride?"

"No, um, Luca did."

Her smile widened like there was something juicy about that notion.

"It's not like that. He treats me like his sister."

"Hmm, well that's a bummer. I was with Jason. I think we got like, I don't know, two hours of sleep at most last night. But O.M.G. It was worth it." She plopped onto her bed dramatically. "I think I'm in love."

I had no response for that. From what little I knew about Elise so far, she fell in love easily and often. And I got the impression her definition of love maybe just meant that she'd hooked up with a guy, but I wasn't in a position to judge.

When she finished telling me way too many details about her night, I moved out to the common area. I watched a movie with my suitemates, caught up on some homework, then texted Luca again.

"Heading out for a walk on campus. Want me to drop off your jacket?"

I waited a half hour, but no response.

Just as I started on my walk, my phone buzzed. I smiled, glad Luca called rather than texted. But then as I went to answer, I saw it was my brother, Matteo.

I answered already, knowing exactly what he planned to say. He was always the one the family would have try to patch things up with me when I was angry.

We spent a few minutes on small talk without him mentioning my dad's birthday, and then he asked what I'd done so far this weekend.

I was about to give my generic "nothing much" response, but then realized honesty would let him know exactly how pissed I was at my parents.

"I went to a party off campus last night, drank way too much, and then snuck a boy into my dorm room," I said.

The line went silent for a moment and then my brother laughed. "Sounds great. What did you really do?"

"I just told you." I paused, then pressed further, determined to give my story credibility. "You should have told me not to drink on an empty stomach. And to stay hydrated. I nearly threw up on the guy."

"Wait, Giada are you being serious? You actually got drunk last night?"

"Yeah."

"Jesus."

"He has nothing to do with this. If you want someone to

blame, blame Dad. If he's going to punish me anyway, I might as well do something worth punishing."

"You're too young to drink, Giada. And boys?" He hissed under his breath. "They should've sent you to a girl's school. Or a nunnery."

"They might as well have if they're never going to let me return home."

"It's not like that, Giada. There's things going on now, everything with dad's business, it's… I don't know. They're being really cautious now."

"Is he still having his party?"

The lengthy silence told me the answer.

"Look, Giada, I get that you're mad, but don't do stupid things just because you're mad. You're the only one you hurt if you get in trouble with some boy."

I rolled my eyes, pretty sure that if I got into *that* type of trouble with a boy, the boy would be the one hurting by the time my family was done with him.

"He was just a friend," I said. "And I'm never drinking again, but Mom and Dad can't keep treating me like a second-class citizen."

"If you're going to be reckless, Dad will send someone to keep tabs on you. If you want your freedom, show him you've earned it," he said.

There was some commotion in the background, so I wasn't surprised when Matteo said he had to go.

"Take care and don't do anything stupid," he said.

"Yeah, you too," I replied. I hung up, finished my walk around campus, then headed back to the dorm for a nap before dinner.

- Luca -

*A*pparently, sneaking into the girls' dorm after curfew counted as two separate offenses. And the fact that I ran from the dorm mom didn't help my case. Nor did the security guard's statement that I "reeked of alcohol." I demanded a breathalyzer to prove my innocence, but apparently I had no such rights at school.

It wouldn't have been so bad if my papà had been back in Italy. When international students got suspensions, it was generally in-house. From what I'd seen, you'd have to be really bad to get banished out of the country.

Anyway, my papà met with the headmaster. They told me to load up my backpack and whatever else I needed for the weekend while the two scariest men in my life discussed my life behind closed doors. When they finished, my papà looked stern, but said nothing. He simply snapped his fingers then sauntered off to the sedan idling out front.

I nodded an informal greeting to the guys up front, Arturo and Tony. They went almost everywhere with my papà. None of us talked for several minutes, and that was just fine by me. Some kids liked to get it over with when they knew they were in trouble, but I was the opposite. The longer my papà had to cool off, the less angry he'd be.

"Mr. Andrews told me they caught you sneaking out of a girl's room after curfew. But you wouldn't tell anyone which girl?"

I shrugged in lieu of answering. I was in trouble regardless… no reason to drag Giada into it.

My papà slapped the side of my head, sparking a high-pitched ringing in my ear. "You will show me the respect of answering me out loud when I ask you a question. Now is that correct that you wouldn't tell them her name?"

"Si, signore," I replied, boldly locking eyes with him.

"What's so special about this girl that you'll take the fall for her?"

"Niente," I said. *Nothing*. And that was true. There was no reason to tell them, regardless of the girl.

"What's her name?"

I pressed my lips together, still maintaining eye contact. I figured it made me look tougher, but it also enabled me to see his hand move before it connected with my cheek this time. I winced, running my tongue over my teeth as if expecting to taste blood. He hadn't actually hit me hard; it was more just the shock of it all.

"I'll give you one more chance to tell me her name, Luca."

I crossed my arms over my chest, stretched out my legs, and turned to face the back of the seat ahead of me. I held my breath, waiting for the next blow, but it didn't come. After a moment, my uncle turned around and clapped my papà on the knee jovially.

"Well done, my boy," he said to me, patting my leg proudly before turning back to my papà. "You didn't raise a rat, Salvatore. That's for sure."

I turned to my papà, confirming that he, too, was grinning. *Huh?* First he was pissed that I wouldn't answer and now they were...praising me? Maybe Gavin was right...Italians were weird.

"So I'm not in trouble?" I asked finally.

The party tone instantly evaporated.

"Of course you're in trouble. If you break a rule, it had better be for a good reason. Fooling around with some girl? Not a good reason. And don't even get me started on how your mamma will react if you get some girl pregnant."

"I'm not even..." I began, but his eyes widened enough to remind me not to interrupt.

"You're a smart boy, and you need to start acting like it. You want to break rules? You want to sneak around? Then don't get caught. Don't be dumb. If I have to pick you up again, it isn't going to be pretty."

From that statement, I assumed that this weekend wouldn't be so bad.

I was wrong.

We drove to a warehouse about twenty minutes from our Staten Island home. I recognized the place as one of the storage facilities my papà used for work sometimes. He handled international shipments, meaning lots of shipping crates and lots of time at the docks. My uncle stepped out of the car when my papà and I did, and the look in his eye told me something bad was going to happen.

But I never would've guessed the truth.

Two more guys met us inside the warehouse. It was dark, and the stench of mildew was overpowering at first. I raised my hand over my nose to muffle the smell.

"You are old enough to know that there are consequences in life, Luca. Everything you do, or don't do, has a consequence. Every choice you make has consequences. Even the tiniest mistake can cost you your life. And I don't know a better way to teach you that lesson, Son."

My papà turned towards the brightly illuminated door. "I'll be back in three hours," he said, presumably to me. Then, he turned to the two guys who were apparently staying behind. He spoke in Italian to them, but his words translated clearly: "No broken bones."

I barely had time to question what he could've possibly meant when the first guy kicked me. His booted foot hit the back of my knee, knocking me off balance so that when the second guy charged at me, I toppled like a domino. I drew my arms in front of my face, blocking the blows as best I could as they kicked me over and over and over.

When there was finally a pause, the one guy grabbed my arms, yanking them both above my head. Before I could even scramble to get my feet beneath me, the other guy punched me right in the face. Pain radiated from my gums to my nose, and with the second hit, my eyes throbbed and I saw stars. When he hit me a third time, the world turned black.

When I came to, I was laying on the damp concrete floor. The room was cold, and the heavy stench of mildew filled the darkness. I appeared to be alone, but I moved slowly, afraid to be wrong. The floor beneath me was slippery and, raising a hand to my face, I realized the puddling on the ground was my own blood. As my eyes adjusted to the dimness of the room, I spotted my backpack and duffel bag alongside the far wall of the warehouse.

I rose slowly to my feet, unsure if my legs would even support me, then made my way to my stuff. I hoisted my backpack onto my shoulders, wincing from the weight of it, and reached into my duffel. On top of my phone, there was a small roll of hundred dollar bills. I would've laughed at the irony of it all if my face didn't hurt so much. Why would my papà leave me money, but let his friends beat the shit out of me?

Real stellar parenting.

I shoved the money into my pocket and did the same with my phone, only after noticing I had an unread text from Giada, apologizing for keeping my jacket.

I grimaced. If I'd been wearing my favorite jacket when I left school, it would be ruined now.

I pushed through the thick door exiting the warehouse, half expecting another guy to jump me and force me back into the damp, dark building. But no one did. I actually didn't see or hear anyone until I got a good fifteen yards or so from the building. Then I noticed a few guys working. I wasn't sure if they worked for my papà, or if they knew what he'd done. They just eyed me warily and I did the same to them.

I walked until I was on a main street, then checked my phone again. There wasn't a bus stop nearby, so I called for a car. I had enough cash to get pretty much any place I wanted to go, and then I could use a credit card to pay for a hotel until it was time for me to return to school.

I wondered what would happen if I went back to school now,

and told them the truth about everything that had happened that day. Would they believe me? And even if they did, would it matter? Based on how much money I suspected my papà gave that stupid institution, they'd probably turn the other way and let him do whatever he wanted to me. What's a little child abuse in the face of a new library?

My phone dinged to alert me that my ride was approaching, so I picked up my bags again. I tried to keep my head down as I climbed in, but the driver's eyes locked on me in the rearview mirror.

"Are you alright man?" he asked, genuinely concerned about either me or his leather upholstery.

"Just great," I replied.

"Am I taking you to the hospital?"

I wished I could see how bad I looked, but then it might just make me feel worse. "No, um, I need to catch a train."

The driver stared at me for another minute before shifting the car into Drive. "Okay, but um, if you want to like go by the police station or something, we could. Were you mugged?"

"No, and I don't want to talk about it. Please just drive."

Thankfully, he did.

I'd cleaned up at the train station and then, realizing I couldn't use my credit card without alerting my papà to my location, I caught the train back to the station nearest school. I paced around the station, trying to decide which of my friends would pick me up and front the cash for a hotel when I saw a familiar face.

He wasn't a student at my school, but he hung out with my suitemate a lot. Actually, I suspected they did a lot more than just hang out, but our campus wasn't so progressive that one could just admit that sort of thing out loud. Anyway, we hadn't even officially met, but Marcus had told me the guy was from Italy, and that had stuck with me. A lot of guys in the area considered themselves Italian, but few actually ever lived there.

I turned away quickly, not wanting him to notice my face and mention it to Marcus, but I was too slow.

"Hey!" he called.

I kept walking in the other direction, hoping he'd give up. He didn't, and when he clapped his hand on my shoulder, pain surged through me.

"Hey, you're uh one of Marcus's roommates, right?" he asked.

"Yeah," I mumbled, without turning.

"What's your name again?"

I blew out a sigh.

He skipped around to face me. "Holy shit, man. Have you seen your face?"

"Yes." I'd tried to clean it as best I could, but parts of it had already formed scabs, and I didn't want to bust those open trying to scrub out the blood.

"Shit, that looks really bad. Do you need anything?"

I hesitated, unsure how much I could trust this guy.

"I've got a car here. You need a ride someplace?"

"Yeah, actually that would be great." I paused. "I'm Luca Marino."

"Alessio Rizzo. Piacere di conoscerti," he said. *A pleasure to meet you.*

That brought a smile to my face. "Where are you from?" I asked.

"Rome."

I nodded and we discussed neighborhoods until we reached the car.

"So are you headed back to campus?" he asked.

"Uh, no. I, uh…" I tried to think of a place nearby to stay. "I was suspended, actually, so—"

"Is your family back in Italy?"

"My mom is, but my papà is in New York. He picked me up on campus earlier today, but…" I shut up when I realized I'd said too much.

"You got in a fight?"

"Yeah."

Alessio stared at me with an uncomfortable thoroughness. "Your hands look pretty clean for someone who got in a fight. Guessing you lost?"

I nodded.

We reached his car, a Kia that looked about as beat up as me. Alessio climbed in the driver's seat, still eying me warily.

"I guess I'll just go to a hotel," I said finally. "I think there's one—"

"Listen man," he interrupted. "I've got one of those too."

"One what?"

"A dad that treats me like a punching bag."

"He didn't…it wasn't…" I blew out another sigh.

"You're welcome to stay at my house for a couple days if you want. It's not as fancy as a hotel, but my mom's hardly ever home."

That offer was surprisingly tempting to me. I didn't want to be alone, but I also didn't want to be with anyone I knew. And it wasn't like I had a lot of options. Except there was one tiny problem. "I'm not, um, well, I'm not into guys."

Alessio made a sour face then laughed. "Yeah man, you're not my type either. I was just offering you the couch."

"That would be great, thanks," I said, feeling ridiculous. "I'm sorry, I just got the impression that you and Marcus maybe had something going on."

"Oh we do," he said. "And that's actually why my dad used to hit me. You know the old theory that you can beat the gay out of someone? Yeah, it didn't work. But no, just because I'm into some guys doesn't mean I'm into all guys."

"Yeah. I'm…sorry." I mumbled my apology then turned to the window. "Does your father still live with you?"

"Nope, he's back in Italy. Mom left him."

"That's good."

"Your parents still together?"

"Yeah."

"Your mom not know what he's like or is she just trapped?"

I hadn't really ever considered that before, whether my mom had a meaningful opportunity to leave my papà and chose not to or if she really was stuck. I didn't for a second believe she still loved him, but that had never really been how their relationship worked.

"She knows," I finally said.

Alessio nodded, then thankfully let the remainder of the drive pass in silence.

CHAPTER 4

THE TRUTH COMES OUT

- Giada -

Saturday church services dragged on and on. I couldn't stop wondering why Luca had never texted back about his jacket, and the fact that I couldn't stop thinking about it drove me crazy. It wasn't like he'd never ignored me before. After our little picnic outside the school kitchen, he hadn't spoken to me for days. So why should I expect Luca to jump at my call after I nearly puked all over him?

The second services ended, I pulled out my phone.

"Just leaving church. Will drop off your jacket now."

I took my time walking back to my dorm, collecting the jacket, then heading over to Luca's dorm. But he still didn't reply. Girls weren't allowed past the first floor living area, so it wasn't like I could just drop it off at his room. Instead, I went inside then texted again.

"Here," was all I said.

I blew out a sigh, feeling like a total idiot. Obviously he didn't need his stupid jacket back that urgently if he couldn't bother to reply.

"Giada?"

I turned in the direction of the voice, but it wasn't Luca. It was his roommate.

"Oh hey," I said. "I was trying to drop this off for Luca, but he's not answering his phone." I held up the jacket lamely.

"He's not here," Gavin said, shaking his head.

"Oh."

"He got suspended."

"Oh," I repeated, feeling my eyes go wide. That seemed like a pretty steep penalty, especially if it had started over a weekend.

"He got busted leaving the girls' dorm way after curfew," he continued. "He wouldn't tell anyone which girl he was with, but…" The look on his face told me he knew exactly whose room Luca had been in.

"Crap," I mumbled. No wonder Luca was ignoring my texts. He must hate me. He went out of his way to help me out and then he got busted.

"He'll be back Tuesday. I can give him the jacket."

"Thank you."

I thrust the jacket into his arms then hurried out. I didn't pause until I got back to my dorm. Alone in my room, I sat down to compose another text.

"Left your jacket with Gavin. He told me you were suspended. Didn't get details, but I assume it is my fault. I am so sorry. If there's anything I can do, let me know."

I was still glaring at my phone moments later when Luca replied.

"No prob," was all he'd said.

I buried my face in my pillow and let out an exasperated scream.

"Uhh you okay?"

I lifted my head to see Blair eying me warily from the hall. I stifled a groan. Out of all of my suitemates, Blair was the one I'd warmed to the least. She wasn't an outright bitch, but she definitely had that look about her that convinced me she talked crap about me every time we weren't together.

"Yeah, sorry. Just frustrated. Guy drama," I explained.

She wrinkled her nose as though smelling something putrid. "Do you have like a boyfriend at church or something?"

I wasn't sure why that possibility disgusted her, but didn't care to get into it. Not today anyway. "No. He's...not my boyfriend. What are you up to today?"

"I have a date later, so Brinley and I are heading out for mani-cures in a bit. You could probably join if you want."

As much as I didn't want to spend an hour with Blair, a mani/pedi was just the thing to relax me and take my mind off of stupid Luca. And besides, Brinley was nice. "Yeah, that sounds great actually. I'll get ready."

- Luca -

*A*lessio lived in a small three bedroom Cape Cod not too far from campus. It was in a nice enough residential neighborhood, one where all the houses had the same size lot and same general style. A carport or single car garage sat beside each home, but a row of older vehicles still lined the street like they were organizing for a junker parade. Alessio parked his car right in front of the house, even though the carport was open. Patches of weeds dotted the lawn, but the flowers lining the front porch were vibrant.

Alessio's mom hadn't been home when we first arrived, so he'd given me a quick tour then left me alone to shower and tend to my wounds. I'd expected to look better after rinsing off all the blood, but the opposite occurred. Bruises dotted my body and places I didn't even recall being hit were swollen. I'd been all ready to sleep on the couch after we'd ordered pizza and watched a movie, but Alessio said I could crash in his sister's room. She attended community college now and spent most nights at her boyfriend's apartment.

Mrs. Rizzo came home after ten, reeking of grease and coffee, and looking bone tired. She was friendly and welcoming to me, and didn't bat an eye at my injuries. She offered me some antibacterial ointment, accepted the pizza and tea her son heated up for her, then escaped to her room for a long shower. I tried not to compare her to my own mother, who had never worked.

The next morning, Alessio's mom had left for work before we were even awake. Apparently, she pulled a lot of double shifts. Alessio and I grabbed breakfast at the diner where his mom worked, then return to his house to play video games.

It was surprisingly easy to talk with Alessio. I wasn't sure if that was because of our shared heritage or because he wasn't a part of my school crew. Regardless, he was one of the most easygoing and least judgmental people I'd ever met. As far as I could tell, he didn't have any agenda except to hang out and have fun. We had the house to ourselves again until shortly after lunch.

From my spot on the couch, I saw the familiar car pull up. "Cazzo!" I swore in our native language.

"What's wrong?" Alessio followed my gaze to the large picture window just as Tony Vito climbed out of the car. "Is that your dad?"

"No," I said, feeling only the slightest twinge of relief. "It's a guy who works for him."

"Ignore him."

"He won't go away," I replied, right as Tony's fist began pounding.

Alessio leapt to his feet. "Go back to my room and lock the door. I'll handle him."

I froze, not sure that was the best solution, but Alessio was already tugging the door open. I had no choice but to scram.

"Hi. I'm looking for Luca," Tony said, his tone unexpectedly friendly.

"I don't know anyone by that name, sorry," Alessio replied.

"Well, his phone is here. So either you stole his phone or you're lying."

"I must have stolen the phone then," Alessio said. "Sorry I didn't catch your name."

They exchanged introductions with almost comical calmness. Then, Tony returned to business.

"Look, I don't got all day, kid, and I need to talk to Luca. So if you want to make this difficult, we can, but—"

"Jesus, I'm here," I called before Tony made a threat Alessio wouldn't forget. I popped my head around the doorway.

Tony pushed forward, but Alessio held him back with the door.

"My mom doesn't let me invite strangers in the house. You can talk to Luca from there," Alessio said.

Tony shook his head, chuckling. "Your friend has some balls, Luca. Too bad your brains aren't as big."

I stepped closer to the door, crossing my arms in front of my chest.

"The next time you are hiding from someone, lose your phone. People can track you," Tony said.

"I wasn't hiding from anyone, but if that's all, you can go."

"Your father wanted me to tell you that you're old enough now to be treated like a man." Tony glanced at Alessio then continued. "He wants to start training you for the family business."

"Not interested."

"It's not optional, Luca. Maybe when you're older, you'll have a choice, but for now…" he shook his head. "It's all about consequences, Luca. You listen, do as your told, stay smart, good things will happen. When he calls, you answer. Understood?"

I scowled but nodded.

Tony reached his hand into his inside pocket, revealing a large handgun tucked in his belt. He pulled a neatly clipped stack of cash from his pocket and held it out to me. I shook my head.

"I don't want his money."

"You're stuck with him whether or not you take the money, so don't be an idiot," Tony replied.

Annoyed, I snatched it.

"Nice to meet you Mr. Rizzo. You've got potential," Tony said, turning and walking back to his car.

"Potential?" Alessio repeated with a frown as he slammed the door. "What an ass. Tell me again how you know this guy?"

I blew out a sigh and stared at the stack of cash in my hand. Normally, I had no problem taking my papà's money. But this time, I wasn't lying when I said I didn't want it. Just touching it made me feel dirty.

"I guess dinner is on me. And whatever else we need," I said, tossing the full stack of bills to Alessio. "Can you keep a secret?"

"Yeah."

"I don't think my papà's business is entirely legal," I said.

Alessio laughed so hard that he snorted. "No shit, Sherlock. You don't spend the first decade of your life in Italy and not recognize a mobster when they knock on your door."

I had no response. As far as I knew, none of my friends had ever actually guessed before.

"Is your dad like a captain, or…?"

I knew what he was asking and the truth was, I had my suspicions but I wasn't sure. It wasn't exactly the sort of thing you could just come right out and ask, especially when your papà was like mine. "I don't know, but I've never seen him work for someone else. All the guys I meet always answer to him."

"Fuck, dude. That's a lot to deal with. Why don't we take this cash and go pick up some girls?"

He swatted my back and then started off into his room like it was a done deal.

I got so focused on deciding whether that plan would distract me or if my mood was too shitty to enjoy it anyway that I didn't process the detail for a full minute.

"Wait, *girls*? What about Marcus?"

"What about him? We're seventeen. It's not like we're married."

"Okay, but...you like guys."

Alessio chuckled. "Yeah, but girls can be fun too. I'm not about to limit myself."

"So...you're bi?"

"I don't know, maybe. Enough with the labels. Do you have anything else to wear?"

I laughed, but went to change. We had a blast that night, and all day Sunday was pretty sweet too. Despite the obvious money struggles, I found myself wishing I had parents like Alessio's. Well, at least his mom. From everything he said, it seemed his father was just as douchey as mine.

Alessio returned to school Monday morning, but I wasn't allowed back on campus until Tuesday. I had fully prepared to simply move into a hotel when he left for school, but Connie, his mom, invited me to stay. Alessio left for school bright and early, leaving his Connie and me alone with a pot of coffee and the rest of the bagels I'd picked up the night before.

Connie was a thin woman, but I could tell she was strong. Maybe not in actual muscle, but definitely in spirit. She gnawed off a bite of bagel, tugged her ragged bathrobe tighter around herself, and eyed me sympathetically.

"Alessio is a good kid," she began, speaking to me in Italian. "But he can get into trouble."

I didn't have a response to that, so I shoved a massive chunk of bagel into my mouth.

"He tells me you're one of his friends from the boarding school in town," she continued, pausing and raising an eyebrow.

"Yes, ma'am. I'm a Junior. Alessio is friends with one of my roommates, Marcus."

Her eyebrow quirked at my use of the word "friends," but she didn't say anything to contradict the label. "You seem like a nice kid, and Alessio has always been an excellent judge of character." Connie paused and snorted sardonically. "He figured out what kind of a man I married far before I did."

I winced and focused all of my attention on the bottom of my coffee mug.

"Sorry. I'm still bitter. Anyway, it's still my job to look out for him. So I guess I'd like to hear it firsthand from you. Are you a nice kid, Luca? Or are you trouble?"

The bread lodged in the back of my throat as I scrambled to come up with a suitable answer. The woman had opened her home to me when I needed it, so I wasn't about to lie. But the truth wasn't going to do either of us any favors, either. I pushed away from the table and refilled my coffee mug, choking down a burning hot sip to dislodge the bagel in my throat. Then I brought the pot to the table and refilled Connie's mug, too.

She thanked me, then focused her eyes on mine to let me know she was still expecting a response.

"I'm trying to be a nice guy, but trouble seems to follow me," I finally said.

She blinked, showing no real emotion over my answer. "Alessio seems to think your father has a lot in common with his own father. He said you didn't get that from a fight."

Suddenly, I felt naked despite my shorts and sweatshirt. I wanted to run away, or at least throw a blanket over my head. Instead, I just ate. After a few more bites, I had the strength to talk again. "I was suspended from school because I walked a girl back to her room."

"Your girlfriend?"

I couldn't help but grin at that thought, but I shook my head. "No, just a girl. A good girl. She had a rough night and I was trying to be a nice guy by getting her to her room, but I got caught. And it was dumb because nothing happened, but nobody would ever believe me if I said that."

Mrs. Rizzo didn't say anything. She simply sipped her coffee and listened with a calmness I found unusually soothing.

"Anyway, I shouldn't have gotten myself suspended. And I'm okay now and I've learned my lesson and whatever, so it's all good. You don't need to worry about me, but I probably am trouble."

She inhaled slowly, then exhaled as she rose from the chair. "Do you have anything you need to do today or would you be able to help out with some little projects around the house?"

I hadn't expected that response so it took me a moment to answer. "I'm not really handy, but I'm free all day."

She nodded and smiled. "Good. I'm going to shower now and get ready for work but I'll show you what I need done before I leave. Sound good?"

"Yeah. Yes ma'am."

She chuckled and started out of the room, then paused and turned back to me, abruptly switching to English. "Don't write yourself off just yet, Luca. The true troublemakers never own up to it."

I thought about that until I heard the shower switch on upstairs. I sure hoped she was right.

- Giada -

I didn't see Luca until Wednesday, when he was leaving the dining hall before first period.

"Luca!" I called. He didn't turn, so I shouted louder. "Luca!"

Then, he sped up. I took off after him, not stopping until I was right beside him.

"Luca, could you seriously not hear me calling you?" I said, reaching for his arm and then stopping, panting. "I can't chase you all over campus to return your coat."

"You could've just left it at my dorm," he said, angling away from me.

"I did, but I wanted to thank you again for helping me out and to apologize. It's all my fault you got in trouble, and then to hear that you wouldn't even tell them which girl you were with—"

"That didn't have any impact on my suspension," he said. "So, don't worry about it."

"Well, I feel terrible. If there's some way I can make it up to you…" I began, but he took off again. I lunged forward and grabbed his arm to slow him down. I was about to lecture him on being rude, but a sharp hiss escaped his lips and he raised his hand to cradle the arm I'd touched.

"Are you okay?" I asked, stepping in front of him to block his escape.

He sighed again, still dodging eye contact. "I just hurt my arm."

I peered up at him. His lip was cut open and his cheek was swollen and bruised. Dark sunglasses covered his eyes but I suspected I'd find more purplish bruises there if I lifted the glasses.

"What happened? Were you in a fight?"

Luca shifted back on his heels, seemingly resigning himself to having to talk to me. "Yeah, but I'm fine. And I need to get to class. So thanks for returning my coat, and no worries on the rest. Alright?"

I couldn't fault the guy for wanting to get as far from me as humanly possible, but I felt horrible leaving things like this. I wished there were something else I could do, some way to make it up to him.

And there was, actually. "I'll pray for you," I said.

Luca's busted lip quirked up a bit and I thought he was going to laugh at me, but instead he just nodded. "I'll see you around."

I ignored him that day in World Religions, then went to the chapel after my last class instead of doing homework like I usually would. Then, at dinner, I sat with Harper, Delaney, and some of the other students from my English class. One guy in particular, Brooks, seemed thrilled for me to sit at their table. We'd talked some in class, but I hadn't before gotten the impression he was super interested in me.

Today, that all changed. Brooks was definitely flirting, so I flirted back. The attention was exactly what I needed to pull me out of my funk. Within a few minutes, my smile came naturally. I didn't need Luca to accept my apology or to explain his behavior to me. He and I were just friends, and apparently not even very good friends. I was stupid for even considering there might ever be more between us, especially when I had other options who weren't moodier than a wet cat.

Brooks was smart, probably a better student than me. And he was cute, with light brown hair and an athletic build I'd expect from a football player, which he was. His clothes were every bit as preppy as his name, but khakis and polos looked good on him.

"I saw you at the powder puff game a couple weeks ago," he said. "I was one of the team coaches."

"Were you coaching the winning team?"

He grinned, an adorable lopsided smile. "Hard to say. We had the lead in the first half, but then the scoring gets a tad wonky, so..."

I laughed, having remembered things getting out of control there towards the end.

"You were with Luca Marino when I saw you."

I nodded, my good mood now evaporating as quickly as it had appeared.

"Are you guys, like, going out?"

I forced a laugh that almost compensated for the clenching in my stomach at the thought. "No, definitely not."

"Oh, okay," he said, looking relieved. "He's kind of…"

I didn't know where he was going with that, and as curious as I was, I didn't need any more drama in my life. "We're old family friends," I said, cutting him off from anything negative he might have been about to say.

"Cool." Brooks gazed down at his plate for an uncomfortably long moment. "Do you have plans to go to Homecoming with anyone?"

I'd totally forgotten the school had a dance coming up in two weeks. I'd been so hung up on my dad's birthday party and stupid Luca and… I realized Brooks was staring expectantly.

"Yeah, I mean I figured I'd go to the game with my roommate Elise," I said.

His cheeks flushed and he licked his lips. "Do you have a date for the dance?"

I held my breath, then shook my head.

"Well, um, I'm playing in the game, so we can't hang out then, but if you'd want to go to the dance with me…"

I smiled. As far as asking someone out, that had been pretty awkward, but also sweet. And as long as I was with Brooks, no one could accuse me of liking Luca.

"I'd love to," I said.

"Cool. Um, a couple of us guys were going to get a limo to take us to the dance but if you already told your roommate you'd ride with her—"

"No, we hadn't really finalized any plans," I interrupted. "For the dance, I mean. We were planning on going to an after-party at that farm, but that's after the actual game I think."

His smile widened. "Yeah, Sullivan's. We should go, I mean, if you're up for it."

I licked my lips and smiled back. "I'd like that."

We exchanged numbers right as it was time to leave for our

next classes. Harper caught my eye and grinned excitedly, clearly having overheard the conversation, but then I turned and saw Blair glaring at me. Hmm. I'd have to figure out what pissed her off later. Now it was time for my art class.

- Luca -

I was in the middle of a video game with Alessio when Gavin popped his head in from the common room.

"Your dad is on the phone," Gavin said.

I shook my head.

"Come on man, he already knows you're here."

I gritted my teeth but stood, wiping my palms on my jeans even though they weren't actually sweaty yet. I dodged Alessio's concerned look and went towards the door.

"Take over for me?" I asked Gavin, handing him the controller.

Gavin hesitated, but nodded. He seemed uncomfortable around Alessio. I wasn't sure if it was because of the whole gay thing or just because he didn't want to piss off Marcus. Although, after watching Alessio dance with a dozen different girls over the weekend, I wasn't sure how sold Alessio even was on Marcus or guys in general. But I liked hanging out with him. I hoped he and Marcus didn't call it quits soon since that would really make it harder for us to hang out.

"Pronto," I said, pulling the phone to my ear. My papà sure had a lot of nerve calling me after what he did. He hadn't even tried my cell phone. He must've known I wouldn't answer.

My papà greeted me and asked how I was doing like he hadn't paid someone to beat the shit out of me and leave me for dead.

"Are you serious?"

He blew out a sigh. "Son, I'm a very busy man, and I don't have time for temper tantrums."

"Tantrums? You…"

"*I* didn't do anything, and we both know that. You need to learn and prepare to take over the family business. What you… endured…is all a part of that."

I clenched my teeth together so hard I half expected to chip one. "So it wasn't a punishment for the suspension. It was just a fun learning experience?"

"Let's call it both. Listen, I have a favor," he continued.

"No." I couldn't believe the nerve of the man. Did he seriously think I'd say yes? Was I that pathetic in his eyes?

He sighed again. "I'm not asking, Luca. Marco Conti called me this morning to express some concerns that his daughter might be eager to act out this weekend. He asked that you keep an eye on her this weekend."

"Keep an eye on her? What does that mean?"

"Exactly what it sounds like, Luca. Make sure she doesn't get in trouble. Don't let her head home. Her father is hosting a large gathering this weekend and he doesn't need any distractions."

"Do you work for Marco Conti?"

My papà laughed as though that were the most ridiculous thing he'd heard all day. "I work for no one, Son. But as you'll come to learn, it's important to have friends in high places. Few things are more valuable than to have Marco Conti indebted to you."

"What if I say no?"

Now his chuckle was softer. "Have you seen the Conti girl lately? If I were you, I'd jump at the chance to spend time with her. But Marco will send someone else to babysit his daughter if you refuse. And you and I can meet up for another discussion about respect and disobedience."

"Sounds riveting, but as luck would have it, my social

calendar is wide open this weekend so I'm happy to babysit your friend's kid."

"Bravo, ragazzo. We'll talk later," he said, hanging up and leaving me wondering whether that was more of a promise or a threat.

As I made my way back into the main room, I saw that Marcus had returned.

"I'm heading down to the dining hall," I said, stepping out of the room.

Alessio followed. "Everything okay?"

I shrugged.

"Let me guess…he denied having anything to do with it?"

"No. He seemed to think I needed to learn to take a beating as part of my future career training. And he wanted a favor."

"From you?" Alessio's face contorted into a near-comical look of disbelief.

"Yeah."

"Did you tell him to go fuck himself?"

"I don't think that's an option. But this favor is one I don't mind doing anyway."

Alessio still clearly thought I was crazy, but he simply shrugged. "Alright. Let me know if you need backup."

I waited until the end of World Religions Friday to ask Giada about her weekend plans.

She frowned, already suspicious by the question. She'd made it clear that she was pissed at me for avoiding her and I couldn't exactly blame her. I'd been less than friendly with her the majority of the week. I wasn't mad at her about my suspension or ensuing weekend; I just had too much shit on my plate to deal with high school drama.

"Tonight? Bowling at the student center and then movie night back at the girls' dorm."

I couldn't hide my grimace at the lame plans.

"Why are you asking if you're only going to make fun of me?" she asked.

"Sorry. It's a reflex whenever someone mentions bowling. What about Saturday?"

"I don't know. Probably church, and…" she stopped talking and glared as I rolled my eyes.

"Sorry. Another reflex. I just can't help it."

She blew out a sigh but the look in her eyes softened. "Look, I had planned to head home this weekend for my dad's party, so I'm already miserable about this weekend. So I don't need—"

"I know, I know. Sorry, okay? I'm trying to cheer you up. I have an idea. Keep Saturday clear, okay? We're going off campus."

"Where?"

"It's a surprise."

She cocked her head to the side. "Luca, I don't want to get you in trouble again."

"No one's getting in trouble. We won't break any rules, okay? I promise."

"Can I invite Elise and Jason?"

"No."

She crossed her arms in front of her chest. "I don't want to go if I won't know anyone. You'll just ditch me and—"

I pressed my finger to her lips. "You know me. And I won't ditch you. I promise you'll have good, wholesome fun and won't think about your jerk father once."

The frown lines on her forehead deepened, but she nodded.

I waited an hour, then texted her to wear her bikini the next day. The weather promised to be unseasonably warm for late September. Not warm enough for swimming, but maybe okay for lounging in the sand. A guy could hope, anyway.

- Giada -

*L*uca refused to tell me where we were heading when we left campus late morning. I'd complied with his request to wear a bikini, but I'd hidden it under denim shorts and a hot pink cropped zip-up hoodie. Public pools had surely closed for the season, but it occurred to me we might be headed to an amusement park.

Our first stop was a diner just off the highway. We made small talk after we ordered our food, but once the meals arrived, I realized Luca was staring at me.

"What? Do I have ketchup on my face?"

His grin widened. "No. I was just thinking that you're cute."

I wanted to throw my napkin over my face. "Cute, like a little sister," I said.

"Not exactly how I meant it. How's your sandwich?"

"Good. So why did you want to spend the day with me if you're still mad at me about the suspension?"

"I'm not mad. Never was. It's just a suspension. It doesn't matter."

"Your parents weren't angry?"

"My papà is always angry. I live to disappoint him."

"So why did you avoid me all week?"

"I was busy." Luca paused, looking pensive. "I have a lot on my mind."

"Like?"

His gaze dropped to his plate. "I don't want to talk about it," he finally said.

"So why spend the day with me?"

Luca's expression changed into one I knew all too well—pity. "You were looking forward to seeing your family today. And I can't make that happen, but what I can do is make today awesome for other reasons."

"I don't need you to waste a day with me because you feel sorry for me."

"That's not what's happening. So hurry up and eat."

I did as I was told, then we returned to the car. Luca played some Italian music in the car, singing along. At stoplights, he'd lean over as if serenading me with these lyrical words I didn't understand. I'd never seen him so carefree before, and his good mood was contagious. By the time we'd reached our mystery destination, I was smiling and dancing right along with him.

He climbed out of the car, reaching for a backpack from the back seat.

I stood and grabbed my stuff as well, looking around perplexed. "Okay, I give up. Where are we?"

"Gooseberry Beach," he said. He reached for my hand, leading me across a large sand dune. I gazed up to see a narrow beach followed by a huge expanse of deep blue water.

Luca released my hand but stopped beside me. I felt his eyes on me, but I didn't look away from the water.

"It's no Mediterranean Sea, but…"

"It's good," I said, turning to him with a smile. "Thank you!" Then, I was so relieved to actually be someplace calming and gorgeous—someplace that maybe, just maybe could take my mind off my stupid family, that I hugged Luca. I threw my arms around his neck and pulled him close.

Luca cut the hug short, shaking his head. "Come on. No need to throw yourself at me."

I rolled my eyes but followed him down to the empty beach. He spread out an oversized blanket and we both kicked off our shoes.

"Now what?" I asked.

A mischievous grin crossed his face. "Tag, you're it!" Luca shouted, tapping my shoulder before sprinting away.

Giggling, I took off after him, nearly falling in the fluffy sand when Luca abruptly changed directions. I successfully tagged him, then took off in the opposite direction. Just as I turned to see if Luca was catching up, he wrapped both arms around me, tackling me to the ground. He shifted midair so he landed first, pulling me on top of him.

Luca grinned up at me, his arms still clasped behind my back. "Well this is nice," he teased.

I scrambled to my feet while Luca laughed.

"I wasn't complaining," he said.

I sighed. "Do you flirt with all the girls?"

His cocky grin widened. "All the girls I like."

So, he did like me. But… also a lot of other girls? I tried to sort it all out in my head, but Luca started chuckling.

"You're cute when you're confused," he said.

I flung my hands in the air and turned to walk closer to the water. When I reached a smooth patch of sand, I plopped down, gazing out at the calm water. Growing up near the Atlantic, and spending most of my vacation time there, I'd never really thought much of the Rhode Island beaches, but this was gorgeous. And if it were about forty degrees warmer, I might actually consider getting in the water.

Luca sunk into the sand beside me. "Why do I get the feeling you didn't take that as a compliment?"

I shrugged. "I'm not offended. I appreciate the honesty. I just…I guess I'm not used to all the games."

"You're in high school. Life should be filled with games."

I raised my hand to my hair, hiding my frown from him.

Luca shifted so he was in front of me, then brushed the hair out of my eyes. "Giada, I do like you. I don't take all the girls out here. Only my favorite. The ones I don't like just get to visit Pebble Beach with me."

I gazed up at Luca. He looked sincere, but those deep brown eyes of his were distracting.

"I get the impression you haven't had a lot of boyfriends," he continued.

"I haven't."

He turned away to face the water for a minute. "There's this story, la principessa e il ranocchio," he began, turning back to me. "The princess and the toad."

"Frog," I corrected.

He shrugged. "There's a saying they get from that story, that you have to kiss a lot of frogs before you find your prince."

I shook my head. I'd heard the expression before, but didn't see the relevance.

"My point, Giada, is that you are la principessa. And I am no frog."

"You think you're a prince?"

He grinned and winked.

"What does that even mean?"

"I'm saying go find some frogs, and then we'll talk."

I considered his words. "I'm going to homecoming with Brooks Adler."

"I heard."

"What if he's my prince?"

"He's not," Luca said with a confident snort that annoyed me.

"What do you have against him?"

Luca shrugged. "Nothing. If I were into guys, he would totally be my type."

"What if Brooks and I really hit it off and start dating?"

"That would be my loss, I guess."

"Are you ever serious?" I asked.

He took his time answering. "Almost always. But it's something about you… you bring out this less serious side of me."

"Really? You're blaming me for the fact that you're an immature clown?"

He playfully tossed a handful of sand in my direction. "I was saying it is a good thing. Being with you makes me happy and carefree."

That statement seemed alarmingly serious coming from him. "Who are you taking to homecoming? Or are you too cool for school dances?" I asked, praying despite the unfairness that he'd say the later.

"Emily Clarke."

My stomach tightened. I didn't know her, but I knew of her. She was gorgeous and a Junior. I could totally picture her being homecoming queen.

"Well, hopefully she's made out with enough rodents for you," I said, sounding even less mature than I felt.

Luca's expression showed no indication of how he felt about my retort. He was quiet for a moment though, as was I. "Can I ask you a question?"

I nodded. "You just did."

He quirked an eyebrow in annoyance, then continued. "The other day, you said you'd pray for me. Did you?"

I hesitated, not sure my fragile ego could take more mockery today. "Yes."

"How? I mean, what do you say?" His expression remained unchanged.

I wasn't sure what to make of his questions. Hopefully he wasn't asking me how to pray in general, because we sure didn't have time for that one. "I keep a list of people I'm praying for. God already knows what people need, so I don't get into specifics. But I asked him to help heal your physical injuries and to help you sort out whatever was on your mind."

Luca dug his fingers into the sand. His injuries were almost completely healed, and in another week he'd be back to his usual perfect self.

"Do you think it helps?" he finally asks.

I shrugged. "It couldn't hurt. And it helps me. I don't like seeing people I care about struggle, but most of the time there's nothing I can do to help. Praying is a simple thing I can do."

Luca didn't speak for a few minutes, then changed the subject. "I'll give you a hundred bucks to go for a swim."

"No way. It's freezing."

"Did you even wear a bikini?"

Boldly, I unzipped the sweatshirt.

"Damn girl," he said, making no attempt to hide that he was checking me out.

I leaned back on my elbows, loving the attention.

"Well, come on then. You got to get in the water for the money."

"I have zero interest in your money."

Luca pouted. "See, this is the problem with you rich girls. Can't get you to do anything for money."

"Not everything is motivated by money," I said.

"Most things are," he replied.

We were both quiet for a few minutes, and then Luca stripped off his shirt and sprinted into the water, shouting what I assumed was the Italian equivalent of "last one in is a rotten egg."

I couldn't help but laugh at his shrieks as the frigid water engulfed him. I had no intention of going into that ice bath, but I did stand and walk to the edge. Luca swam around for a few minutes, and then when it was clear he was coming out, I grabbed his towel and walked it to him.

He jogged towards me, shaking the water from his hair much like a dog. I held the towel out, but instead of taking it, he dove into my outstretched arms, hugging me.

I shrieked at the sudden onslaught of cold, wet limbs tangling around me.

"Ahhh," he trilled. "You're so warm."

"Luca! You're making me wet," I scolded.

He pulled back, grinning. "If I had a quarter every time a girl told me that."

His mischievous grin told me he expected some dramatic response, but I didn't know why. I couldn't imagine he often hugged girls after jumping in a lake.

"Come on, nothing?" he asked.

I shrugged.

Luca shook his head. "You're too sweet and innocent to get my dirty jokes."

"I don't even understand what you're talking about," I finally admitted.

"I know, Tesoro. And that's a good thing." Luca stepped closer, and this time when I shivered, I was sure it was from his proximity and the way he was looking at me and not from my damp shorts or bare stomach.

He leaned in and the world grew silent except for the pounding of my heart.

I braced myself for the kiss I knew was coming, but right as I was about to close my eyes, Luca inched to the side, brushing his lips across my ear.

"Find. Some. Frogs," he whispered.

I shoved him back and turned abruptly. "I'm going for a walk."

"Don't get lost!" he called after me.

I held my middle finger above my head as I made my way down the shoreline. All of the nervous energy racing through my limbs had gathered deep in my core. I needed to get away from Luca, to walk until the unsettling warmth filling my belly.

We spent another hour or so lounging in the sand when I returned, then we dusted off and headed back towards campus. We stopped at an Italian restaurant on the way home, but still itchy with sand and woefully underdressed, we ordered our food to go and ate it while seated on the hood of Luca's car.

By the time he dropped me off at my dorm, I was exhausted, happy, and past due for a shower.

"Thank you for keeping me company today," I said. "It helped."

"I'm glad. What do you got going on tomorrow?'

"Church and then some volunteer stuff. Maybe homework."

"Ooh, thrilling. Sweet dreams, Princess!"

CHAPTER 5

THE PRINCESS AND THE FROG

- Luca -

Homecoming week passed in a blur of school-sponsored spirit days and unofficial festivities, culminating with the game Friday. Lots of the school's big money alumni showed up for the game then stayed Saturday for campus tours and a big fancy dinner, so the students all had to be on our best behavior that weekend until the dance.

Emily and a friend tagged along with me and the guys to the game, but I couldn't help but notice Giada a few rows down, sitting by two of her roommates and that Jason guy one of her friends was dating. Aside from one shy wave, she seemed completely unaffected by my presence. I couldn't stop watching her, though.

I'd kept an eye on her the day after the beach date, like I'd promised my papà, but from a distance. That day was supposed to be a favor to him, and somehow it had been the best day I'd had in…I didn't know how long. Giada was just so sweet. Everything she said and did was so…kind. And innocent.

On paper, she and I had so much in common, but in reality, we couldn't be more different. Giada had spent the day at church Sunday, and she seemed happy about it. Actually, she always seemed cheerful. Even when she was supposedly sad.

Maybe her unending positivity was what intrigued me so much.

I watched as Giada laughed at something her friend said, and her entire face lit up. Giada was truly beautiful when she smiled. I wanted to be the one to make her smile like that. And I really wanted to kiss her.

I almost had at the beach, and she knew it too. I could tell Giada wanted it every bit as much as I did. But that was only because she hadn't yet realized I was not a nice guy.

"Earth to Luca!" Emily said, giggling in a way that made me wonder if she'd been drinking.

I turned to her, still in a daze over my Giada-fantasies.

"Everybody is heading to Sullivan's Farm tonight after the game. Should we go?"

I cringed at the way she said the word "we," like now that I'd invited her to homecoming, we were bound together for life. But I nodded anyway, flashing her a fake enthusiastic grin before turning back to Giada. I wondered if she would go to the farm, and if so, if she'd get drunk like last time. Probably not, I decided. While lots of people said things like "I'll never drink again" after overdoing it, Giada probably really meant it.

I shook my head, dragging my hand through my hair. If Giada went to the farm tonight, she'd probably be with Brooks. Her date for the dance. He would be the one in charge of getting her home safely, not me.

I turned back to Emily as she started cheering for something that had happened on the field. I clapped too, then leaned right over and kissed her without another thought. She looked surprised, then happy.

As it turned out, Giada was at the farm that night, and she was with Brooks. We'd won the game, so he and the other jocks were celebrating by drinking. A lot.

I had enough fun with Emily and my friends to keep my mind off Giada almost the entire time, but I had to say something to her before it got too late so she didn't think I was avoiding her again.

Giada had walked closer to the fire, and from the way she'd wrapped her arms around herself, I could tell she was cold. Brooks was back by his friend's truck, but still well within sight of us all. I wondered why he hadn't offered her a jacket.

"Hey," I greeted.

"Hey yourself," she replied. "Having fun?"

I nodded, surprised it was actually the truth. "Did you enjoy the game?"

She lifted her shoulders in a noncommittal shrug. "Football isn't really my thing, but I had fun with Elise and some of my other roommates."

"Wasn't your date playing in the game?"

Giada cast a gaze in his direction. Brooks was talking with a friend, but watching us out of the corner of his eye. "He was. And they all seemed pretty pleased with their performance."

"They won," I said. "You know that, right?"

She flashed me the spicy look she always gave me when I teased her, then glanced around us. "Your date is cute," she said, without a hint of jealousy.

I glanced back at Emily, who was talking to her friend but staring at me in a distinctly stalker fashion. "Yeah," I said, turning back to Giada. "Listen, you're not riding home with him, are you? They've all been drinking a lot, and—"

Giada shook her head, laughing. "No, Dad. We have a designated driver already on standby."

She didn't say who it was, but I trusted her.

I stared at Giada for another minute, appreciating the way the light from the flames danced across her smooth skin, casting shifting shadows. Then I patted her on the shoulder blade like we were teammates. "Have fun with your frog," I said, winking.

The second I walked back to Emily, she roped her arms around my neck and jammed her tongue into my mouth. I wasn't about to complain about a hot girl making out with me, but I couldn't help but wonder if she was trying to stake out her territory.

- Giada -

Campus was quiet Saturday. All of the students were either tired or hungover—or both, so I followed the trend and spent the early afternoon napping like everyone else. In the evening, the girls' dorm was a wash of chiffon and lace, and the variety of perfumes saturating the air made it hard to breathe.

Brooks and I were sharing a limo with a few of his football buddies and their dates, and we all stopped off for a quick dinner first. Breathalyzer tests were administered at the entrance of the dance, with signs promising the tests would be repeated at the exits. Apparently, the school administrators didn't realize most kids had drunk too much the night before to bother bringing booze to the dance.

I'd settled on a bold red dress with skinny straps and v-neckline with lace trim. The bottom flared out into an A-line shape and hit mid-thigh. The gown was definitely sexier than what I'd wear for a party with family, but not too sleezy.

Brooks was a great date—attentive, complimentary, and fun. He was a surprisingly good dancer, too. We spent the first half of the dance on the dance floor, then snagged a table to devour some of the yummy desserts. Once we'd eaten more than our fill of chocolate, I excused myself to go touch up my makeup.

On the way out of the bathroom, I slammed into Luca.

"Gotcha," he teased, grabbing my wrist and tugging me around the corner before I regained my balance.

"Were you stalking the women's bathroom?" I asked once we were alone.

He wiggled his eyebrows devilishly. "I saw you from across the room in that red dress and had to get a closer look."

I smiled and twirled in a circle to give him the full view.

"Bold choice in color, Giada. I like it."

"Thank you." I loved the way red brought out the espresso shade of my hair and my olive-toned skin. I gazed at Luca, noticing his suit had the expensive look of a true Italian designer outfit. Knowing him, it probably was, but either way, I couldn't help but appreciate the way it fit him. "You look nice, too," I finally said.

Luca grinned. "I was watching you dance."

"Creepy."

Luca ducked his head towards my neck. "You even smell good, too. What is it about you?"

I inched backwards. "Where's Emily?"

"Talking to her friends."

"I saw you guys making out last night."

"Jealous?"

"No. I'm here with Brooks."

Luca licked his lips, still staring at me with such an intensity that I felt my temperature skyrocket.

"Why'd you have to wear red lipstick?" he asked.

"It matches the dress," I replied, annoyed. "If you dragged me over here just to criticize my makeup…"

He gripped my hip, and the sensation of his fingers on my body forced me to stop talking. "You look beautiful. Like always.

But I can't kiss you while you're wearing red lipstick or then I'll be wearing red lipstick."

My whole body froze when he called me "beautiful." It wasn't the first time someone had paid me that compliment, but it was the only time the word had such a visceral effect on me. I had to remind myself to breathe, then processed the rest of what he'd said. "You can't kiss me because I'm here with Brooks."

"Details, details," he whispered.

I shook my head and snapped out of the trance. "Go back to your girlfriend."

"Not my girlfriend," Luca replied, but I'd already pulled away.

What was his deal anyway? He made it abundantly clear he thought of me as a little sister. Now he wanted to tease me and flirt with me while he was on a date.

"Screw you," I mumbled.

"Wait, Giada!" Luca called.

Against my better judgment, I turned.

"Are you mad?" Luca actually looked confused.

I swallowed hard and stomped closer. "Yeah, a little bit, Luca. You can't just mess with my head all the time. I get that I'm not some mature, worldly person like you, but I'm not an idiot. You don't get to flirt with me and look at me like that and make comments about kissing me. You," I said, accenting my word by poking him in the chest with my pointer finger. "You were the one who told me to date other guys."

His lips parted like he was going to say something, but I stormed off before he could. I had a date waiting for me who actually wanted to spend time with me and wasn't embarrassed by me.

- Luca -

J wasn't sure what to make of the encounter with Giada. I'd thought we were both having fun, flirting and playing around. I thought she liked me, though probably not as much as I liked her. I didn't know why she was mad, but I didn't like it. Giada had stormed right back to Brooks and not glanced in my direction once the rest of the night.

She actually looked like she was having fun, which I guess should've made me happy if I weren't such a dick.

Emily was all over me from the second I returned. She wanted to dance, and luckily they played two slow songs back to back, enabling me to obsess over Giada without drawing any attention. When the next fast song came on, Emily wanted to keep dancing, but I had a better idea.

"I bet if I paid the limo driver, he'd let us have it to ourselves for a bit."

Her eyes widened as she smiled. "We can't get back in if we leave. Another half hour?"

I agreed and settled for a break back at our table instead. I sipped my woefully virgin punch and gazed over in Giada's direction. She was dancing with her date, and his hands had settled dangerously low on her back. I didn't even know the guy and I had an overwhelming urge to punch him.

"So um, what's the deal with you and that new girl?" Emily asked, her voice clipped.

"Which new girl?" I asked, despite knowing exactly who she meant.

"I don't really know the froshies," she began, emphasizing the pejorative term we all used for the freshman class. "But I think her name's Giada."

"Oh, yeah. She's a Sophomore actually. But what about her?"

"I don't know. Did you two, like, used to date or something?"

"Nope."

Emily seemed surprised by my quick response. "Oh. Well, you just seemed…close for having just met."

"We grew up together, I mean, our families were close. She's a friend. Do you know anything about the guy she's with?"

Emily followed my gaze to the dance floor. "Brooks? Not really. I mean, that's pretty savage for her to ask him to the dance though. He and Blair just broke up like the last day of school."

"Blair?" I remembered hearing the name before but sure couldn't place her.

"Yeah, Blair Rutlidge. She's one of Giada's suitemates. She and Brooks went out like all last year. Rumor has it they weren't really over for good."

I cringed, familiar enough with girl drama to know that probably wasn't good news for Giada's reputation on campus.

"Not the best way to make friends at a new school, taking your roommate's man," Emily continued.

"Yeah," I mumbled, grateful when the music changed and Emily dragged me back to the dance floor.

Thirty minutes and fifty bucks later, I was alone in the back of a stretch limo with Emily Clarke. I felt bad for the driver, not just because he clearly knew what we were up to despite the dark tinted windows, but also because he was desperate enough to agree to my offer for only fifty bucks. I'd been prepared to go over a hundred.

Once we were alone, Emily launched herself at me, straddling my lap. Her perfume filled the small interior quickly, but I didn't care. We kissed until our lips were both sticky from her thick lipstick, and then I reached around and unzipped the top of her dress. She tensed when my fingers first brushed along her bare skin, but she didn't stop me from fully exploring her breasts with my hands, then mouth. She reached between us, her hand quickly settling on my zipper.

We were both breathless as we shifted, then I unzipped my pants and she hoisted up her dress. I stroked my finger up her thigh to her hip, pausing to take note of the thin fabric of her thong. Her hand reached into my pants, eliciting a sharp hiss from me as her cool finger touched my hot flesh. She grinned mischievously and I knew that I could have her right then if I wanted. And part of me really, really wanted that. But part of me was still annoyed and confused about everything else.

For once, my conservative side won out.

"Em, we shouldn't," I said, my voice ragged.

She paused. "Do you have protection?"

Like every other guy at every high school dance, I did. But her question gave me an easy out.

"No, I'm sorry."

She pulled back, the look in her eyes telling me she clearly wondered why I'd dragged her out to a limo if I wasn't prepared. But then she smiled.

"That's okay," she said, sliding off my lap and onto the floor of the limo. She knelt between my knees, grinned, then dipped her head down. She took me in her mouth, using her hands to help. Her hair cascaded around her face obscuring my view of her. I was tempted to watch, certain what she was doing looked nearly as amazing as it felt, but instead I closed my eyes, filling in the gaps with my imagination. I let my head fall back against the seat.

- Giada -

*T*he morning after homecoming, I slept late before enjoying a long, luxurious shower. Well, as luxurious as it could be in a shared space that inspired me to wear flip flops while bathing. But I had just shampooed my hair when the water turned ice cold. I shrieked loudly, almost as an instinct. Rinsing as fast as I could, I aborted the plan to luxuriate in the shower longer.

I switched off the faucet, rang out my frigid hair, then poked my head out of the shower to grab my towel. It was gone. I tugged the gross curtain back further and confirmed neither my towel nor my robe were anywhere in sight. I groaned.

"Super funny!" I called, assuming whomever had stolen my stuff was waiting outside the door, laughing. If I hadn't been so cold, I would've waited another minute to drip dry. As it was, I didn't want to wait. Bracing myself, I climbed out of the shower then poked my head around the door. My room appeared empty, so I made a mad dash through it, grabbing my blanket to dry off with. I was about to get dressed when my door swung open.

Blair stood in the entrance, holding my towel. She glared at me and dropped it on the floor, her face emotionless. "Ansley took this. I guess she was confused since apparently us suitemates are now stealing each other's stuff. Anyway, you can have it back. I don't even want to touch a skank's towel."

In less than five seconds, I figured out Blair was pissed about Brooks, but she left before I could say anything. *Whatever.* I couldn't make her see reason and I sure wasn't about to apologize when I'd done nothing wrong.

Regardless, the two weeks after Homecoming were awful. Blair continued lashing out at me for "stealing her boyfriend" and Erin and Ansley both teamed up with her. On Tuesday, when I went to apply my weekly pore-refining charcoal face mask, I found that the contents of the small jar had been replaced with blue slime.

On Friday, I squirted a dollop of my usual strawberry shampoo into my palm, then recoiled at the chemical scent. I rinsed my hand, then used by body wash to suds up my hair instead. When I returned to my room, I confirmed my suspicion. Someone had filled my shampoo bottle with a hair remover chemical that was popular for keeping bikini lines smooth.

I sighed and chucked the bottle into the trash, determined not to engage in their dumb games. Besides, aside from the spiteful pranks, Blair, Ansley, and Erin all kept their distance.

While they were busy avoiding *me*, *I* avoided all contact with Luca outside of class. It wasn't hard, since Emily was almost always glued to his side. As much as Luca's behavior perplexed me, I was glad he was still with Emily in light of all the rumors that they'd had sex in the back of a limo during the dance.

Brooks had kissed me after the dance, and it was a good kiss. I mean, I thought it was. I'd only been kissed twice before, and neither was particularly bad or great. I wasn't repulsed, but didn't feel sparks, either. I suspected true sparks only happened in romance novels and sappy movies, but that was aside from the point. I had fun hanging out with Brooks, but I was way too young for a boyfriend and certainly didn't like him enough to stir up shit with my roommates.

When Brooks asked me out again, I'd told him the truth. I said I really liked him, but needed to focus on school and wasn't looking for a serious relationship. I also told him it would've been nice if he'd mentioned that he used to date my suitemate, but he'd simply responded that they were "ancient history." Obviously, Blair didn't view the timeline the same way. Anyway, I asked Brooks if we could just be friends. He said okay and seemed fine with that, but then he was super awkward around me the next several days.

Oops.

I had more important things to focus on anyway—Halloween. Elise, Brinley, Delaney, Harlow, and I were dressing as the Spice Girls. As most fashion-minded the person in the remaining group, I was in charge of designing our costumes. I brainstormed ideas, then sketched up each one before spending hours selecting the perfect materials. I hired some help with the sewing, but the entire process was thrilling. By the last week of October, our costumes looked great and I'd found my future career—fashion design.

The school hosted a huge on-campus Halloween party every year, filled with bad, spooky music, over-the-top décor and special effects, and copious amounts of candy. Best of all, there was a costume contest, which we were guaranteed to win.

We spent the first part of the evening taking photos, then dancing as a group. I asked Brooks to dance to one song, mostly so he'd know I wasn't blowing him off, but also to show Blair that her cattiness wasn't getting to me. Later, I danced one slow song with Andy and another with Jack, then Holden, Conrad, and finally Keaton.

The event felt the way a high school dance should feel—fun and not at all serious. By the time the costume contest was announced, I was riding a serious sugar buzz and fully in love with all things high school. I made a mental note to never attend a school function with a date again. Everything was way more fun—and way less rife with drama— when I just enjoyed my friends.

Our Spice Girls costumes did win the contest—but only second place. First place went to Harley Quinn, which was a great costume but totally cliché and obviously store-bought. Still, I was happy with our prize, and proud when Elise bragged that I'd designed the costumes during her unnecessary, over-the-top award acceptance speech.

"You deserved first place," a deep, heavily accented voice said as I made my way back to the candy table for the third time.

I knew without looking that it was Luca, so I kept walking and didn't turn to face him until I'd unwrapped a KitKat. He looked hot, as always, but clearly hadn't dressed up.

"What are you supposed to be? A bad sport?"

Luca scowled then reached into his pocket, retrieving plastic vampire teeth and popping them in his mouth. "Dracula," he said. "The fangs glow in the dark."

I nodded, still unimpressed. That did at least explain Emily's costume. She wore a long blank wig and a black and purple dress that made her look like a creepy prostitute. I suspected she had fake teeth to match Luca's.

"Did you really make those?" he asked.

"Yes."

"That's really cool."

"Thanks." I tried to think of a reason I needed to go, but came up blank.

"Have you been avoiding me?"

"No," I said quickly. "Okay, maybe. School has been busy, with midterms and all, and there's been some drama with one of my suitemates."

"Blair?" he interrupted.

I felt my eyes narrow in surprise that he knew this. "Yes. How did you—"

"Emily told me you stole your roommate's boyfriend."

I rolled my eyes. "Pu-lease. They broke up last year and I had no idea they'd ever even met when I agreed to go to one stupid little dance with him."

Luca laughed and I remembered I was supposed to be explaining why I was avoiding him, not why he should be grateful be a male.

"I just don't have a lot of time for games. And I don't know what you want from me or why you keep hunting me down just to reject me, but—"

"I have never rejected you," Luca interrupted.

"Right," I said with an overdramatic eyeroll. "Just like you don't have a girlfriend. But it's fine, because I actually understand what you were trying to tell me back at the beach and I completely agree. I do not have the kind of experience you're clearly looking for in a girl, and hopefully I never will."

"What is that supposed to mean?"

"I heard all about you and Emily having sex in the back of a limo. And that might be your idea of a fun homecoming activity, but…"

I stopped talking as Gavin chose that precise moment to join us. I could tell Luca didn't welcome his presence, but he couldn't exactly banish his friend, not with his girlfriend standing twenty feet away and shooting him daggers.

"I didn't have sex with Emily in the limo," Luca said.

"Yeah, she just sucked his…" Gavin began, shutting up as Luca shot him the scariest look I'd ever seen. "I'm going to get more punch," he said, walking away.

I flung my hands in the air. "Luca, is that honestly any different in your mind? And what kind of a guy tells the whole school about it? Even if she has zero self-esteem and bad taste in boyfriends, she still deserves some respect."

"I didn't tell anyone. People just figured it out," he said.

"You don't have to defend yourself to me, Luca. It doesn't matter to me what you do."

For some reason, Luca actually appeared hurt by my words. But I didn't have time to dwell on that because Emily came up then, wrinkling her nose at me like I was some rodent in her path.

"Hi Emily," I said, flashing her the most genuine smile I could muster. "Cute costume." I swiveled and walked off before either of them could say anything to further ruin my night.

- Luca -

I felt like a total jerk after talking to Giada, and then Emily went all psycho on me and accused me of flirting. No matter how many times I told her that Giada and I were just old family friends, she still whined. I broke up with her on Tuesday. The rumors surrounding our breakup were still prevalent enough on Saturday that I was willing to leave campus for the weekend with some guy my papà sent to pick me up.

I figured I was either going to get beat up or participate in another drive-by. Either way, it would probably be less stressful than dealing with girl drama.

"Hi Luca," my driver said. "It's been a while. I'm Tomasso." He stood beside the car, wearing casual pants and a dark brown leather jacket. He looked familiar, but I had the feeling I'd only met him before in Italy. I greeted him with a nod, then climbed into the front seat.

"Is this alright?" I asked, buckling my seatbelt. "I mean, if you want to beat the shit out of me, I'm closer this way."

He didn't answer.

I tried a different method of getting answers out of him. "I actually have things to do back at campus, so if there's someplace close by we could go for you to beat me up. Unless there's some other guys meeting up with us to help you out."

I glanced over at his hands, which looked pristine. He definitely was not the guy who beat up people for a living. Maybe this wasn't another beating after all. Maybe my papà was trying something new. "Ooh are you going to dump me in the middle of nowhere with only a compass and a granola bar and see if I can find my way back to civilization? That could be cool. Not sure how it would help me in this line of work, but…"

Tomasso gazed at me, his eyebrow raised.

"So what's your role in this whole organization? You're not just a driver. You look like you could be an accountant or some shit."

He still didn't answer. His silence was infuriating.

I sighed. "You know, when parents hit their own kids, it's called child abuse. The police get involved. I haven't actually heard of too many cases where the parents pay someone else to hit their kid, but I'm pretty sure that's frowned upon too."

Still nothing. I wondered if maybe he just didn't understand.

"Parla inglese?" I asked.

He cracked a smile at that. "Si."

"So my papà pays you to stay silent."

He sighed. "Strength comes from adversity. Your struggles will make you stronger."

I gawked at him. Seriously, he finally spoke and *that* was what he said? "Wow. That's inspirational. My problems are all solved now. You should print that on a poster with a picture of a cat."

At the stoplight, Tomasso turned to me. "You're a tough kid, Luca. Everyone sees that. But you could be tougher. And not everyone agrees with your father's plan, so you need to be prepared."

I wasn't sure what he meant by that, but I didn't have much time to ask. We pulled into a deserted looking parking lot. Sweat coated my palms, and my throat was dry. I wished I'd brought a drink, although, I'd already had so much coffee that I'd probably piss myself if someone kicked me.

Tomasso led me to the front of an abandoned-looking strip mall. When we walked in an unlabeled door, I nearly keeled over at the sight. Row after row of guns filled glass cases ahead of us.

We checked in, chose our weapons, then went to a lane.

"What are we doing?" I asked, mystified. Surely my papà wasn't going to shoot me. And I didn't believe the redneck behind the counter had any affiliation with my family.

"Shooting," he said, as if it were obvious. "You know how to shoot a gun, right?"

"Of course." I'd learned to use a gun when I was ten.

"Well, now you're gonna practice."

We practiced until my shoulders were sore and my fingers started to form blisters from the trigger. We practiced with everything from a Glock, a Smith & Wesson, a 44 Magnum, and when we got bored of handguns, we tried out some pistols. Tomasso had impeccable aim, and while he didn't talk much, when he did, it was to share a useful tip.

Tomasso drove through a burger joint on the way back to campus. "Want anything?" he offered. I ordered a burger and fries. Relief flooded my system as I saw he was, in fact, driving me right back to campus.

"Your dad values discipline," he said as we neared the long winding road that led onto campus.

"No shit," I mumbled between bites.

"But that isn't what he wants from you now," Tomasso continued. "He needs to see that you are tough—physically and mentally, that you can handle the life awaiting you. And he needs to know that you have the makings of a great leader."

"And those would be…?"

He frowned, shaking his head dismissively. Apparently I had to figure that out on my own.

"He's testing you now. He needs to know your potential before he lets you in on the full business and starts really training you."

"So I just have to survive all the crap he's doing to me and I pass the test?"

Tomasso pulled into the circular drive facing the administration building and shifted into Park.

"Do you think that's what your father would do, if he were in your shoes?"

I shrugged. I tried not to think what that asshole would do.

"A leader doesn't let people walk all over him. A leader fights back."

"You want me to fight my papà?"

Tomasso sighed, making no effort to conceal his disappointment. "No. I don't mean literally. But there are no rules to this game, and yet you seem willing to follow the ones he's made up without a struggle. And that doesn't seem to me like what a leader would do."

I took the hint and exited the car.

- Giada -

*E*veryone knew when Emily and Luca broke up. I tried to ignore all the gossip, but that proved even harder than avoiding Luca himself. Elise and I spent the next weekend shopping, then I kept busy the rest of the week finishing my volunteer project for the church. I was trying to convince Father Harris to let me organize a holiday party for the children's hospital, too. Focusing my attention on that was much easier than trying to decipher Luca's random moods.

Unfortunately, about a week into my campaign to completely ignore Luca, Mr. Cobb assigned me and Luca to work together on a project. Each team had to prepare a presentation on religion in their assigned country. He assigned us Italy, so I assume he paired us together because we were both Italian. The project was worth a third of our grade, and involved a significant amount of work, but I could handle it alone. I told Luca that after class.

"What? No, we're supposed to be partners."

"Luca, it's not a big deal. I'll do the project and send it to you and you can…I don't know, add some pictures or something."

He jumped in front of me, blocking my path. "Giada, I literally spent fourteen years of my life in Italy. I may not be a straight A student, but I am an asset to you in this project."

"More like ass!" Grant shouted, brushing by us both.

I sighed. "Fine. But if you so much as think about flirting or making an inappropriate comment, I'm finishing it all solo."

Luca agreed to my terms and we met that night in the library. I took charge, dividing up the work and developing a timeline for us to complete each step. Luca stuck to the agreement and didn't flirt, but he did mock my organization. We worked until close to curfew, getting way more accomplished than we needed to, given that deadline wasn't until the last day of class before Thanksgiving.

Despite that, we met again the next day and were similarly productive. On the third day though, I was distracted.

"We're going to finish by next week at this rate," I told him. "Can we just skip tonight?"

Surprisingly, Luca looked bummed. "Yeah. Do you have other homework?"

I shrugged. "Some." Now that Elise spent her evenings on the phone with Jason, I had plenty of time to work on homework after curfew. "I just can't focus. I'm trying to convince Father Harris to let me organize a holiday party for the children's hospital and I don't know how to show him I'm up to the task."

I waited for Luca to mock me for stressing over a charity project, but he didn't. Instead, he flipped to the next page of his notebook.

"Do what you did for this project," he said. "Make a list of all the tasks and divide it up. Show him when you need to finish each task and how you'll make it happen. He'll agree. You're hard to say no to."

I refrained from pointing out that *he* seemed to have no problem with telling me no. Instead, I focused on his suggestions. With Luca taking notes, we made the master list for all party planning tasks. I came up with a budget and a list of tasks we'd need volunteers for, and then I assigned dates for figuring out all the other details.

We were nearing curfew when we finished.

"Why are you being so nice to me?" I asked.

"Because I like you."

I made a face even though I'd sort of set him up for that one.

"I'm not flirting. I do like you. You're a good person and I like being around you. I'd really like to be friends."

His over-the-top puppy dog expression undercut his sincerity a tad, but I still believed him.

"I would like that too," I said, tearing out the notes and sticking them into my calendar. "Now I just need to figure out how to raise that much money and then plead my case to Father Harris."

"You could just write a check," Luca suggested. "Or I could."

"I don't have access to that kind of money!" After factoring in food and drinks, decorations, entertainment, and small gifts for each of the kids, I'd reached five thousand as a decent budget number.

"I find that hard to believe. But I can get you that much by Thanksgiving if you want."

I tried to decide whether he was being serious or not, then let my mind wander for a moment as to how he had access to that much money. I shook my head, not needing to venture down that rabbit hole.

"Fine. But tell Father Harris you've already raised half the money. That'll help your case for sure."

I thanked him and went back to my dorm to type up the notes. I emailed my proposal to Father Harris that night, and by morning, he agreed to my plan. I texted Luca in the morning to tell him the good news and thank him for his help. He didn't reply until I saw him in person after English.

"Congratulazioni," Luca said, pulling me close for a hug that probably bordered on flirting. "Shall we meet tonight to celebrate? I was planning to order pizza."

After weeks of campus-dining, pizza sounded amazing, but I wasn't going to be that easy for him to trick into our old patterns. "We can celebrate after the party is a success. I'm up for pizza tonight but only if you help me figure out the menu and the entertainment for the party."

"It's a deal," he said, smiling.

We spent the majority of the weekend on our project, finishing it a full week before the due date.

"Can we celebrate finishing the project?" Luca asked as we left World Religions class together on Monday.

"What do you have in mind?"

"Dinner?"

I raised an eyebrow.

"Not a date. Just dinner. I've been craving arrabiata sauce all week though and you'd appreciate the best Italian restaurant in town more than anyone else here."

Shoot. Luca had quickly figured out the best way to get time alone with me—food. Specifically, good Italian food. I couldn't turn that down, not when it was Taco night on campus. Even the smell of the cilantro they used was disgusting.

"Fine."

CHAPTER 6

FRIENDZONE

- Luca -

caught myself whistling in the shower before the dinner with Giada. We'd been clear that it wasn't a date, but I didn't care. I loved spending time with her, hearing her voice, seeing her smile. And I couldn't wait to hear those sexy sounds she made when she savored Italian food.

I went with dark gray slacks, a light green fitted button-down shirt, and my favorite loafers—without socks, of course. If anyone accused me of dressing up, I could blame it on the Italian thing. Being raised in a country where men actually put some effort into looking good, I struggled with the typical American guy uniform of jeans and tee shirts every single day.

I leaned against the wall outside of Giada's dorm until she came out. I pretended to be distracted by something on my phone, but in reality, I spotted her the second she appeared. She'd worn a flowy dress with tall brown boots and a denim jacket. She'd totally dressed up. She looked gorgeous, even with the scowl on her face as she looked at me.

"You look nice," I said.

"You changed clothes," she said, her tone accusatory.

"Uh, yeah. Just played football—Italian football, so I needed to shower. And it's not exactly the food court," I replied, motioning for her to follow me to my car. "Besides, you changed, too."

"I'm a girl. I'm supposed to spend time getting ready to go out, even when it is just for a casual dinner with a friend and not even a little bit like a date."

"Wow. Sexist much?"

"No, it's the truth. Guys only dress up when their mom makes them or when they're going on a date. I have brothers, remember?"

Her assessment accurately described all of my suitemates, but that didn't make it any less sexist. "That may be true for American men, but not Italians. We like our fashion just as much as the ladies. Textiles are huge in Italy," I paused while we both climbed into the car. "Not just any label is going on this body."

She laughed so suddenly that she snorted. "You can't expect me to believe you know labels."

I turned to her, aghast. "I do, and I'm offended you've never noticed my wardrobe before."

From the way her cheeks flushed, I was confident she had, in fact, noticed. But instead of just accepting defeat, Giada pressed further.

"Who are you wearing tonight then?" she asked, clarifying when I looked confused. "Which designers made your outfit?"

I glanced down at my clothes. "Canali, Ricci, Prada, and Bottega Veneta."

Giada narrowed her eyes as though still not believing me. "What's the Prada?"

I pointed to my shoes.

"Oh." She crossed her arms over her chest. "Okay, I'm impressed. Also, nice shoes."

"Thank you."

"You don't always wear Italian designers though, do you?"

"Yes." I paused, then explained. "They're the best, plus my papà is a big supporter of the local economy."

She sighed. "That jacket you left at my dorm was Gucci. That should have tipped me off. Most guys our age don't really care about fashion."

"I'm not most guys."

"No," she agreed. She reached for the dial to turn on the radio, signaling she was comfortable enough to make herself at home in my car. "Does your music have to be Italian too?"

I chuckled. "No."

She found some top forty hits type station and relaxed back in her seat. "Are you familiar with Boglioli?"

I nodded, certain I owned several shirts and probably a suit by the designer.

"Their winter line is amazing. Very unique twist on classic pieces."

We slowed to a stop at the light and I snuck a peak at her. She looked happy and relaxed. "You really are interested in fashion design, aren't you?"

"I'd love to make a career out of it."

"You should get an internship somewhere in Italy. I'm sure my papà has some connections if you're interested."

Now she laughed. "My father won't let me drive myself to the local grocery store. I seriously doubt he'd let me leave the country without a babysitter."

I laughed, then switched the topic to our classes for the rest of the short drive.

As we parked and walked up to the restaurant, Giada was careful to keep several feet distance between us.

"Are you heading home for Thanksgiving, or do you travel?" I asked.

"Home," she said, her smile widening. "I think this has been the longest I've gone without seeing everyone."

"You really like your family, don't you?"

"Most of the time, yeah," she said as we followed the hostess to our table. "My dad and I don't get along like we used to and Angelo can be kind of a jerk, but I love being surrounded by all the people at home and how connected everyone is. There's always someone cooking something, always someone to talk to, someone to sit with by the pool."

"That does sound nice," I agreed.

"What about your family?"

I glanced at the menu to confirm the dish I wanted was still available then quickly shut it. Giada already knew the basics about my family, having met them all at some point. But, it had been a while. "Well, I'm an only child and my papà is pretty much always a dick. But I do get what you're saying about the extended family and that is all nice."

"I'm sorry about your dad. Are you spending Thanksgiving in Staten Island?"

That was a touchy subject. "Well, sort of. That's where I'm headed when school closes, but my parents fly back to Italy Thursday morning, so I'm probably just going to hang out alone the last couple of days. Or head back to school early." I made a mental note to check whether the dorms even reopened early. I'd already confirmed Alessio was out of town, so I couldn't go there.

"Your parents are leaving you alone on Thanksgiving? That's terrible!" Giada's expression was filled with disbelief.

"It's an American holiday. They apparently didn't realize the timing of it all. It's fine. I'm not going to starve."

"The whole point of Thanksgiving is to be surrounded by people. You can't spend it alone." She paused. "Oh, you should come spend it with us. My dad would love that! So would my brothers, I'm sure."

"I don't..." I began, then stopped myself. I was unable to think of any reason why *I* wouldn't like that but a thousand reasons why *she* shouldn't.

"Don't say no. Just think about it so you're all ready to say yes when you get the official invite."

The waitress came to take our orders but Giada still hadn't opened her menu. I started to ask for a few more minutes, but Giada insisted she was ready and asked me to order first.

"You're not going to look at your menu?"

"Nope. I want whatever you're having."

I stared at her for a moment to confirm she was serious, then told the waitress what we wanted.

"Bold move," I said to Giada once we were alone.

"I trust you," she said, her eyes shimmering.

"You shouldn't," I replied.

She smiled as though I'd been joking. I wasn't.

The rest of the dinner was good. Not just the food, but Giada. Despite her stubbornness, she was easy to talk to and a lot of fun. I felt like I could be myself with her, or at least more like myself than I'd ever been with Emily. Or even any of my suitemates, for that matter. And it didn't hurt that she was so easy on the eyes. Although, maybe the whole friendship thing would be even easier if she weren't so damn hot.

- Giada –

Since dinner with Luca, I hadn't been able to concentrate on anything else. We'd had fun together, and I felt surprisingly comfortable talking with Luca. Everything between us continued going smoothly the rest of the week. We chatted between classes and whenever we ended up at the same table in the dining hall. He sent me funny memes and smartass texts, I forwarded him random news articles about his beloved Italian designers.

Luca had quickly become one of my best friends.

But that was the problem.

The more time I spent with Luca, the harder it was to distract myself from the still-vivid image of him sopping wet and shirtless, skipping towards me from the ocean. I needed to get my brain on board with the whole friendship thing. Luca clearly had, so why was I struggling so much?

I was supposed to finish the invitations for the Children's Hospital party that evening, and Luca had offered to help. I would have rejected the offer, but Luca had a car, which made him my most convenient option for getting to the printer to pick up the invitations. I'd bought a few reams of cute ribbon so we could roll each invitation and tie it like a royal decree, which of course went perfectly with the party's Royal Holiday theme.

I didn't see Luca at lunch that day, which was just as well. I spent the entire time panicking about ruining our friendship with my stupid crush. I needed a distraction. Luckily, Art was my first class after lunch, and that always calmed me. We were finishing a unit on the art of ancient Greece, and I had been sketching an ornate urn Mrs. Libby had placed on one of the tables.

One of the best parts of Art was that we could move around the class as we saw fit, plus we were allowed to talk quietly as long as she wasn't in the middle of a lesson. I was so focused on the finishing details of my drawing that I didn't notice someone had stepped up beside me until he cleared his throat.

I jumped, dropping my pencil, then turned to see Liam, a Junior in the class.

"Sorry," he mumbled, bending to pick up my pencil for me. "That's amazing. You have a really good eye for the details."

Liam was flattering me, since I really wasn't one of the best in the class, but I didn't mind. I thanked him, then paused my work while we chatted for a minute. I hadn't gotten to know him very well yet, but he seemed nice enough. He was in Luca's grade, so I wondered if they had any classes together. I considered asking him, but before I could, he started speaking again.

"Listen, I know it's the last weekend before we all head home for Thanksgiving so everyone is really busy, but if you don't have anything else going on Friday night, maybe we could go to a movie or grab some ice cream or something."

I sucked my bottom lip between my teeth, instantly piecing it all together. He'd never struck me as nervous or awkward before. He was totally asking me out. Although, I didn't want to get my hopes up for nothing. I already had enough 'friends' with four-letter names starting with L.

"Um, like with a group of friends, or like just the two of us?"

"I was thinking just us," Liam said, holding so still that he had to be holding his breath.

I pulled my phone from my backpack and scanned my calendar. I already knew I had nothing I couldn't skip Friday, but I didn't want to look too pathetic. "Sure, that would be fun," I said.

Relief flooded his face. "Yeah?"

"Yeah."

"Giada!" Mrs. Libby called from across the room. "Phone!"

I cringed and shoved my phone back into my bag. "Sorry!" I called back, blushing.

Liam smiled and it was adorable. "Well, I uh, should get back to my own masterpiece. Want to meet up at 6:30 on Friday, outside your dorm?"

"Sounds good."

As I watched him walk back towards the replica sculpture he'd been sketching, I breathed in with relief. I didn't need to stress about Luca now. I could just daydream about my date with Liam.

- Luca -

I'd been looking forward to spending the evening with Giada the entire day, but then some schmuck in my Economics class ruined it all by gloating that he was taking her on a date that weekend. It wasn't that I minded her dating someone, but why him? Why choose a guy that would brag about it? How well did she even know him?

I managed to assemble invitations for the charity party thing for about twenty minutes before I just had to bring it up.

"So, I heard this rumor that you're going out with Liam this weekend," I began, keeping my eyes focused on the ribbon I was tying so she wouldn't think I cared too much.

"A rumor, huh?" the twinkle in her eye told me she wasn't buying it.

"Alright, Liam told me. Not specifically me so much as our whole Economics class. He was bragging about it."

Giada smiled.

"Why does that make you smile?"

"Umm because it's good to hear he's excited to go out with me. It's nice to know someone considers me brag-worthy."

I snorted. "Giada, everyone thinks you're bragworthy. Even if the guys didn't all have some sick fascination with you since you're 'new blood' at the school this year and all, they'd all still want to go out with you. That doesn't mean you have to say yes to everyone."

"I don't say yes to everyone! I like Liam."

"Really? You don't even know him."

"I do too. He's in my Drawing class."

"Tell me five things you know about him."

Giada thought about it for a moment then held her fingers up, adding one each time she mentioned another trait. "Okay, he goes to school here. He likes art. He's rich."

"That doesn't count. That was implied by the first one."

She rolled her eyes and continued. "Fine. He has great hair. He's a Junior. And he has great taste in girls."

I could only shake my head. "That's ridiculous. You're going out with the guy because he's rich and has great hair?"

"No, I'm going out with him because he's cute and he asked me to go out and it sounded fun. I have nothing better to do Friday night."

"We might have stuff to finish up for the party."

"Yeah, like you're going to spend your Friday night helping me." She rolled her eyes, then pushed her hair behind her ear. "The whole point of the date is to get to know someone. It's not like I'm marrying the guy, so you can stop worrying about it."

"That is not what I'm worried about." I paused, unsure of how to make her understand. I had a newfound appreciation for her brothers' constant frustration. She was difficult to keep safe. "I just don't trust him alone with you."

"Is he a serial killer?"

I made a face, although frankly he could be, for all I knew.

"You're being ridiculous," she said matter-of-factly. "Besides, he really can't kill me on Friday because he already told everyone he was taking me out."

"Giada, look, he's just… he's older than you. He's in my class."

"So?"

"If you're going to go out with a guy that much older, you might as well go out with me," I finally blurted out. Then I clenched my jaw, certain she'd banish me for breaking the no-flirting rule. But instead, she laughed.

"Well, if you'd asked me out for ice cream and a movie Friday night, maybe I would have. But now we'll never know." She smirked and then shoveled the rest of the papers into a tote bag. "I think we're done. I'll check in with Father Harris tomorrow and then we can meet up on Sunday to finish up?"

I nodded grumpily.

She smiled. "Arrivederci Luca."

My breath caught in my throat a little. I didn't think it was possible for someone to sound so hot simply saying goodbye in my native tongue, but it was.

"Hey, tell Liam I said hi when you see him in Economics tomorrow," she added, flipping her hair over her shoulder and sauntering out.

My head dropped to the table and I groaned in frustration.

- Giada -

The date with Liam was a bust. He picked the movie, some dumb futuristic action film about robotic insects. When we arrived, he sauntered right past the snack counter without even asking if I wanted anything. Reasoning that we'd both just had dinner, I waited until the previews were finishing before telling him I was going to go grab some candy. I expected Liam to jump up, apologize for not thinking of that sooner, and go buy it himself. Instead, he'd looked at me like I was insane and said he thought we were getting ice cream after.

So, I skipped the candy, even though that was literally the only good part of a movie. He draped his arm over my shoulders, which would have been romantic, except he didn't even glance at me once the whole movie. Plus his arm got heavy after a while. After the movie, we did get ice cream, as promised, but we ran out of things to talk about before we'd even finished our cones.

Liam might've been planning to kiss me, but I successfully dodged his attempts, promising him I'd see him in class Monday, and then dashing into my dorm where Elise and I giggled over every horrific detail.

Luckily, the weekend still had potential for redemption. Elise, Delaney, Harlow and I headed out to Sullivan's on Friday, indulging in a true fall gathering organized by some of our classmates. We roasted hot dogs and smores, stumbled through the corn maze, and then as soon as the sun set, we turned up the music and brought out the booze.

Well, I didn't have any role in that part, but I wasn't about to complain. Colton had been flirting with me the whole night, and now he'd seemingly made it his mission to teach me how to consume gelatin from a miniature plastic cup with no spoon.

"You have to squeeze the bottom of the cup and then use your tongue to get it out," Colton explained.

I eyed him warily, considering that maybe he was messing with me, but then I noticed everyone else seemed to be employing that odd tactic. I did as he said, cringing when the first clump of the gooey red substance hit my tongue. Then slithered down my throat. I paused, then decided it was good.

"Tastes like regular Jell-o," I said.

Colton grinned mischievously. "That's what's so great about them! Next time I'll get my brother to bring us some pudding shots."

He was talking to me, but the people behind us appeared to hear, too, and cheered. I finished my miniature plastic cup of gelatin and tossed it into the trash. Perusing the options, I went for a blue one next.

"Giada! It's our song!" Elise called from across the way.

As far as I could tell, every brown-eyed girl considered that her song, but I wasn't about to turn down a chance to dance. I squished the rest of the blue Jell-o into my mouth then joined her. Despite the unseasonably warm temperatures for mid-November, the air was chilly, especially now that the sun was beginning to set.

Elise and I followed our usual dance routine of twirling in circles until we were dizzy then holding hands and shimmying, lasting through "our" song and two more. Then, we were both thirsty.

"Is there any water?" I asked. "Or coffee?"

Colton laughed and handed me another blue gelatin shot. I didn't feel any effects from the alcohol of the first two yet and really, I reasoned there couldn't be much alcohol in such a tiny concoction anyway. When Elise and I went back to start dancing, we noticed that more people had started to arrive, and a few more had joined us on our makeshift dance floor.

Colton and his friend Beckham came to join us while we danced, and I realized Colton was actually a decent dancer. As his hand grazed my ribs before settling on my hip, I giggled, ticklish. He made a confused face, so I leaned forward and explained.

"Oh, you're ticklish?" he said, waiting to pounce until I confirmed it with a nod. Colton tickled me all over until I could barely breathe I was laughing so hard. He wrapped his arms around my waist and lifted me off my feet and both of us were giggling and breathless when he finally released me.

"I will totally get you back for that," I promised, wagging my pointer finger at him.

"You better," Colton replied with a wink. Then, he gazed behind me at some guys that seemed to be vying for his attention. "Be right back," he said.

Colton took off to chat with his buddies, so I turned back to Elise. We both danced, twirling around as an excuse to check out whether any new people had come since we last looked around. I was surprised to see Luca hanging out in the corner. Earlier in the day, when I'd asked him if he had any plans, and all he'd mentioned was some work for his dad. Apparently work had ended early.

I didn't recognize the guy standing with Luca, a guy with a similar build and dirty blond hair, who seemed to be about our age. The guy appeared to be talking to Luca, but Luca wasn't paying any attention. Luca was staring straight at me. I couldn't quite recognize the look in his eyes, and I certainly didn't want to give him time to decipher mine.

Luca looked hot, as always. The worst part was that he always achieved that look in a way that came across as totally effortless, like he just stumbled into designer clothes that perfectly accented his slender, defined form. His dark-rinse denim fit tighter than most guys wore, and instead of a fall flannel, he'd layered an olive green Henley over another shirt or two. If I looked closely enough though, I could make out the cut of his biceps beneath the fabric.

I snapped out of my daze and offered Luca a flirty half wave before turning away. We'd been doing really good at the whole friends thing lately. I couldn't quite fool myself into thinking that was actually what I wanted with Luca, but I also wasn't going to keep setting myself up for rejection.

Thankfully, Colton came back then, offering me another blue Jell-o shot.

"I think this is my fourth," I admitted. I had no interest in a repeat of my first night at Sullivan's Farm where I'd gotten totally drunk. "How strong are they?"

"It's mostly gelatin," he assured me.

I tapped my plastic cup against his then downed the mixture. I didn't think slimy food was ever going to be my favorite, but this combination was growing on me.

Elise grabbed my arm. "Ummm, Giada, we have to talk real quick," she said.

The sudden serious expression on her face stumped me. Just a moment before we'd been laughing and having fun. What could have possibly happened in such a short time? I followed her closer to the fields where it was quieter to find out.

Elise barely waited till we were away from the music to talk. "Liam is telling everyone you gave him a hand job during the movie," she blurted out.

The idea was so preposterous that I barely followed what she was saying. "Why would I do that?"

Elise rolled her eyes then focused them on Blair. I hadn't even noticed she was at the farm that night. "I bet it was her idea."

"Why would Blair try to spread that rumor?" I spoke the words aloud before realizing I knew exactly why she'd spread that rumor. Even after I stopped seeing Brooks, she hadn't gotten over the fact that we went out once, ages ago. Clearly, she was psycho. But that didn't explain Liam's motivation.

"Why would Liam go along with it?" I asked.

Elise shrugged. "Look, I'm sure no one believes it. I just thought you should know."

I blew out a sigh and gazed over to where Colton was waving for me to rejoin him. But now I had to question his motives. Did he like me, or was he being nice to me because he thought I was his best chance for no-strings sex?

"Thanks for telling me," I said to Elise. "I'll handle it."

- Luca -

I hadn't expected Giada to be at the party, although I should've known better. Despite her good-girl persona, she never missed a good time. Giada was friends with everyone, and she was a magnet for any event involving dancing. She sure looked good spinning around and shimmying, and she clearly loved dancing, especially when she had an audience. I wondered if this was similar to the preacher's kid phenomenon—a lifetime of behaving and not getting enough attention had led her to seek out attention like a drug.

I wasn't the only guy watching her, but that didn't bother me nearly as much as seeing Colton and Beckham dancing with Giada. From the way Giada was smiling and laughing, I guessed she was enjoying their company, but then again, maybe it was just the attention she relished. Colton stepped forward, bringing his groin way too close to her for my taste.

"I should say hi," I said to Alessio, who was already distracted by the beer.

I approached slowly, waiting until Giada pulled back from Colton enough for me to catch her eye.

"Hey," I said, grinning.

"Hey yourself," she replied, shimmying her shoulders as she spoke.

Colton shot me a dirty look, but he could kiss my ass. I wasn't about to let the evening pass without talking to Giada.

"I didn't think you were coming," I told her, intentionally not raising my voice over the music.

"What?" she called.

I crooked my finger for Giada to come closer. She rolled her eyes, as did Colton, but Giada slowly sashayed over to me. I tried to hide my smug grin.

"I said I didn't think you'd be here today," I repeated.

Giada shrugged. "You're the one who said you were running errands for your dad or something lame."

"Well, I finished early." I glanced behind me to see if it would be a good time to introduce her to Alessio, but he'd disappeared. "You look like you're having fun," I said.

She smiled sweetly. "Good. That's the idea."

I digested her words for a moment. "To look like you're having fun or to actually have fun?"

"Ideally both. I mean, I *was* having fun for real. I aced my science test Wednesday and we just have five more days of classes until we get a full week off. What's not to enjoy?"

"Sounds good to me. So are you saying that you're no longer having fun just because I walked over here?"

"No. You're fine. Elise just told me there's some dumb rumor circulating about me."

"I haven't heard it."

She wrinkled her nose. "Yeah, well if you go near Blair, I'm sure you will. God, she is such a bitch."

I already knew why Blair was annoyed with her. Everyone at school knew, although most agreed it was petty. "Want me to have a chat with her?"

Giada shrugged. "No. What she's saying is stupid and it isn't true. I would not do that. I'm just going to show her that she can't ruin my day with her childish antics."

"You wouldn't do what?" Already, a pit was forming deep in my core.

"I wouldn't do what they're saying I did with Liam. On our date."

My stomach tightened. I could guess what the rumor was without knowing the details. My hands curled into fists, itching to punch something. Or someone. My heart raced and my limbs practically vibrated with the anger coursing through them. I tightened my jaw, realizing I needed to snap out of it. Giada would not be impressed by my wild temper.

I stared at her for a moment to try to distract myself from my growing fury. She'd twisted her silky hair into some loose bun on top of her head, but several long tendrils had fallen free, begging to be touched. Her bold eyes sparkled like the distant stars ahead, and a rosy hue filled her cheeks. She fidgeted beneath my intense gaze, then her tongue darted out to wet her full lips.

"Why is your tongue blue?" I asked.

Giada gazed up at me from beneath her dark eyelashes in a way that could only be described as coquettish. "Jell-O," she finally explained.

I had noticed the table of shots, but was a little surprised she'd partaken.

"I thought you gave up drinking," I reminded her.

"I thought you gave up flirting with me," she retorted.

Ouch. "This is not flirting."

"Fine, but seems awfully convenient that you just had to talk with me as soon as you noticed someone else flirting. If I didn't know any better, I'd think you were trying to scare off Colton, or mark your territory or something."

I leaned closer, not wanting to admit she was right. "Giada, are you asking me to pee on you?"

She swatted my chest and made an adorable fake annoyed face. "Jerk."

"Where's Liam?"

A flicker of panic crossed her face as she looked around, and I actually laughed aloud.

"I don't see him, Giada. I was asking you where he was. Geez, date went that badly?"

"It wasn't bad. It just…wasn't great."

I rolled my eyes. "I could've told you that you guys had nothing in common. Oh wait, I did. You ignored me."

Her eyes narrowed. "Do you want me to say you were right? Fine, you were. Liam is not my soulmate. And the fact that he isn't denying this stupid rumor isn't helping his case. Now if you'll excuse me, I have dancing to do. Enjoy the show."

I groaned silently then watched her head off to rejoin her friends. After a moment, Alessio came up beside me.

"So that's the Conti girl, huh?" he asked.

I paused, trying to determine out how he'd guessed that, but then again, Alessio was smart. He figured out everything. And he could read people even better than I could, which was saying a lot.

"Yep."

He didn't say anything, but he was nodding his head and eying her happily when I turned to him. I swatted his arm, certain his thoughts weren't pure.

"I see what all the fuss is about now, that's all," he finally said.

"There's no fuss. I'm just…looking out for her, like my papà asked."

Alessio laughed. "That's a tough gig, looking at her all day," he said right as Giada and her friend leaned towards each other and did some sort of shimmy move that flashed us an indecent view of her chest. "Seriously, when are you gonna grow a pair and get with her?"

"It's not like that," I insisted.

"If you're about to tell me you don't like her…"

"It doesn't matter if I do or not. Our dads are friends. Or associates or something, I don't know. And besides, she's… younger," I finally said, for lack of a better word. "She's a good girl. She goes to church every week by choice. And she does all this charity stuff."

"Okay, but it's not like you're the devil."

I shot him a look.

"Think of it this way. Someone is going to corrupt her. It might as well be you." Alessio pinched an orange Jell-o shot between his teeth and darted away before I could smack him again.

- Giada -

By the time Elise and I made it back to our dorm, I was sleepy and had the slightest twinge of a headache. I'd definitely gotten a little buzz from the shots, but thankfully not as bad as the last time I'd drank alcohol.

I showered to wash the scent of smoke from my hair and then rejoined Elise in our room.

"Do you think Colton is into me?" I asked, determined not to think about Blair, Liam, or anything rumor-related.

Elise shrugged, then twisted her hair into a loose bun on top of her head. "It's hard to say. He's a total flirt. He was definitely all over you tonight, but I think that's just him."

I sighed, agreeing with her assessment. "He's a lot of fun, but I'm not sure he's my type anyway."

"Why not? He's cute?"

I answered with a shrug. He was cute, but he had blond hair, a bit longer than I'd prefer, and he had a bigger stature than most of the guys I went for.

"Are you going to confront Liam about this stupid rumor?"

"I don't think so. He knows it isn't true, obviously, and we know Blair was the ringleader behind it all anyway, so what's the point?"

"Clearing your name?"

I sighed. I knew what Father Harris would say. Or any priest, really. It didn't matter what anyone at school thought about me. God knew what sins I had—and hadn't—committed, and the rest shouldn't matter.

"What I want is to get even," I began, surprising even myself when I heard the words come out of my mouth, especially after my conscious thoughts had been so pure. "I mean, I just want Blair to stop messing with me, but I also don't want to cause World War Three."

"Yeah, that's a tough one," Elise agreed. "So what's the deal with you and Luca? Are you two ever going to go out?"

"What? No."

She flicked off the lamp by her bed, bathing the room in darkness. "Oh come on, you obviously like him. And the way he was watching you when you were talking to Colton, he was totally jealous."

I settled my head against the feather pillow. Luca did look jealous. And the way he'd interrupted when I was talking to Colton, he'd basically cut into our dance without even asking. Except then, instead of joining me in a dance, he just talked. Luca hadn't even flirted with me.

"I don't know," I finally said. "I don't think he likes me talking to other guys, but I don't think he wants to go out with me either."

"You guys are too cute together to stay just friends forever."

I sighed. We would make such a cute couple.

Elise was quiet for a moment then continued. "Do you think you'll go out with Colton?"

I took a beat to shift gears, and boys, in my brain. "I don't know. Maybe? He didn't ask me out or anything."

"It's not 1812. You could ask him out."

"Yeah, but…"

"But you're too busy crushing on Luca?" Elise supplied.

I groaned. She'd hit the nail on the head. Luckily, I didn't have to figure any of it out now. We had one more week of classes and then everyone would head home Friday. Spending time with my family and catching up with Matteo especially would distract me from all of the boy drama at school.

Well, until Thanksgiving Day, I supposed. Luca had accepted my invitation to join us for the big meal, and then he was staying at our house until Sunday. *God.* I had no idea how I was going to get through four whole days with Luca without throwing myself at him or otherwise mortifying myself.

CHAPTER 7

HAPPY HOLIDAYS?

- Luca -

At the start of Thanksgiving break, Iacopo picked me up from school. He seemed to be in a good mood. He played music, albeit crap from the seventies, and he attempted relatively normal conversation with me.

I, on the other hand, was a mess. The closer we got to home, the more dread filled me. I hadn't seen my papà since the day at the warehouse. I sensed he considered all of that water under the bridge, but I did not share his attitude. I also didn't know if my mom knew what he'd done, or how either of my parents would react if I told her.

"How much does my mother know?" I asked Iacopo.

"About?"

"Papà's business."

"She's never taken much interest in it, but I assume she knows everything." He paused and turned to me, flashing a Cheshire cat grin that revealed two gold teeth. "Everything the IRS knows anyway."

I rolled my eyes at his dumb joke and pressed onward. "Does

she know Papà paid some guys to beat me up?"

Iacopo took his time answering, and when he did, his tone and expression had changed dramatically from his last statement. "Now how would she know some crazy story you just made up?"

I blew out a sigh and turned to the window. Iacopo had a point though. If it were between me and my papà, she'd believe him every time. She'd side with him every time.

"Is he in a good mood at least?" I finally asked.

Iacopo chuckled at that. "As good of a mood as ever. And I think he's pretty happy with you for once."

I cringed at his qualification. "Why?"

"You're headed to spend the weekend at the Conti manor. That's good news for business."

"Right. Because that is all that matters," I mumbled, turning towards the window.

"Chin up, kid. Your family *is* your business. You should be grateful for that at least."

I wasn't sure how that was supposed to reassure me, but it didn't matter. I leaned back against the headrest and dozed off for the rest of the ride.

Once at home, I was relieved. My papà was pleased with me, as Iacopo had promised. My mom was even more excited to see me, and apparently had decided to spend the entire week feeding me. One day, my papà brought me in to his club with him. This time, it was a dance club—not the one that had strippers. Other than that, he actually let me relax at home. Papà had a lot of questions about my friend Alessio, but nothing that raised eyebrows. I supposed even good parents would want to know about the family their kid crashed with for a whole weekend.

My mom's oldest sister and her husband were in town from Sicily, so I saw my cousins on my own turf for once. I took them around town and showed them some of my favorite hangouts. Everything felt refreshingly normal. Giada texted me a few times, and I was no longer even anxious about spending the last few days of break with her family.

But as Iacopo drove me to the Conti residence, I realized I could have miscalculated how stressful the visit might be. I remembered the wide metal gate and the massive yard surrounding the circular drive leading up to the house, but I hadn't anticipated quite that big of a crowd. There were easily fifteen cars parked along the drive.

As Iacopo slowed to a stop, a man in a suit jacket came out to greet us.

Or possibly to shoot us. It was hard to say, given that he was dressed like all the gangsters my papà had paid to beat me up. Iacopo rolled down the window, followed the man's directions, then parked off to the side. The guy smiled and chitchatted with Iacopo for a moment, then Iacopo popped the trunk and nodded for me to get out.

"You need help carrying this in?" he asked me.

"No, I can manage," I said, eying the house skeptically. I was tempted to ask him why I felt like I was entering enemy territory, but I wasn't sure I wanted to hear the answer. I slid my backpack straps onto my back, draped my larger duffel bag over my shoulder and loaded my hand with the bag of food my mom insisted I give to the Contis.

I nearly dropped everything as a loud, deep voice called my name.

"Luca! Welcome, my boy. Benvenuto."

I turned, relieved that I recognized the speaker as Marco Conti himself. "Buongiorno," I said, smiling widely.

"Grazie, we got it from here," Mr. Conti said to Iacopo, dismissing him. Then he turned to a guy that didn't look much older than me. "Lorenzo, come help Luca with his bags."

"It's fine, Mr. Conti. I can…" I started, but the guy already had taken everything.

Luckily, Giada appeared then. She was flanked on both sides

by older men. One I recognized as her brother and the other I couldn't identify.

"Hi Luca," she said sweetly. She wore a mustard colored dress, brown boots, and oversized cold earrings. She looked like a magazine photo of Thanksgiving spirit. Every muscle in my body ached to hug Giada, but she seemed so reserved that I figured I should be, too.

Her brother stepped forward, offering his hand.

"Hi Angelo," I said. "How's it going?"

He nodded curtly, then moved over to his dad, who nodded in response to whatever question he'd asked.

"I'll show you to your room," Angelo said, swiveling away.

I took off after him, barely glancing at Giada as we passed.

"We won't eat until six, but we do drinks and appetizers around five," Angelo was saying. "So if you need to shower or change or anything…"

He cast a dubious look in my direction.

I glanced down at my outfit of trousers and a button-down shirt. Not formal, but certainly not casual, either. "Do you all usually dress up more than this?"

"No. You're fine. I just thought you Italians always wear suits," Angelo said.

He moved quickly on the tour through the house, so I barely could take in the basic layout of the home, let alone the details or the many people filling it. "My papà does," I said.

Angelo stopped abruptly at the top of the stairs and pointed. "Second room on the right is you."

"Thanks." I started in, unsure if he'd follow. He did, but stayed outside of the room. "Where's Matteo?"

"Downstairs probably. His room is just past yours. I'm the one on the end."

"And Giada is…" I pointed across the hall, just guessing.

Angelo scowled. "Why do you need to know where my sister's room is?"

I had no response. It seemed like an obvious question, but the way he was looking at me made me feel like a pervert. "We go to school together, you know. We're friends."

"Aren't you a Senior? She's a lot younger."

"One year. I'm a Junior." Technically since we both had summer birthdays and I'd started school a year before she did, it was nearly two full years. But whatever.

He eyed me warily, then nodded. "I'll let you get settled. Just come down that stairway whenever and you'll find your way around."

"Cool," I said, then added, "Looking forward to catching up. It's been a while since we've hung out."

Angelo turned and still seemed uncertain, but then he smiled. "Yeah."

- Giada -

Aside from my birthday, Thanksgiving had always been my favorite holiday of the year. So far, this year was on track to meet that expectation for sure. Angelo came home the same day as me, so after catching up with him and Matteo most of the day Saturday, our immediate family went for dinner. I couldn't remember the last time the five of us had done that, and it was so nice.

After dinner, my mom insisted we all walk along the water to burn off some of the dinner calories. I hadn't really worn shoes for walking, but we didn't go far, and it turned out to be a good thing. My brothers scurried on ahead with my mother and my dad hung back by me. He apologized for not letting me come to his party. He told me it was the worst birthday he'd ever had because I wasn't by his side, but that he'd received some threats from disgruntled customers or something and he couldn't bear the thought of putting me at risk. My dad sounded sincere, so I accepted the apology.

That night, Matteo and I stayed up late streaming some of the new Christmas movies, all of which were such garbage that they were actually a bit funny. My dad took Angelo to work with him, and when Matteo and I finally switched off the TV and went to bed, they were still out.

The next morning, we went to church, and I loved seeing all of the familiar faces from my old parish. By dinner, my entire extended family arrived, and us ladies cooked a huge feast together while the men discussed "business" in my dad's office. The next few days were spent decorating the house for the holidays and shopping.

Everything was perfect.

Luca arrived shortly after noon on Thanksgiving Day, but in typical Conti fashion, we all skipped lunch in anticipation of the big meal later. My brothers had latched on to Luca the moment he arrived, and he was seated at an entirely different table from me at dinner, so we didn't really have time to even talk.

After dinner, I played board games with my cousins and brothers—another family tradition for Thanksgiving week. Luca and I were on the same team, along with Matteo and my cousin Vinny, but we barely got a chance to talk. My cousin Giulia was also on our team, and even though her husband was on the opposing team, I noticed Luca paying more attention to her than me.

The next morning when I awoke, the house was relatively quiet. My aunt Sofia was in the kitchen sipping coffee when I first came downstairs, but after a few minutes, she took off on some errand with my mom and Aunt Bianca. I relished the moment of quiet, cringing when I heard footsteps on the stairs. A moment later, Luca popped his head around the corner.

"Good morning," he said, gazing around with a confused look on his face.

"Morning. Coffee?"

He nodded eagerly, so I poured him a mug and sat it beside mine, feeling only slightly embarrassed about my attire. I hadn't wanted to get dressed for the day until I knew what we were doing, so I'd stayed in my comfy red pajama pants and matching tee shirt. Luckily, I'd at least put on a bra.

Luca, on the other hand, looked like he was fresh off a magazine shoot. He wore dark jeans, rolled up once at the ankles, and a teal button-down shirt with grey stripes. The jeans fit him just right and he'd rolled up the sleeves of the shirt enough to show off his muscular forearms. He somehow managed to look casual and dressy all at once, but mostly all I could focus on was how hot he was. I dropped my eyes to his feet, deciding it was safer to stare at his blue sneakers.

"Do you ever wear socks?" I asked.

He joined me at the breakfast bar and sipped his black coffee before answering. "If I'm headed to the gym. Otherwise, no. But do you really want to start down this path?"

"What path?"

"Commenting on each other's current attire?"

I gazed down, noting the pattern all over my pajamas—a cheerful polar bear offering a mug of cocoa to his penguin friend. Maybe not the most mature design, but it wasn't too terrible. "Whatever," I mumbled, eager to change the topic. "You sure seemed to hit it off with my cousin last night."

Luca nodded, then frowned. "Which cousin? You have like a million."

"I don't," I replied, and it was true. I had only seven actual first cousins. But I could see how it felt like more. And it probably didn't help that we occasionally referred to other family members as cousins. "Giulia. You know she's married, right?"

He snorted. "Yeah, I met her husband. Also, she's old. What's your point?"

"No point." We sipped our coffee in silence for a moment, and then I asked him about his time with his family. We located a box of leftover pastries, refilled our drinks, and continued catching up while we ate. Just when I was about to suggest I get dressed and then show Luca around town some, Matteo barged into the kitchen.

He nodded his greeting to me, then turned to Luca. "You ready?" he asked.

Luca rose to his feet without another glance in my direction. "Yep."

They were gone before I could even ask where they were off to. Luckily, my mom and aunts came back in and suggested a spa day, so I changed into my spa clothes and left on my own adventure.

- Luca -

After spending the entire day with Matteo and his cousins, I was eager to unwind back at the house. Instead, I barely made it out of the foyer before Marco Conti cornered me.

"I never properly thanked you for helping me out that weekend," he said.

"Oh, it's no problem. I was happy to do it," I replied, eager to change the subject before Giada overheard us.

"It made a big difference. I worry about her sometimes. She's so impulsive..." Marco trailed off as though some specific memory was stressing him out, but then he didn't elaborate. "I've asked Lorenzo to drive her around and keep an eye on her when she's here, but when she's at school, well, I worry."

I nodded, not sure what to say to that.

"I'm glad you're at school together, is all. Giada can be a handful. There was a lot going on that weekend, and with it being my birthday, I just didn't need one more thing to worry about. You keeping an eye on her was very reassuring."

Giada appeared behind me as if magically transported. Her expression was as clear as day. "You asked Luca to babysit me on your birthday?"

"Giada, it's rude to eavesdrop. And I don't think you need a babysitter. It was just…"

She sighed and rolled her eyes before storming out.

Mr. Conti flung his hands up. "See what I'm dealing with?"

I nodded, offering my fakest smile, then hurried down the hall. Giada was nowhere to be found. I checked the sunroom, since that seemed to be her favorite hangout, then headed up to her room.

I knocked lightly.

"I'm busy," Giada called through the door.

I opened the door anyway.

"Are you deaf? I'm busy. Go away."

She didn't appear busy, perched on her bed inspecting her fingernails. I shut the door behind me and sat on her bed.

"He doesn't really think you need a babysitter."

Giada glared up at me through her eyelashes. "He does, too. That is literally Lorenzo's job."

She had a point.

"Okay, well, *I* don't think you need a babysitter. That's not what I was doing that day."

"So you're telling me my dad didn't ask you to keep an eye on me?"

I hesitated. She obviously already knew the truth, but admitting it seemed like certain death. "*My* papà asked me to, but I was glad to have an excuse to hang out with you. I could've just watched you from campus if I really wanted to."

Giada rolled her eyes. "Please go. I don't need a babysitter now. There's probably bars on the window so I can't escape anyway."

I sat on the bed beside her, inching backwards until my back pressed against the pillows along the upholstered headboard. "Not a babysitter. Really, what kind of parent would leave their kid with me?" I paused and grinned, hoping she'd laugh at my shadiness. "How about a friend? I think you could use one of those."

Giada shook her head. "Friends don't hang out simply because they're told to."

"What was I supposed to do, Giada? Tell my papà no?"

"Yes."

I winced. *That* had backfired. "I didn't want to tell him no because I wanted to hang out with you. It was the perfect excuse."

She turned away. "I'm asking nicely. Please leave me alone."

"No, not until you tell me why you're so mad." Out of all the shitty things I did on a regular basis, this one didn't seem that bad.

She swiveled back to me and I couldn't help but see the glistening tears forming in her eyes. "I'm not mad, okay? I'm hurt. I feel…stupid. I actually thought you took me to the beach that day because you wanted to, not because someone made you. That was probably the most fun day I've had this semester, and to find out it was all a lie—"

"Me too," I said.

"What?"

"It was the best day of the semester for me too."

Giada frowned. "You should've told me the truth, that my dad or your dad or whoever told you to stay with me. Letting me think you like me if just cruel."

"I do like you."

"Not like that," she said with a sigh. "I mean, like interested."

"I am interested in you," I insisted. "You are fascinating."

Somehow that only seemed to annoy her more.

"Giada, come on. You're being crazy. I wanted to spend time with you. Why can't you just believe me?"

She pressed her pillow against her face and muffled a frustrated scream. "I don't know, Luca. I'm not insecure with anyone else in the world, but you just make me crazy."

I flashed my dimples. "Wanna play cards?"

She agreed reluctantly.

We'd just started our second game when there was a knock and Giada's bedroom door swung open. Matteo poked his head in, then his eyes quickly widened.

I stared at him, waiting to say something, but he took his sweet time.

"Am I interrupting something?" he finally asked.

"Yeah, a cut-throat game of rummy," I said, eager to correct any of his misconceptions.

His eyes flashed down to the cards, then back to his sister. "Pretty sure the 'no girls in your bedroom' rule for Angelo and me means you can't have boys in your bedroom. Especially not on your bed, with the door closed."

"Uhh you're in here," I pointed out.

His eyes narrowed.

"It's just Luca," Giada finally said. "You want to play?" She held up the deck of cards to her brother. He shut the door behind him, nodding.

"Deal me in."

As much as I'd enjoyed the time alone with Giada, I was relieved when Matteo joined us. Being alone with Giada in her bedroom was hard. She'd changed out of her adorable pjs and into some plain black leggings and a grey sweater that dwarfed her small frame. I knew from brushing up against her that the fabric was every bit as soft as it looked, and everything about the casual outfit made me want to snuggle up with her like she was a kitten. She smelled like a freaking cupcake and she wore only the slightest hint of makeup, which made her look even more beautiful than usual.

At school, I'd wondered if part of my interest in Giada was

fueled by my competitive nature, like maybe seeing all the other guys hitting on her made me think I should do the same. But here, I had zero competition. And she sure wasn't trying to impress me.

And yet I wanted her more than ever.

- Giada -

By Saturday evening, I was about to murder Luca. He'd spent the entire day with my brothers—again—and then when he got back to the house, he ignored me. He sat directly across the table from me at dinner but did everything he could to literally never look at me once.

It was ridiculous.

I already knew he was a player, but I hadn't realized our whole friendship was a big ruse to him. Now, it was obvious that given the choice between Matteo and me, he'd pick my brother every time. Not only that, but now I had to wonder why he even paid attention to me at school. Was he just messing with my head?

I definitely hadn't misheard him when he said he was interested in me the day before. Granted, I hadn't asked him to elaborate, so he could've meant interested like a friend, but still. *Any* level of interest should earn me at least a few minutes of his apparently precious time.

Annoyed and desperate for some space, I went into the kitchen and busied myself making hot cocoa. I wasn't a great chef, but my mom had taught me an amazing cocoa recipe. The recipe called for warming the milk on the stove, and something about the slow, deliberate method of crafting the drink soothed me. The recipe made four cups, so I topped each with whipped cream and then carried some out to each of my brothers, then Luca.

Matteo's gratitude was sincere, even as he groaned with delight upon the first sip.

"Wow, Giada who knew you could cook?" Angelo teased.

When I handed Luca a mug, he literally just thanked me. He didn't even glance up.

That was it. I was done.

I gritted my teeth together and stomped out of the room with my own mug. I sipped slowly, enjoying the quiet of the kitchen. After a moment, I heard footsteps. Not eager to chat with any more relatives, I ducked out onto the patio.

I'd barely made my way to the far corner when I heard the door open then shut. I turned to see Luca eying me warily. He clutched his tan jacket, extending his hand slowly like he feared I was a cobra ready to strike.

Already shivering, I snatched the coat from him, thrusting one arm in and then feeling even more annoyed when Luca stepped closer to hold the back of the jacket so I could get my other arm in more easily. Once I was warm, I turned around and pretended to be fascinated with the dying mum occupying a cracked pot on the side of the patio.

"Why are you ignoring me?" Luca asked.

I swiveled to face him, my annoyance ratcheting up another notch. "Me? You haven't glanced in my direction once all day," I said. I knew Luca could be dense, but that was unbelievable. "Actually, you've been avoiding me since the moment you got here. I thought you were going to strain your neck trying to avoid looking at me."

"You want me to stare at you while I'm eating?"

"No, but—"

"Your parents were sitting with us. And your brothers. And a billion other relatives. What do you want me to do?"

I rolled my eyes. "Be nice to me. Act like I'm your friend and not some annoying little sister."

"Annoying little sister?" he repeated, skepticism filling his eyes.

"That's how every single person in there treats me. You are supposed to be different. You said you were interested in me." My stomach muscles tensed as the words left my mouth. I hadn't really intended to say that out loud. Judging from the look on Luca's face, he hadn't expected me to, either.

"Yeah, well, you're fifteen. So maybe unless I have a death wish, I won't act too *interested* in front of your father and brothers."

I hated rolling my eyes again so soon after the last time, but his ridiculousness called for it. "Dramatic much?"

"Me? You're the one giving me the silent treatment because I'm not seducing you in front of your parents."

"I don't want to be seduced!" I shrieked. "Not here, not at school, not at all. I just want some consistency. If you're my friend, fine. Be my friend everywhere. But you don't get to flirt with me at school just to make all the other girls jealous and then ignore me when we aren't someplace you have a reputation to protect. For someone who says you want to be my friend, you sure aren't acting like it."

Luca laughed. I assumed it was my word choice that amused him, but I never could tell with him.

"I don't want to be your friend anywhere," he finally answered.

I blew out a sigh. "Well, at least you're finally being honest," I said, turning on my heel.

Luca grabbed my arm before I distance myself. "Giada, you misunderstood. I have enough friends, and the way I feel about you isn't how I feel about friends." He paused, licking his lips. "I'm not playing games with you at school. I'm not using you for attention or whatever. I like you. A lot. And I'm trying to ignore my feelings, but it's hard."

Luca looked completely sincere, and I hated that. It was so much easier to be annoyed with him than to accept that, maybe, this super hot boy actually felt about me the way I felt about him. I glanced past him towards the house. From our current location on the patio, anyone could walk out and see us, but unless they opened the blinds, we were fairly protected from view from inside. That awareness made me feel bolder. I took a step closer to Luca.

"I don't believe you."

"What's not to believe?"

"I think you're playing with me. You know I have a crush on you and you're using that to mess with me."

Luca's lips curled upwards and he stepped closer, too, bringing the tantalizing scent of his aftershave right up to my nose. "You have a crush on me?"

I gritted my teeth together. I'd realized it was risky to admit that, but I hadn't anticipated him throwing it back in my face so quickly. Now my only choice was to own it. "You know I do."

"I'm glad."

"Why?"

Now he looked confused. "Because I have a crush on you too."

"And we're back to square one," I replied, throwing in my third eye roll in as many minutes.

"Go on a date with me when we get back to school," he said. "A real one. Please?"

"Why back at school? Because you don't want anyone here to know you're interested in me?"

"No, because today is almost over and I'm leaving tomorrow."

I started to come up with another argument when his arms shot out. He placed his palms on either side of my face and pressed his lips to mine. By the time I got over the initial shock that Luca Marino was actually kissing me, I was already kissing him back.

Suddenly, I understood all those stupid expressions about weak knees and butterflies.

I felt ALL of it. My entire body warmed despite the forty-degree temperature, my legs threatened to stop supporting me, and my stomach felt swirly like I'd been on a rollercoaster.

Luca's tongue darted between my lips and I couldn't resist letting my own tongue brush against his. One of his hands shifted to my back, pulling me closer, and goosebumps spread down my arms as his chest pressed against my own. Luca tasted like chocolate. His mouth was still hot from the cocoa we'd drunk. And even with Luca's jacket wrapped around me, I could feel his heartbeat thumping against my chest.

I could've kissed Luca for days. Actually, I had a feeling I might literally try that sometime. And I'm not sure how long we actually did kiss, but there was a crash inside the house and I jumped back.

Luca didn't move his hands from my cheek and kept staring at me while his breath steadied. After a minute, he smiled and released me.

I stood there, dumbstruck. I had no idea what to say and wasn't sure my legs could even carry me if I tried to move, so I didn't.

"Don't question me, Giada. I do like you. Too much, probably. But there's no rush. We've got all the time in the world," he said, winking before adding, "Unless your dad shoots me."

Luca made his way to the French doors leading back into the house and then paused, tilting his head for me to go inside first. Still breathless from the kiss and speechless from his words, I did.

CHAPTER 8

MORE GAMES?

- Luca -

I didn't sleep a wink Saturday night. Every fiber in my body was acutely aware that Giada was directly across the hall from me, likely snuggled up in some adorable animal-print pajama that somehow looked insanely hot on her despite itself.

I kept replaying the kiss in my mind. Every second of it had been perfect. It was everything I'd pictured about kissing her, and more.

After the kiss, we had joined Matteo and some of the younger cousins for a few more games. Angelo and the older guys had all taken off, leaving a calmer, more playful vibe in the house.

We started with charades. Giada was equally terrible at giving clues as she was deciphering them, but we were on the same team, and after her first turn, she sat right next to me on the floor. Our outstretched legs were side by side, and when she rested her hand on her thigh, I did the same with my own, letting our fingers brush against each other.

She'd moved her hand quickly, but as soon as Matteo stood to take his turn, Giada flashed me a knowing grin. Her smile floored me, and I made it my mission the rest of the night to casually touch her or look at her whenever her brother's attention was diverted.

The next morning, I waited to leave my room until I heard Giada's door open, hoping to casually bump into her in the hallway. I couldn't help but smile when I saw she was already dressed in jeans and a long sleeve v-neck shirt, complete with necklace and bracelets. Given that Giada had stayed in her pajamas well past noon the day before, I assumed I was the motivation for her dressing up.

Color flooded her cheeks the moment she saw me, and she shifted her gaze to the floor.

"Fancy running into you here," I joked, trying to lighten the awkwardness. The way we were standing, I was blocking the hallway. I didn't move until Giada finally gazed up to look at me. When she did, I felt my smile widen. She looked beautiful, even first thing in the morning. "Good morning," I said, my voice cracking even though it was barely above a whisper.

"Hi," she replied shyly.

Before either of us could say anything else, Matteo burst out of his room.

"Hey guys, I was hoping to catch you before you ate. Angelo and I were thinking we should do brunch, just the four of us, before you all head back to school."

Giada and I exchanged a glance, then she nodded.

Lorenzo drove us in a white Lexus SUV. Angelo rode in front, which left Giada wedged in the middle of Matteo and me. Every time Giada shifted, her body brushing up against mine in a slightly different way, I tensed. All morning I looked for an opportunity to kiss her again, but there was never a time when we were actually alone. Even when it was time to head back to school, we missed our chance.

The same guy, Lorenzo, drove us. Giada offered me the front

seat, and I refused. It was the gentlemanly thing to do, but I'd hoped she'd opt to just ride in the back beside me. She didn't. And when we arrived at school, they dropped me off at my dorm and then drove to Giada's. I didn't want to come off as a stalker, so I waited an hour and then sent a simple text thanking her again for letting me crash their family holiday.

"Anytime," she'd replied, accenting her response with a medley of emojis.

I took a deep breath, then typed the rest. "So, about that date… I'm guessing you'll have homework or unpacking stuff tomorrow, but how's Tuesday dinner?"

She responded with…a thumbs up. *What the fuck?*

I tossed my phone onto the bed then began unpacking.

I overslept the next morning and missed Giada at breakfast, but I made sure to run into her in the hallway whenever I could. Each time, I played it cool, and she did the same. I wasn't sure what game we were playing, but I couldn't help but wonder if we were both losing.

Luckily, Giada ended the duel first. At lunch, Giada marched right over to my table and stopped beside me. I appreciated the bold move, and yet, it felt like another time when Giada was close enough for me to kiss her, but when it would be totally inappropriate for me to do so.

Not that I'd never made out with a girl in the cafeteria, but this was Giada. And even if she was down with that eventually, we weren't there yet, and maybe I'd never want that. Giada was not the type of girl you shared with the general public. When I finally got the physical affection I'd been craving from her, I wanted her attention on me and only me.

"This seat taken?" she asked, one brow quirked.

"It is now," I replied, tugging her wrist to lower her to the bench beside me. "How's your day going?"

She shrugged. "Not bad. Yours?"

"It's looking up," I said. I snatched a handful of her fries, knowing she hated them. I turned to Grant across the table to catch the tail end of his story while I chewed, but casually dropped my hand to Giada's thigh under the table. I felt her muscles tense at my touch, but then she relaxed. Even better, she didn't move.

"Why do you get fries if you don't like them?" I asked her when Grant finally stopped rambling.

"You looked hungry and I remembered you griping about the portions."

I gave her thigh a slight squeeze. "Thanks. So what sounds good tomorrow?"

"What's tomorrow?" Grant asked.

I turned and flashed him my most obvious butt-out glare, but Giada simply laughed.

"Italian, duh," she said. "And why didn't you tell your roommate?"

I wasn't sure why, actually. "I don't know. Maybe in case you come to your senses before then and reject me?"

She laughed again then turned to Grant. "We're going to dinner tomorrow."

"Oh, can I come?"

"No!" Giada and I both answered at the same time.

"Not that kind of dinner, man," I clarified.

A look of confusion washed over Grant's face as he looked from me to Giada then back to me. I could tell the precise moment he figured it out, as his eyes widened and he broke out in a huge grin. "Wait, like...are you two going on a date?"

I turned to Giada just in time to see her a soft rosy hue color her cheeks.

"I want to get to Art early. I'll see you in an hour," she said.

I reached my hand up as Giada stood, letting our fingertips meet for a moment before she turned and walked off. As I turned back to Grant, his eyes were still huge.

"Seriously? You guys are dating now?"

"Not exactly, but…" I let my voice trail off, aware I was smiling like an idiot anyway.

"I feel like you maybe left some things out when you were telling us about your break," Marcus said, jumping into the discussion. "You said you spent a few days at her house, but I was picturing you in the guest room…"

"I asked her out, and we're doing dinner tomorrow. That's all," I said. But I couldn't stop grinning at the possibility of something more.

- Giada -

J'd selected my outfit for dinner with Luca the day before our date, and yet it still took me nearly two hours to get ready.

I wore an olive-green, long-sleeved dress that hit mid-thigh. paired it with my taller suede boots so that only an inch or two of bare flesh would freeze. I styled my hair into gentle waves, spending nearly an hour to secure each strand so that it appeared natural.

"I can't believe you're finally going on a date with Luca," Elise commented, lounged across my bed snacking on popcorn while I fastened my final bracelet around my wrist.

"It's just dinner," I said, trying to convince myself it wasn't a big deal.

She giggled. "Sure, dinner with the boy who says he likes you *too* much. Gah! How romantic is that?" Elise rolled onto her back, spilling popcorn all over my duvet. "Can you imagine if you guys did actually end up together someday? This is the date you'd be telling your kids about."

My stomach swirled uncomfortably. "Can you stop? I'm already nervous enough."

Elise made her way to her feet and circled around me before nodding. "You look gorgeous. And don't worry. You guys have been friends forever so just forget it's a date and pretend you're eating dinner with Luca your friend."

I decided to follow her advice.

Luca met me outside my dorm. He greeted me with a cocky grin, then complimented my outfit. Of course, he always did that. Luca looked good—he wore black jeans and a long-sleeve fitted shirt and a jacket that probably cost more than my dress —but again, he always looked good. All of the initial details helped me feel comfortable. I clutched my purse strap in both hands, so he didn't hold my hand. And I opened my own car door.

We sat in the corner of the restaurant, close enough to enjoy the warm glow of the fire without the sweltering heat. I let Luca order for me again, and he surprised me by choosing different dishes than the time before. Conversation flowed easily, and for the majority of the meal, I actually did forget we were on a date. I felt like I was out to dinner with a friend.

Well, dinner with a ridiculously hot friend that made me dizzy whenever he looked at me.

When the waitress brought dessert menus, I fully expected Luca to shoo her away since I'd barely made a dent in my entrée. Instead, he gazed at the list for a minute and then looked over at me. "We definitely need some tiramisu, and maybe cannoli?" Luca waited for me to nod before returning the menu to the waitress.

I couldn't help but contrast his attitude towards desserts with that of Liam. I wondered if Liam had realized how many points he lost simply by depriving me of sugar. Luca barely touched the desserts himself, so it was obvious he had ordered them for me. He even offered to order coffee, but it was too late in the day for caffeine, especially since I hadn't slept much the night before due to my excitement over the date.

Luca paid and then we drove straight back to campus. I'd had fun, but something felt…incomplete.

"That seemed a lot like the last time we went to that restaurant," I said. I intended it as a compliment, but quickly panicked that Luca wouldn't interpret it that way.

"Yeah. It is the same, right? A dinner with a friend or a dinner with a…" he paused and glanced at me, grinning like a kid on Christmas as he added, "Girlfriend?"

My heart thumped rapidly, blocking all rational thought. All year, whenever I'd seen him with a girl, he'd denied having a girlfriend. But now, one kiss and one dinner with me and he was using that word? I was confused.

"I think the only difference is that now I get to hold your hand," he continued, reaching for my hand and then turning back to the road. "And kiss you."

At the mention of kissing, my mouth ran dry and I began to sweat. Suddenly, Luca's car felt like it was a million degrees. I cracked the window.

"You too warm?" he asked, pulling his hand away to adjust the temperature. I felt his eyes on me as he reclasped my fingers, running his thumb along the back of my hand.

I was still dizzy, hot, and thoroughly overwhelmed when we arrived back at school. Luca parked the car, then turned to me. Before he could say anything, I flew out of the car. I had to have I looked like a crazy woman, but I didn't know what else to do.

I'd been thinking about kissing Luca for exactly a week now. Well, it had crossed my mind before, but the last week, the images had been particularly vivid thanks to the actual kiss we'd shared. I wanted nothing more than to do it again, but what if it wasn't the same? What if he realized he didn't like me? Or that I was a terrible kisser?

"Giada," Luca said, startling me with his proximity. "Did I scare you off?"

"No, I…" I had no idea what to say.

Luca gripped my elbows in his hands and stared straight into my eyes. Despite the intensity of his gaze, I actually felt myself relax.

"It was the kissing comment, wasn't it?" he asked.

I hesitated, my eyes already locked on his perfect pink lips. Then, I nodded.

"If you don't want to kiss me..." he began.

"I do," I interrupted.

His lips were on mine before either of us could say anything else. The kiss started gently, with our mouths barely touching, but within a minute, my lips relaxed and parted softly. I felt his tongue tracing along my lower lip, working its way towards the seam, and I angled my own tongue to meet his. We might have kissed for minutes or hours, I wasn't sure, but it felt like an eternity and still not long enough.

"You're good at that," I said, so breathless that my voice came out like a whisper.

Luca gently brushed the hair off my cheek. "It's only good because it's with you."

My legs were weak and my pulse was still probably in the range usually reserved for a sprint. All I knew was that I wanted to kiss him more. So I did.

This time, the slam of a door from a nearby car caused us both to jump apart. I cringed, hoping it wasn't a teacher.

"I should go inside," I said. *Before I do something stupid.*

Luca grinned. "Grazie bellissima."

- Luca -

*D*espite my best efforts, I was late to breakfast the next morning. I tried to catch up with Giada, but she was already on her way out. If I wanted time to grab any food, I couldn't chase her. I settled for eye contact and a smile instead. As soon as I caught her eye, she smiled shyly, then held up her wrist as though showing me that even according to her invisible watch, I was tardy.

For lunch, I made sure to arrive early. I filled my tray then plopped down at my usual table, with my usual crew. More fifteen minutes passed without any sign of Giada. I stood, craning my neck to see if anyone was still in line, but she wasn't there. Then I swiveled around and surveyed the rest of the cafeteria and spotted her already seated at another table with her roommate and her roommate's boyfriend. Two other sophomore boys were across from them.

When Giada noticed me staring, she smiled and raised her eyebrows, as though nothing was off. I tried to decide if she was avoiding me. Suddenly, a hand smacked my arm. I turned to see Grant scowling.

"What are you looking for?"

"Nothing," I said. It was the truth. I'd found her.

"I think his newest girlfriend," Gavin taunted.

"She's right over there," Grant said, pointing to her.

I swatted his hand down. *God.* Could he be any more obvious? "Not my girlfriend. We had literally one date."

Grant rolled his eyes and exchanged a look with Gavin. "You've been obsessed with her all semester."

I started to argue with him, but recognized the futility. "Did you want to ask me something or were you just wanting me to rub in the fact that I can get dates and you can't?"

The whole table laughed, including Grant, who, luckily, was a good sport about being teased.

"I was going to see if you wanted to go to the mall tonight. But if you're too busy hanging with the ladies…" he began.

"Nope, I'll be there. I need new athletic shoes." I didn't, but I needed a reason not to spend every free moment with Giada. I shoved one last bite of my sandwich into my mouth and then stood. "I'll see you in Science," I said, walking off to dump my tray.

Once my hands were free, I went straight to Giada's table. Elise greeted me before Giada did, which told me that Giada had definitely blabbed about our date. My eyes dropped to Giada's tray, which held a chef's salad, a cup of diced melon, and a yogurt. She appeared to have eaten as much as she wanted and was now simply poking at the rest of it with her fork.

"Can we talk?" I asked.

She nodded, but made no move to leave her table. I motioned my head to the side, then perched on the table behind her. Giada popped a piece of honeydew into her mouth, then stood and joined me. She sat on the bench about two feet away. I swung a leg over to straddle the bench so I could face her, then scooted closer.

"Hi," she said, color rushing to her cheeks.

"Hi. Are you avoiding me?"

A crease appeared between her eyes. "No. Why?"

"You didn't sit with me."

Giada glanced over at my table. "There wasn't exactly room."

"We would've made room. Or you could've sat on my lap," I said with a wink.

She ignored the last part of my sentence. "Elise was with me. I couldn't just leave her alone."

"Yeah, she looks so lonely without you," I teased, nodding towards the table where Elise was now making out with Jason.

Giada cringed.

"Did you tell her about our dinner?" I asked, leaning closer. Giada smelled like a cupcake and it was the most distracting thing ever. I was overwhelmed with the urge to lick her just to see if I tasted the vanilla.

"Maybe," she teased.

"You had fun," I phrased it like a statement, but I was hoping for confirmation. She delivered.

"I did. You?"

I raised an eyebrow and nodded. "Especially that part at the end. We should do that again. All of it, I mean."

Giada licked her lips before dragging her teeth across the bottom one. Then, she nodded her agreement.

"I've got plans with Grant tonight, but um, maybe tomorrow?"

"Church," she replied.

She paused just long enough for me time to feel disappointed that she was ditching me for church before she offered a substitution. "Friday? I promised Elise and some others that I'd go bowling with them. But there's always room for one more and I'd love if you came with me."

I detested bowling, but couldn't refuse when Giada invited me. And she'd said the L word, albeit not exactly in reference to me. I felt myself nodding before I realized I'd made a decision.

"Yeah, alright. Text me the time and I'll meet you."

Her smile widened. "I should head to class. I want to check my homework before it's due."

I was about to pout over her ditching me already, but she continued.

"Walk me there?"

I nodded, popped to my feet, then helped her up. I reached for her hand, then grabbed her tray with my free hand.

- Giada -

Now that the weather was too for outdoor tennis, I didn't run into Luca during last period, when we both had PE. And since Luca was headed off campus with Grant, I didn't expect to see him at dinner.

Luca had texted after curfew, wishing me sweet dreams and including a picture of new shoes he'd bought when he was with

Grant. He included the caption "not for use with socks," which made me giggle.

I'd replied with a simple "sleep well."

His response, which didn't come until the next morning, made me blush.

He wrote, "I didn't. I spent most of the night thinking about kissing you. Now I'm tired and grumpy."

"Coffee cures all," I replied, pressing my palm against my stomach. At the mere mention of kissing, I felt all woozy and anxious.

Science—my first class of the day, wasn't much help. The substitute played a video on careers in chemistry, leaving me nothing to do but daydream about Luca. Next was Trigonometry, which at least forced me to pay attention. But still, I couldn't wait for lunch, even though I wasn't even sure if I'd see Luca then.

I was one of the first ones out of my math class, so I had not expected to run into Luca—literally or otherwise.

"Oof," I said, dropping my notebook upon impact.

Luca bent to retrieve the notebook. I reached for it, but he held tight. "I think I should get a kiss for being such a gentleman," he said.

I felt my eyes widen. "Here?" We were less than a foot from the classroom. Dozens of students were in the hallway and any number of teachers could poke their head out of their classrooms at any moment.

Luca licked his lips, clearly amused by my panic. He gripped my elbow and tugged me around the corner near the top of the stairs. It still wasn't private, but it felt infinitely more so than the main hall. "Better?"

I leaned forward, offering him a quick peck on the lips. Luca breathed a laugh and pressed his hand into my lower back, dragging me back to him. He kissed me like we'd kissed after our date, but ended it after a minute.

"That was better," he said, his voice coming out like a sigh.

"I'll see you at lunch," I stammered, offering him my sweetest smile before starting on my way.

"Hey!"

I turned to see Luca holding up my notebook. "Oh, right." I grabbed it from him and scurried off. That boy seriously made me lose my mind.

My next class was boring, and I couldn't stop thinking about Luca for long enough to concentrate on anything Mr. Kellerman was saying anyway. Well, not just thinking about Luca generally. I was thinking about kissing him. Like, kissing Luca was all I could think about. Probably, that had been his plan, to give me a small taste of what he had to offer and then send me into the boring world of American History. I stifled a frustrated groan and flipped through my textbook.

Luca sat with me and some of my friends at lunch, and we got so caught up in talking that neither of us actually ate anything. And then, when I saw what time it was and started to panic about being late to Art, Luca offered to return my lunch tray so I could get a head start. I thanked him, thinking how sweet it was. Just as I was about to dash off for class, he grabbed my hand, raised it to his lips, and kissed my palm, right in the middle of the cafeteria.

Heat rushed to my face and I scurried off without saying anything. I'd really never heard of kissing someone on the palm. Was that even a thing? Back of the hand sure, but the palm? Except… it was hot. The palm of my hand was so sensitive and something about the whole experience felt way too intimate.

I had hoped for at least a few minutes before World Religions to catch up with Luca and say something about my weird behavior in sprinting off after the kiss, but he rolled in seconds before the bell. He mouthed the word "sorry" then took his seat one row back and to the side of me. All throughout class, I felt his eyes on me, and whenever I dared to glance to my side to confirm my feeling, Luca would grin, wiggle his eyebrows, or wink.

At first, I felt self-conscious, naked almost, under his unending stare, but after a while, I started to enjoy it. I still couldn't concentrate, but then the awareness that the cutest guy in school was ogling me brought a pleasurable warmth to my belly.

With ten minutes remaining to class, though, Luca finally dropped his gaze to his desk, writing. I turned back to the front of the room, reminding myself I had no right to feel hurt that he got bored of staring at me. A moment later, a small wad of paper hit my shoulder.

I glanced down as the paper hit the floor beside my desk, cast a glance back to confirm it was a note from Luca, then subtly bent to retrieve the note. I had successfully gotten the folded paper into my hand when I felt Mr. Cobb's eyes on me. He approached slowly, holding out his hand.

"I'll take that," the teacher said. "This is neither the time nor the place to pass notes."

My face burned with embarrassment as I handed the note to him. I expected him to dump it in the trash, but instead he proceeded to unfold the paper. A wave of nausea hit me as I dared to glance back at Luca, who appeared calm as ever.

Luca shrugged as though it was no big deal to get busted breaking the rules, but then, of course *he* wasn't the one who got caught with the note.

Mr. Cobb stared at the note for just long enough for me to pray it wasn't horrifically inappropriate, then he scowled and turned to Luca. "Well, if there was any doubt who the author of this delightful note was, I suppose that is now resolved. Save the Italian for your foreign language class, Mr. Marino," he said, placing the note beneath a binder of lesson plans on his desk.

Mr. Cobb's comment confused me, but I was too embarrassed to turn and look at Luca again. Instead, I hid my face under my hair and focused on my notes the rest of class. When the bell rang, I half expected Mr. Cobb to say something to Luca and I, but he didn't. And I didn't wait around for it, either. I shot out of my desk and flew through the classroom door before Luca even caught up to me.

"God that class was boring," Luca said, casually throwing his arm over my shoulders as he fell in line with my pace.

"That was mortifying! What was on the note anyway?"

Luca smirked and reached into his pocket, retrieving the offending note.

"How'd you get that?"

"Swiped it from his desk," Luca replied with a shrug. "You'll have to translate, but that should keep you entertained next period."

I glanced down at the crumpled paper. The note contained five sentences, all in Luca's familiar, scribbly penmanship. Every word was in Italian. I shook my head, trying to figure out why Luca write me a note in a language I couldn't read. I was very eager to start translating.

"I'll see you for bowling," Luca promised, dropping his arm and turning the opposite way down the hall.

- Luca -

When I walked into the student union building, my eyes struggled to adjust to the bright fluorescent lighting. The old building resembled a medieval castle from the outside. While the majority of the inside matched that vibe, the school had attempted to modernize the section which housed the bowling alley as well as a miniature movie theater and some other lame activities. The result was cringe-worthy at best, insulting at worst. Just because we were students didn't mean we couldn't appreciate good architecture.

The moment I reached the bowling alleys, my eyes twitched

and I felt a twinge of a headache start already. Apparently, "cosmic bowling" consisted of regular old bowling, but with strobe lights, a disco ball, and neon words piercing the darkness and distracting you from the God-awful music. Once I'd gathered my bearings, I spotted Giada's group. Two girls were bowling, and a couple kids appeared to be dancing while waiting for their turn.

I didn't have to look too closely to recognize Giada. The way those jeans clung to her curves, I'd recognize that ass anywhere. Especially since her arms were raised above her head as she wiggled like a genie. As I approached, she stopped dancing, tossed her head back and laughed.

I couldn't help but smile. Giada was the happiest person I knew, but no matter how often she laughed or smiled, I was sure I'd never get sick of it.

I just didn't see why she had to be enjoying herself so much with Colton.

I stepped up behind Giada, roping my arms around her waist so suddenly that she jumped and shrieked. I leaned back, lifting her off her feet, relishing her squeals. When I set her down, she turned to face me.

"You came!" Giada looked equal parts happy and surprised. "I never pegged you for the bowling type."

I gazed around again, wincing from the pathetic surroundings. "I'm not, nor will I ever be, but I wanted to see you."

"Aww, you're so sweet," she cooed. Giada leaned in and I thought she was going to kiss me, but instead she just rest her head on my chest for a moment. Then Colton called her name.

"You're up," he said.

"Watch and learn, boys," Giada taunted. She selected a ball then sashayed to the head of their alley, swinging her hips much more than necessary.

Giada knocked down five pins on her first try, then rolled a gutter ball on her second shot. Still, she jumped and cheered for herself, evoking the same enthusiasm from the other players. Her roommates gave her a high five and Colton pulled her in for a hug.

"Giada is literally the worst bowler I've ever seen," Elise confided in me. I agreed, but was too busy shooting daggers at Colton to even think straight.

Giada broke free and walked back to where I was standing. "I think I'm improving," she said to me, completely serious.

I started to ask her a question when my phone rang. It was my papà's ringtone, which made my chest tighten painfully. After I missed a call from him the other day, Papà made it perfectly clear I was to answer every time he called.

"Shit," I mumbled. "I need to take this." I turned and slouched away without making eye contact. I answered the phone as I pushed through the double doors to exit the bowling alley. The cold night air smacked me in the face and felt about as rough as I suspected the call would be.

Sure enough, Papà launched into his lecture before I even said hello. He barked at me in Italian, his voice growing louder and more animated with each sentence. I pulled the phone away from my ear to spare myself the volume, but snapped back to attention when he informed me he needed to see me at his club that night.

I exhaled, wishing I could release my anxiety along with my breath. "Papà it's after seven here. I have a curfew. I can't get there tonight, even if you send a car." I clenched my abs, praying this tactic would work, then continued. "I'm happy to help out with whatever tomorrow, but—"

He called my bluff, cutting me off and agreeing. "You can do some work with Iacopo during the day and then head over to the club at night."

I acquiesced, despite my better sense. I disconnected the call and squeezed my eyes shut, desperate for answers. I knew he was mad because I had rejected his call the other day. He'd called in the middle of my date with Giada, and I'd forgotten to call him back until lunch the next day. He didn't even have anything important to tell me, but according to him, that wasn't the point. I needed to learn respect, and apparently that meant being at his beck and call no matter what.

On the plus side, he hadn't mentioned Iacopo dragging me to some abandoned warehouse to get jumped by a bunch of thugs. I reasoned he wouldn't want to bring his son into one of his clubs looking like a losing streetfighter anyway, so probably I wouldn't get the shit kicked out of me, at least.

A hand brushed up against my bicep and I nearly jumped out of my shoes. My eyes flew open right as my phone cracked against the pavement and I came eye to eye with Giada.

"Shoot, I'm sorry Luca. I didn't mean to startle you," Giada said, crouching down and grabbing my phone. She wiped it on her coat then inspected it. "The screen didn't break." Her tone was hopeful, but uncertainty filled her eyes as she gazed up at me.

Her chocolate eyes sparkled, and the streetlight above us cast a soft glow across her face that made her skin look shimmery. She looked even more beautiful than usual, and she was looking at me. I had assumed Giada would stay inside the warm building, laughing and playing with Colton and her other friends, but instead, she was out here in the frigid night air, with me.

"It's cold out here," I said. "Did you need something?"

She hesitated. "Just wanted to check on you. You were gone a while."

"That was my papà," I explained, holding up my phone then cramming it in my pocket. "I figured you'd stay inside with your friends. You seemed pretty cozy with Colton there."

Giada tilted her head to the side and reached her hand back to my bicep as though trying to steady me.

I shivered, but it was more from her touch than the lack of coat.

"You jealous?" she asked.

I stepped closer and slipped my hands between her coat and her fitted sweater. Without any space between us, I was warmer, although maybe not just from body heat. "If I say yes, will you warm me up?"

She smiled shyly, but didn't pull away as I slowly leaned in to kiss her. The kiss started tentatively, our lips barely touching. Even like that, though, kissing Giada felt amazing. Eventually, one of us deepened the kiss, but I didn't really even know who. Every sensation was exquisite. I'd never before felt such an intense rush of emotions just from a kiss. All I knew was that kissing Giada made me forget all of the other shit going on in my life. As long as I was kissing her, life was good.

"Hey!" a deep voice called.

Giada pulled back instantly, but my hand lingered in her hair.

"Move it along!" the voice continued.

I cringed. That voice definitely belonged to the campus security guard. As far as I could tell, he had been hired solely for this purpose—breaking up couples happily making out anywhere around campus.

I stepped back from Giada, then thought better of it and gripped her hand before she could bolt.

"Sorry," I said, waving to the security guy with my free hand. Then I led Giada back towards the student union entrance to the bowling alley.

Giada's friends were already finishing up their bowling match, so we said goodbye to everyone, and I offered to walk Giada back to her dorm. We waited a few minutes to make sure the security guard was gone, then started out the door, hand in hand.

"What was your dad calling about?" Giada asked, breaking the magical spell.

"He just wanted to remind me that I'm an epic disappointment and tell me he wants me to come home tomorrow."

Giada stopped walking and turned to me, pouting. "I had been hoping you were going to ask me out for another date."

"I'll be back by Sunday to help you with the party stuff. We could go out after that?"

She smiled and resumed walking, which meant we reached her door a minute later. We both stopped, then turned to face each other at the same time. A beat passed, then our lips crashed together. After a moment, Giada pulled back, likely afraid of getting busted again. I held tight to her hand for another minute, then released it, still smiling.

Giada started up the steps to her dorm then paused. "Luca? I don't think you're a disappointment."

She skipped up the remaining stairs before I could think of a response.

By some miracle, I was able to get some sleep that night, despite the uncertainty about what my Saturday might entail. When Iacopo did come to pick me up, Lodovico was with him too. I wasn't sure if that was a good sign or not, but after we endured a couple of boring hours driving around town collecting various payments owed to my papà, I decided I was probably safe.

At nightfall, they said my papà wanted to see me at his club. That alone didn't surprise me, but when we pulled up to 4th and Main, I was shocked. It was the same club I'd gone to the last time- the one with the half-naked women dancing.

"Uhh, this is where my papà wanted to meet with his underage son?" I clarified.

Iacopo leaned closer to the windshield, squinting as if trying to see whatever might possibly be objectionable.

"Just don't stare at the titties when your papà is talking, okay Luca?" Lodovico advised.

I laughed, but followed him into the building. We bypassed the main floor, heading straight to my papà's office. When they didn't join me, I started to worry. My papà was seated at his desk, in the middle of a phone call. Stationed just outside the door was Daniele Pagano, one of my papà's personal bodyguard's. Immediately inside the office, flattened against the wall, was Maximo Fonatana, another member of Papà's personal security detail. He'd been with my papà for as long as I could remember, and I hated him more each day. He never smiled, and I didn't trust him.

My papà motioned for me to sit down, so I did. I tried to conceal my boredom while he finished his call, but apparently I failed because the first thing he did upon hanging up was comment on my scowl.

"Sorry, but I can't help my face," I said. "It's genetic."

A hand smacked the back of my head before my papà could even respond.

"Hey!" I turned to Maximo, who simply shrugged.

"You show your father respect," he said.

"You keep your hands to yourself," I replied.

"Luca! It doesn't have to be this way," my papà said. "Why can't you just listen to your papà?"

I took a deep breath, trying to guess what the right answer might be. "I'm sorry. I'll try harder," I finally said.

My papà nodded his approval. "This family is based on loyalty. The family comes first, always. That means you answer your phone when I call, but it also means that nothing else ever comes before your duty to this family. If I say jump, you jump. You don't ask why, you don't say 'in a minute.' You obey. Immediately and without question. Capisci?"

I didn't understand at all, actually, but it seemed pretty clear I was *not* supposed to ask questions. So I nodded.

Papà looked pleased by this, and motioned to Maximo. He opened the door and a moment later, Daniele reappeared along with Lodovico. They were dragging along a third man. The guy was already in bad shape, with his eyes swollen nearly shut and his lip bleeding.

My stomach rolled as I tried to imagine what my papà planned next.

I turned to my papà as Lodovico stepped out of the office, shutting the door behind him, apparently taking over guard duty on the outside of the office. My papà handed me an aluminum baseball bat.

"This man is one of my bartenders here," my papà explained. "We learned yesterday that he's been stealing from us."

I clenched my teeth together, sending up a silent prayer for the guy. I actually remembered him now that I thought about it. He was the guy who'd served me the last time I was there. You'd think he would've figured out then that the place wasn't the best work environment, after seeing an underage kid drinking at the bar, covered in fresh bruises.

"As far as we can tell," Papà continued, "He's stolen from us at least ten to fifteen times. So I'd like you to hit him with the bat, at least ten to fifteen times." He smiled calmly at me as though he hadn't just told me to beat a man with a fucking baseball bat.

I swallowed the growing lump in my throat.

"He's already bleeding," I said after a lengthy silence. The words had barely left my mouth when an arm forced me forwards, slamming my face against the wall.

"Down boy," my papà said with a chuckle.

Maximo released me, glaring.

"To refresh your memory, we just discussed how you are to obey without question. Do you understand what I've asked you to do?" my papà asked.

"Yes," I said, my throat painfully dry.

"Go on then."

I tightened my grip on the baseball bat, but made no attempt to move. After a moment, I turned to my papà. "I'm not hitting him."

Any hope I'd had that this was some sort of test of my morals disappeared when I saw the instantaneous change in my papà's expression. Anger and disappointment painted his face even before he sighed then nodded to Maximo.

Maximo reached for the bat and stupidly, I let him have it. I wasn't foolish enough to think they'd let the poor guy go, but I did think they'd at least do the job for me.

I wasn't even a little prepared when Maximo swung the bat at me, cracking it into my ribs. I instinctively clutched my arms around myself, but then the second hit slammed into my elbow, which was almost worse. I lunged for Maximo, but Daniele grabbed my arms, quickly restraining me.

I could tell Maximo wasn't using his full strength, but I didn't exactly feel gratitude for that fact. He counted out loud, in Italian, to ten. One count for each time he slammed the bat into my flesh. When he reached "dieci," my papà calmly told him to stop.

The moment they released me, I bolted from the office. I half expected someone to stop me, so when I made it all the way to the back lot, I had no further plan. The lot was mostly empty, save for a handful of cars which likely belonged to employees. It wasn't the safest neighborhood to wait for a car, but I supposed I had no choice. I pulled out my phone to call for a ride, groaning out loud. It couldn't be a good sign that my body already hurt this much. That asshole might have broken a rib.

If I hadn't been dizzy with pain, I might've actually laughed at the thought of my papà's reaction upon hearing that his loyal thug fucked up and broke a bone.

I could barely stand up straight, so I didn't notice the SUV pull up until it stopped in front of me. I would've run, but I couldn't. My body was done.

I glanced up as the passenger window rolled down.

"Get in," Iacopo yelled from the driver's seat.

I replied that he could go fuck himself, except I said it in Italian, which was much classier.

"I'll take you back to school," he promised.

"I can't go back to school like this."

"Alright, I'll take you to your friend's house." He paused. "You'll never get a car to pick you up here."

He was right, and by this point, the pain was too much. My options were to get in the car with Iacopo or curl up on the pavement and pray for a swift death. I lumbered over to the SUV and climbed in, clutching my arms around my body like my intestines would fall out if I stopped.

I struggled with the seatbelt, and Iacopo reached over and fastened it for me like I was a little kid. Then he held out his hand, which contained two chalky white pills.

"What is that?" I asked.

"Does it matter? It'll help with the pain."

"I need water."

He reached over me, pressing a code on the glove compartment box, then flipping it open. "Should be a bottle in there somewhere."

There were two bottles of water, but also three stacks of money and a Glock. I stared at it all, then grabbed a water and shut the compartment. "Take me to Alessio Rizzo's," I said. "I don't have the address, but I can tell you how—"

"I know where it is," he interrupted, casting me a concerned side eye. "I knew you wouldn't do it. Lodovico thought you would, but…"

It took me a moment to figure out what he was talking about. "You knew what my papà planned and you didn't give me a heads up?"

"I work for him, not you."

We were quiet for several minutes, then I got ballsy. Maybe it was the drugs, or maybe it was the realization that I truly had nothing to lose. "So he tells you to beat someone up, and you just do it? No questions asked, no hesitation?"

He took his time replying. "You already know the answer to that. But before you start judging me, maybe wait a decade, and see what you think then. You're in for a rude awakening if you think the next stage of your life is going to be all soccer games and shopping trips."

"Whatever," I mumbled. I shut my eyes and didn't open them until we reached Alessio's. As the car rolled to a stop in front of my friend's house, I realized I hadn't told him I was coming, and it was after midnight.

I swore, then texted Alessio.

Iacopo retrieved my backpack and duffel bag from the back seat and then set them on the curb. As a light switched on inside Alessio's house, Iacopo climbed back into the car and drove off, leaving me alone.

CHAPTER 9

MISSING IN ACTION

- Giada -

After spending Saturday at church for the regular service and then finalizing party prep, I was grateful to have Luca's help with the finishing touches Sunday. Well, mostly I was excited about our date. So I was more than a little disappointed when he texted that he wouldn't be back to campus until Monday.

All day, I'd been sending him cutesy pictures of the various decorations and favors—all of which he'd helped pick out and pay for. And now, he couldn't even be bothered to "like" any of the pictures.

Instead of nagging Luca, I sent a super supportive text, letting him know I hoped his dad wasn't making the weekend too miserable and that I couldn't wait for him to see the decorations at the party room.

Luca didn't even reply.

I didn't see him at breakfast or lunch Monday morning, and when I texted him to see if he had gotten back yet, he said he had. But then he was MIA in World Religions. I sent another text, despite how stalkerish I was starting to feel, and Luca said he wasn't feeling well. I replied that I hoped he felt better soon.

After school, I was meeting Elise outside the chapel. Since Luca had ditched me, Elise had promised to help me go over the final details for the charity party, which was happening that weekend. In typical Elise-fashion, she was late.

"So I guess you've given up on pretending you're not after Luca," a nasally voice said from behind me.

I turned to come face to face with Emily, Luca's homecoming date. I took a breath and opted to take the higher road. "Hi Emily. Cute top. What were you saying about Luca?"

"Thanks," she said dryly, clearly not buying the authenticity of my friendliness. "I was just recalling how you said you weren't interested in Luca."

I plastered my biggest smile to my face, remembering that I was the one with the cute boy in my corner. I didn't need to engage in the mean girl antics when I'd already won. "Yeah, crazy how quickly things change. If you'd asked me a month ago, I wouldn't have ever thought I'd agree to date Luca Marino, but he's pretty persuasive."

"*He* asked *you* out?" Skepticism filled her voice.

I nodded, omitting the part about the most perfect first kiss ever…and all the equally perfect kisses since that day. "We spent some time together over Thanksgiving and were able to talk about everything. What he had to say about us as a couple made sense, so I agreed to give it a shot. Definitely glad I did. I think our friendship makes our current connection stronger."

Emily's expression now was a mixture of disgust and confusion. "Yeah, um, I hate to tell you this, but I don't think you and Luca have the same sort of, uh, connection in mind. He's a teenage boy. They all want the same thing. And trust me when I tell you that Luca's no beginner when it comes to fooling around. I speak from experience."

At that, I'd officially had enough. Kindness was overrated.

"Yes, I heard about that whole…limo debacle. Classy," I said, wrinkling my nose. "But if that was what Luca wanted, don't you think he'd still be with you or someone like you, and not me?"

Emily rolled her eyes. "Guys like the chase. But eventually, if you're not willing to give him what he wants, he'll go to someone who will. I'm just warning you."

She turned on her heel and stormed off before I could say anything else. I gritted my teeth together and made a face at her back. I wondered how she knew I wasn't doing anything more than kissing with Luca. Surely he hadn't told her. Elise knew, as did my other suitemates, but…

I groaned aloud as I realized Blair must have told her. God, it sucked having a roommate who hated me. She and Emily had probably formed an anti-boyfriend snatcher alliance or something to gang up against me.

"Um what was that?" Elise asked, sneaking up from the side.

"Ugh! That girl is horrible."

"Emily?" She didn't seem to agree initially, but then recognition washed over her. "Oh right, she and Luca… Yes, she is absolutely awful."

"She doesn't even care that the entire school knows what she did in that limo."

Elise locked her arm around mine at the elbow and we began to walk towards our dorm. "Don't let her get to you. She's just jealous. Everyone knows he liked you back when he was with her, so it makes sense for her to try to get back at you now."

"I know, I know. And I'm the one with the boy, so I just need to shake it off."

"Exactly."

I blew out a sigh.

"What?"

"She implied that if I didn't eventually put out, Luca will dump me. Or maybe cheat on me," I added, realizing it was unclear which she'd meant.

Elise cast a gaze in my direction and shook her head. "I keep forgetting you're a virgin."

She said it like it was so surprising. I supposed that teens at boarding school tended to engage in that sort of behavior earlier than they might if they were still living at home. In a lot of ways, we were like adults, or at least college students. But in terms of age, we weren't. I wasn't even sixteen yet. No one could convince me it was weird that I hadn't yet had sex. I honestly didn't even see what the big deal was. People here acted like that was a bad thing, but it wasn't. The Church said my virginity was a gift, something to be saved and treasured. Personally, I liked that idea.

"Do you think Luca knows?" Elise asked.

I shrugged. "I'm not sure. He knows I'm not as experienced as him, but…"

Elise frowned for a moment before resuming her chipper tone. "Well, it doesn't matter now anyway. You guys just started going out. He obviously likes you enough to take it slow. And by the time he's ready to take things to the next step, who knows? You might be ready too."

"Nope."

"You don't know that."

"I'm not having sex until I'm married."

I turned to Elise just in time to see her eyes widen. "You're joking, right?"

"Afraid not."

She stared at me for a minute, then shook her head again. "You are full of surprises, Giada Conti. Honestly, when I first met you, I pegged you for a party girl who'd slept with like half a dozen college guys and maybe a couple teachers. Of course, I also thought you would be a total bitch, but that was just based on your wardrobe."

"What's wrong with my clothes?"

She laughed and waved her hand dismissively, then waltzed into the chapel.

With Elise's help, I finished everything for the party. That was a good thing, since Luca didn't show up to class Tuesday either. All Luca and I would need to do over the weekend was decorate and then show up to enjoy the festivities.

I called Luca Tuesday evening to check on him. I was toying with ordering some chicken soup delivery or something else to cheer him up, but realized I didn't even know what illness he had. Since girls weren't allowed in the boy's dorm and the school was quick to isolate anyone when sick anyway, it wasn't like I'd be able to actually see him. Still, I could at least have his roommate run something up to him.

When he answered, I heard the dinging noise a car made when keys were inserted, and then a voice in the background.

"Luca?" I asked, almost thinking I'd called the wrong number.

"Yeah it's me. What's up?"

"Are you off campus now?"

"Uh huh. Just running an errand with a friend," he said in a confusingly casual tone.

"I thought you were sick."

"Oh." He paused for an eternity. "Well, um, no. I was tired when I got back, but then I just had a lot of work to do. Sorry. I'll um be in class tomorrow."

I was so annoyed I couldn't see straight, but instead of lashing out, I just ended the call. "Okay, guess I'll see you then."

I ended up seeing him before then. I finished lunch early, then waited outside the door he'd go in for his science class. If Luca didn't show up at least a few minutes early, it would make me late for my art class. But, my art teacher wasn't super strict, so I reasoned it was worth it to have a minute to catch up and figure out what was going on with Luca before we had class together.

Luckily, he came along five minutes early. I jumped off the bench where I'd been waiting.

"Where have you been?" I should've been mad, but I was so relieved to see him that I skipped the lecture.

His eyebrows dipped as his lips parted, but then he turned to the side, looking at Grant as he answered. "I just had some stuff to take care of."

His indifference annoyed me. "You could've called."

"I texted."

I sighed and dropped my gaze to my feet. Maybe this was his subtle way of breaking up with me. First he ditched me for our date, then he claimed to be sick, then he avoided me like the plague. I listed the reasons aloud, staring pointedly at Grant until he took the hint and left us alone.

A moment passed, then Luca stepped closer. "Giada, I'm sorry. It was…I had a rough couple of days. Stuff with my papà just, wasn't good. And I guess I was avoiding you but only because I didn't want to talk about it and I'm not ready to forgive him and you would've made me feel bad about that. I missed you though."

Luca reached for my hand, his fingertips brushing against mine.

I relented, letting Luca take my hand in his. His free hand stroked my hair, tucking the shorter strands in the front behind my ear. His hand lingered next to my face, soothing my anger. I inhaled slowly, smiling at the sweet, sporty scent of his cologne or aftershave or whatever it was.

Luca took one more step, dipping his forehead towards mine.

"I'm sorry you had a bad weekend," I finally said, surprised that it was true, that suddenly my concern was more him and not my own annoyance.

"A kiss would make it better," he replied, grinning.

I rose to my toes, kissing him lightly. As always with our kisses though, it quickly intensified. He dropped my hand, reaching his arms around my lower back instead. I followed suit, shifting my hands to his back. I pulled him tightly against me, loving the closeness after even such a short time apart.

Luca stiffened suddenly, his lips going limp. He quickly recovered, trying to play it off, but I'd felt it.

"What's wrong?" I pulled back.

"Nothing." Luca didn't meet my eyes.

I paused, certain I'd noticed something. But he didn't say anything else, so I squeezed his back, determined to let it go.

He grunted and pulled back.

"Luca?"

Without hesitation, I walked around him, yanking his shirt up. Angry purplish-blue bruises coated his back and ribs. "Jesus!"

He swatted my hand away, tugging his shirt down. "We're in the middle of campus, Giada. You can't just undress me."

"What is that? Were you in a car accident?"

Luca shook his head, then glanced around as if there were spies.

"I'm fine, Giada. Just some bruises."

I stared at his face, noting nothing out of the ordinary. Maybe he looked a little more sleepy than usual, but that was it. Then, I reached for his hands. He let me inspect them both, and they were pristine. He certainly hadn't hit anyone, so maybe he was telling the truth about the accident. "Is it just your back?" I finally asked.

Luca head moved from side to side. He hesitated, then lifted up his shirt in the front, revealing similar bruising along his ribs.

"Oh Luca, I'm so sorry. What happened?"

He shoved his hands in his pockets and stared at his shoes. "My papà had asked me to deliver all this stuff for him and I was rushing so I could finish up early and I fell down a flight of stairs. And then my papà called me clumsy, so, um what's that expression, adding insult to injury?"

I nodded, wishing I could push Luca's dad down a flight of stairs. What kind of a sociopath said shit like that to his kid?

"It looks worse than it is."

I made a face, certain he must feel awful. "I'm so sorry," I repeated, having no other words for it.

"Thank you. You should probably get to class though, don't you think?"

I checked the time on his watch and nodded. "Yeah. I'll see you next period."

Luca lifted his head and reached for my hand. He pulled it closer and gave me one more slow, sweet kiss, then turned and went into the building.

- Luca -

I couldn't believe Giada actually bought my stupid story about the stairs. Did she really think I was clumsy? I was glad Alessio had made me think up a plausible explanation for the injury though. It was definitely nice to stop avoiding Giada.

I'd spent the rest of the weekend on Alessio's couch. His sister Ginevra had been home so I didn't get a bed, but that was just as well. I barely moved all day Sunday. I left the couch to go to the bathroom and that was it. Alessio's mom worked a double Sunday, so she never realized I was hurt. Ginny definitely knew something was up, unless she was just that nice to all of her younger brother's friends, but she didn't say anything. And Monday morning, after Alessio left for school, Ginevra was the one who had driven me back to school.

Part of me wanted to just take off. I could start saving cash, max out my credit cards, then make a run for it. I could live on my own in Italy or something. I'd need a fake ID for that to work though, and at the end of the day, I wasn't sure I could even live that way.

Yeah, it sucked being at the beck and call of a papà who seemed to think I was a punching bag. But that didn't happen too often. The other 85% of my life was pretty sweet. And leaving would mean saying goodbye to everything, including Giada.

I wasn't so sure I'd find another girl like her. Not in Italy, not anywhere.

Final exams were coming up, so Giada refused my offer to take her to dinner that night but instead made plans for us to study together in the library on Thursday and Friday night. I balked at the idea of wasting my weekend at the library, but Giada was right. I'd gotten behind and needed to catch up. Failing and one of my exams would give my papà more than enough reason to stick his gangsters on me again.

Giada was heading off campus to do some Christmas shopping Saturday, and while she already had a small group of girls going with her, I decided to tag along too. I recruited Marcus and Gavin to come with me so I wouldn't be the only guy.

Giada held my hand in front of her friends, and even let me kiss her in front of an audience now. And for that, I was grateful, because I couldn't be near her and not touch her. We separated for about an hour, her taking off with the girls to some jewelry and lingerie shop while us guys stopped for food. When the girls came back, Giada snuck up behind me and pressed her hands over my eyes.

"Guess who," she taunted, as if I hadn't already figured it out by her sweet smell and soft fingers.

Turning swiftly, I tugged her sideways onto my lap instead of answering. She shrieked, drawing the attention of a dozen or so nearby diners. "I'm not good at guessing games," I replied, kissing her before she could protest. To my delight, she kissed me back, even leaving her hand on my cheek, right up until our friends groaned.

"Get a room!" Elise shouted.

"I could go for that," I said, my voice low enough that only Giada could hear.

She shot me a look then squirmed off my lap. "Have you guys been sitting here the whole time?"

We all nodded in unison.

Giada flashed me her best pouty face. "You didn't have any shopping you needed to do without me around?"

I laughed out loud, realizing what she was hinting at. "Tesoro, there is absolutely nothing in this mall that I would deem worthy for you," I finally said.

She blushed. "Tesoro?"

Now it was my turn to flush. I hadn't realized I'd actually said that out loud, but it was too late to take it back now. "It's an Italian term of endearment," I explained.

"Meaning?"

"Treasure."

All of the girls "awwwed" in unison, and then Elise spoke. "Yeah, well Giada just bought your present in the Gucci shop and she spent way too much."

Giada shot her a dirty glare that brought a smile to my face. I loved how sweet Giada was, but her scrappy side was fun, too.

"Go on, Luca and I will catch up with you guys," Giada said, waiting until our friends had started off to steal the seat beside me. She had several bags, but pulled the Gucci one onto her lap. "I got you two things, but I want to show you one now. That way, if you really hate it, I can go return it before we head back to campus."

"I couldn't hate anything you picked out."

She grinned mischievously and reached into the bag. When she pulled out a pair of white socks with the Gucci logo around the ankle, I laughed out loud.

"Okay, so maybe these are a tad more expensive than normal socks, but go big or go home, right? And if you're going to wear socks, you can't beat these."

I nodded, still chuckling. "I love them. I might even wear them sometime," I said, leaning in to kiss her again.

"So I should not return them?"

I shook my head, then leaned forward to peer into the bag. "What else is in there?"

"No peeking," she said, snapping the bag shut.

Giada let me carry the rest of the bags for her while we finished shopping, but she kept that one clutched tight in her hands the entire time. I'd already picked out what I planned to get her— a pair of Damiani earrings. The brand was trendy and Italian, so it seemed fitting. They weren't cheap either, so it was reassuring to see she shared my same lack of budgetary restraint when shopping.

The next day was filled with more Giada. We went to the children's hospital shortly after lunch to decorate and set up for the party. Elise and Jason came too, since Giada had recruited them to help out as well. The party itself went from 4-7, and included food, a magician, balloon animals, dancing, face painting, and tons of treats for the kids. The entire thing was a huge success, and seeing the happiness on all those kids' faces, I could actually see why Giada had wanted to do something like that.

After the party, we stayed to clean up. Curfew had long since passed by the time we drove home, but we were in no rush. Father Harris had informed the school our absence was excused.

We stopped for milkshakes near campus, getting our food in the drive thru then parking in the back of the lot to enjoy our treats. I'd eaten a fair amount at the party, but Giada had been so busy playing hostess that she'd barely touched a thing.

"You must be exhausted," I said. "And starving."

She shrugged. "It was so worth it. Did you see how grateful those parents looked?"

"Yeah. You are a really good person, Giada Conti."

"You are too," she insisted.

I frowned, but didn't disagree.

"What? You are? You didn't have to spend your whole day there, especially not a week before finals. You did a really good thing today, and I don't know why you act like it's out of character for you. You're a good guy, Luca Marino."

I reached over and squeezed her hand. *If only she knew.*

- Giada -

Thanks to my stupid classes, I didn't have time to see Luca on Monday. But Tuesday, we met outside my dorm. The plan was to walk around campus and grab coffee by the student union, but for the first fifteen minutes, we just stood outside the building making out. I could've happily kissed Luca all day, forsaking my beloved coffee, but we were interrupted.

"Slut!" snarled the nasally voice.

I jerked back from Luca and saw Blair stomping past us, her stupid combat boots making me wonder if she was off to war.

Luca lifted his sunglasses and flew to his feet as if ready to fight, but I gripped his hand tightly. He turned back to me, a bewildered expression filling his soft, silky eyes.

"Did I hear her right?" he asked.

I stroked his cheek with my free hand. "Let it go. That was just Blair. She's still pissed about the one time I went out with Brooks."

Luca furrowed his brows. "Does she speak to you like that often?"

"No. Mostly she ignores me. But she seems to have teamed up with Emily and decided I'm a boyfriend-stealer."

His frown deepened and he sat on the stone half-wall behind us, letting his sunglasses drop back down over his eyes. "She started that rumor about you and Liam too, didn't she?"

"Yep." I sat beside him, gazing at my nails absentmindedly. "She also stole my clothes and towel while I showered one day. Oh, and she put Nair in my shampoo."

"Nair?"

"It's a cream that makes your hair fall out."

Luca cringed. "What a petty bitch."

I was about to agree, when he continued.

"I think she has the same science teacher I had last year. I could get a copy of the old test and hide it in her room, then leave an anonymous tip for the dean that she's cheating. We could get her kicked out of school before Christmas."

I lifted his sunglasses, desperate to decipher if he was being serious. His deep chocolate eyes peered back at me, without any hint of sarcasm.

"No!"

His eyebrow quirked. "No?"

"Of course not. Luca, you will absolutely not do anything at all to her."

"I don't mind. Blair deserves it."

He wasn't wrong about that part, but that wasn't the point. "*I* mind. And you should too."

Luca pressed his fingers against my hip, holding me close. "Giada, she was a total bitch. You can't just let her get away with that."

"No one is getting away with anything," I reminded him. "But it isn't my job to punish her. Or yours," I added, after his lips parted to protest.

"Oh, because God is going to take care of the mean girls?" Luca snorted. "Don't you think He has more important stuff to worry about?"

When he put it that way, it did sound a little ridiculous. I dropped my gaze to my shoes, but quickly looked up again when Luca pressed a kiss to the crown of my head.

"I'm a good person," I finally said. "And nothing Blair does will change that about me. If she wants to be a jerk, I can't control that. But I can control whether she drags me down with her."

He sighed and dropped his hand from my hip. "Kill her with kindness?"

"Something like that."

"What if I slip some laxatives into her lunch without telling you? Then Blair shits her pants, but your soul is still pure."

The image of Blair sprinting to the bathroom did bring a smile to my face. But it was still a no for me. "I don't need to get revenge on Blair. She doesn't matter. I have you. I'm happy."

Luca pouting was the most adorable sight I'd ever seen. I reached for his hand, twining my fingers around his.

"You're too good for this world, Giada," he said, raising our joined hands to his lips for a kiss.

The next week and a half flew by. I divided my time equally between Luca and studying. When possible, I incorporated Luca into my study time. That proved to be harder than I would've expected, though. Luca was the ultimate distraction. Being a year older and having already taken my current English, Science, Math, and Social Studies classes, Luca should have been able to help enormously in those subjects, but he was more focused on making out than tutoring me.

In his defense, he would answer questions when I asked. But he usually demanded payment for his wisdom in the form of kisses. And while he probably would've accepted one tiny kiss as payment, it was really hard to stop after just one.

"Ugh!" I groaned. "This is terrible."

Luca's face paled. "Terrible? Do we need to practice more?"

I bit back a laugh. "We definitely do not need to practice more. I don't even think that is possible. But what I meant was this, our study tactic. You already said your dad will kill you if you flunk, and I'm pretty sure mine will react the same. I need solid B's to avoid a lecture. B's require me to actually study."

"But it's like osmosis. When we kiss with our textbooks open, you absorb the material even better than if you actually read it," Luca insisted

He leaned in for another kiss and I pushed away from the table.

"Nope. You are studying here. I will go back to my room to study. Once we each get half our exams done, then we can go out for a dinner to celebrate. Okay?"

Luca wrinkled his nose and mumbled something in Italian, but he nodded. "Can I give you my present then?"

"Yes." I leaned in to kiss him goodbye, intending to just press a kiss against his forehead. Instead, he kissed me hard on the lips and then tickled my side, eliciting a sharp squeal from me.

The librarian peered up and cleared her throat.

Luca and I both laughed.

It wasn't much easier to concentrate at the dorm. Everyone was in various stages of preparing for the holidays, packing to head home, and studying. I lugged all of my books and notepads to my bed, popped in headphones, then began studying.

The way the school structured finals, we had a long weekend to study for the first exams, and then two tests each on Monday and Tuesday. Wednesday was a free day intended for studying, and then the final four exams were spread out over Thursday and Friday. In reality though, many people used the free Friday and Wednesday to party, shop for Christmas, or pack for their winter break.

Despite the distractions, I finished my first four tests. And while I still had four remaining, they were in my easier classes. Art had a final project, which we could complete during the scheduled time for our examination. Tennis had some stupid strength and endurance progress test that one couldn't exactly study for anyway. Interior Design also had a project, but it was fun and I'd been working on it during my study breaks for other classes and could easily finish during the allotted time for the test. So that just left World Religions, and since Luca was in that class, obviously it made sense to study with him.

We met at the library again, committed a good two hours to

studying, then went to a movie. Luca let me pick the movie, so I chose a cutesy Christmas romance that I probably would've loved if we'd actually paid attention. But we spent the entire movie making out. I was so busy kissing Luca that I didn't even finish devouring either of the candies he insisted on buying me.

After the movie, we went to our favorite Italian restaurant. Luca spent the first few minutes trying to teach me Italian, then once we ordered, we exchanged our gifts. He loved the Gucci scarf I'd bought him, and the Damiani earrings he'd chosen for me literally gave me flutters in my stomach. It was the perfect date.

Until dessert.

Somehow, I'd managed not to think about the reality of our situation until then… the fact that in two days, Luca was heading back to Staten Island and then flying out to Italy, where he would spend the next three weeks. I was staying on campus Friday evening for a holiday sleepover with my suitemates, and then heading home Saturday morning. I'd be in Connecticut until after Christmas, and then we were heading to the Caribbean for a week.

I was going to be apart from Luca for three full weeks.

"Che cosa?" Luca asked when he saw my face. Then, he laughed, shook his head, and switched to English. "What is it? What's wrong? Is the tiramisu bad?" He reached over with a spoon to taste it.

I tugged the plate out of his reach and smiled mischievously. "Tiramisu is never bad. I just realized I'm not going to see you for three whole weeks."

Judging from the lack of change in his expression, Luca had already figured that fact out himself. "You are going to have a wonderful Christmas. It's one of your favorite holidays and you'll have so much fun with your family. And then you get to go on a cruise. There'll be sunshine and turquoise water and all the tiramisu you can trick them into serving you."

As Luca teased me, I dipped my spoon back into the creamy dessert and held the bite out towards him. When he leaned closer, I smeared it on his nose.

"Well played," he said, wiping his nose with a napkin.

"I swear, two out of three years we go to Italy for the holidays. Why is it the one time I desperately want to go there that my family decides to float around some islands?"

"You wouldn't want to see me anyway. I'll be busy with family stuff and my papà's work and I'll probably be grumpy the whole time."

I sighed. "Will you text me while we're apart?" While I awaited his response, I spooned another bite of tiramisu for him, and this time, I actually fed it to him properly.

"No," he said after swallowing. "I'll write you traditional Italian love letters and you'll spend your entire break translating."

I stuck out my tongue at him right as the waiter returned with the check.

Luca paid and then smiled at me. "I'm going to miss you, Tesoro."

CHAPTER 10

THE CAT'S OUT OF THE BAG

- Luca -

While everyone else on campus was stressed about final exams, I would've happily continued testing for the full month. What I dreaded was returning home.

By some miracle, my papà managed to act like a real father the entire break. Although, truth be told, I didn't have much interaction with him. He had returned to Italy earlier in the month, so it was just my mom and me on the lengthy flight from New York to Sicily. As a bonus, my papà spent a week in Rome before flying down to join us in Sicily right before Christmas.

With my entire family around, my life felt normal. I could pretend, at least, that my focus was on whether I'd get the presents I'd hoped for and not whether my papà would order me to beat up a complete stranger again in the near future. I missed Giada and I really missed Alessio too, but in Italy, I felt at home in a way I rarely did in the U.S. I wasn't sure if it was the customs or the language; something about life in Italy was just easier.

My papà had already told me I'd be spending my summer working for him as an apprentice of sorts. As winter break drew to a close, I found myself dreading the summer much less than I had been before the holidays.

Once I returned to New England, I caught up with Alessio. He told me he'd gotten in a fight with Marcus and wouldn't be hanging around our dorm anymore. I didn't press for details, but that was a definite bummer. Alessio and I had gotten so close over the past few months that I'd considered him my best friend at school, and rarely remembered he didn't actually attend the school.

Alessio was the only person who knew what my papà had done to me. I'd told him all the details, and I trusted him when he said he'd never tell anyone else. Alessio also understood the nature of my family business, perhaps more than I did. He was the one who researched the local mafia and helped me identify some of the major actors in the area. As far as we could tell, my papà was the head of one of the six major crime families in the area. Marco Conti was another.

Alessio had mapped out which areas each family controlled in general. My papà had a hold on Staten Island, where we lived, but also in upstate New York. The Conti family ruled all of Connecticut. A third family seemed to be in charge in New Jersey, and the remaining ones were smaller factions in Manhattan. Not surprisingly, my family had the strongest ties with Italy.

"There's more in Italy, I'm sure, but I'm having trouble researching all of that. Your father is active in Sicily and also Rome, but I don't see much news of him in Naples," Alessio explained.

I shrugged. That made sense. Whenever we were in Napoli, it was generally just a stopping point between Palermo and Roma. "There's always been several different families in Napoli. And I think the entire North is controlled by a different group." I paused. "You don't need to look into this anymore though. It's my problem, not yours."

"You need to know what you're getting into though."

"It's not like I have a choice either way," I reminded him.

Alessio narrowed his gaze. "Does it matter? Would you honestly choose to leave the family if you could?"

"In a heartbeat."

If this surprised my friend, he didn't say so. "Someday it'll all be yours, Luca. Then you won't have to put up with your papà or any of his bullshit. You'll make the calls. They will all answer to you."

Alessio said it like all that was a good thing, but I wasn't so sure.

Giada returned to campus late Sunday, so we barely had time to catch up before curfew. We spent lunch Monday kissing in an empty hallway behind the student center, and thankfully we still had World Religions together. But that wasn't enough.

"Meet up with me tonight," I said, trying to figure out where we could actually meet on campus where we wouldn't freeze to death.

"I haven't unpacked anything. Tomorrow?"

I groaned but agreed.

The next night, I took Giada to a nicer seafood restaurant overlooking the water. I figured it wouldn't hurt us both to break up our routine of always going to the same Italian place. The food was amazing, so I got to enjoy listening to all the enticing sounds Giada made when enjoying delicious flavors. And the ambiance was nice too—very romantic. But it was further from campus, so it was already nearing curfew as we returned to the car.

"If we left now, I could get you back in time for curfew," I said, squeezing her gloved hand as we walked to the car.

"Was there another option?"

"We could blast the heat in the car and just hang out here for a bit. You know, enjoy the view and catch up. But that scenario might get you back to campus late."

Her lips slowly spread into a smile. "You just want to sit in the car and…talk?"

"Yeah. What else is there to do in a car?" I teased, certain we were both thinking the exact same thing.

"Sure. Let's talk."

I opened her car door and waited until she'd climbed in before shutting it. Then I scurried around and, as promised, blasted the heat. It wasn't the first time we'd stayed out past curfew and generally, no one really noticed on a weeknight unless we were really late. Upper classmen had a later curfew, so as long as we returned before that curfew, no one was likely to notice that Giada wasn't technically eligible for that later curfew.

"What should we talk about?" I said, smiling coyly. "Vacation? Christmas? Classes?"

"We could talk about my new Chapstick. It's papaya."

A beat passed before I figured out she didn't actually want to discuss her new lipwear. "I bet it tastes good. Can I try some?"

She smiled and launched herself across the gear shift, bringing her arms around my neck and her lips squarely on mine. I couldn't actually taste anything resembling papaya, but that was just fine with me.

I thought we'd only kissed for a few minutes, but when we paused to catch our breath, I realized it had been nearly an hour.

"Huh," Giada said, clearly noticing the same fact. "That went fast."

I swore under my breath and buckled my belt. "I have to get you back." I drove as fast as I could, slowing only when we reached the school. I parked in the back corner of the lot, killing the lights as we rolled into the spot and then tiptoeing out of the car. We didn't see anyone around as we approached her dorm, so I thought we'd made it. I gave Giada a quick kiss goodbye then watched her go inside before returning to my own dorm.

- Giada -

$\mathcal{M}$y dorm mom was waiting for me directly inside the dorm when Luca dropped me off after our date. She'd crossed her arms over her chest, shook her head, and mumbled, "I hope it was worth it" before explaining my parents would be called in for a meeting with Dean Andrews.

My initial thought was that it *had* been worth it. The school was strict about possible "moral" violations like breaking curfew, so that was why they required the stupid parent meeting. But as far as I could tell, there really wasn't much in terms of additional punishment. And after going three whole weeks without kissing Luca, I'd have suffered through a lot more than a lame lecture to get to kiss him like that.

I hadn't expected both of my parents to come to the meeting, so that was rough. Apparently, since my dad hadn't yet been to campus, Mom thought it would be a good opportunity for him to see the place in person.

I sat in a chair to the side of the dean's desk while my parents were shown to the comfy couch in the corner of the office. Mr. Andrews pulled up a chair to sit adjacent to them after shaking both of their hands.

"Mr. and Mrs. Conti, I don't want to waste your time, so I'll get right into it. We at the Academy have truly enjoyed getting to know your remarkable daughter. Her teachers all praise her academic work and the priest who works with our campus chapel tells me she spearheaded some sizable charity projects and made quite the impact in our community. But all of that said, we have a strict moral code here at the Academy, and we take our role of serving *in loco parentis* very seriously here."

Mr. Andrews paused to take a breath and my dad turned to me, scowling. I felt my face burn even redder, and I was dreading the moment where my parents learned what I'd been caught doing.

"We know parents are putting a lot of trust in us to supervise your children as you would at home, so this type of violation always merits a candid, in-person discussion involving all parties."

I felt my eyes widen. Surely they weren't going to drag Luca and his parents in here as well...were they? I didn't even think his parents weren't in town now. But even having Luca present for this discussion would make this torturous experience even worse.

"Your daughter violated a weeknight curfew. She also left campus, which is a privilege only our upper classmen hold."

"The students can't leave campus?" my mother interrupted.

"Our Freshmen and Sophomores can leave campus on the weekends, but during the week we ask that they remain on campus except for medical appointments, participation in religious activities, and any other specific activities arranged in advance by the family."

My mother nodded then turned to me. "Did you know that?"

"I go to church on weekdays," I said, not exactly answering.

My mother was satisfied with that response, but my dad narrowed his eyes. "Giada Francesca, were you aware of the rule?"

"Yes," I said in a sigh.

"And you left anyway?"

"I planned to go to church when I left, but I decided not to. It didn't seem like a big deal at the time, and..." I paused in lieu of pointing out that no one would've known where we'd gone if we hadn't spaced the curfew. "And we lost track of time. I'm sorry, and it won't happen again."

"We?" my dad repeated.

I dropped my gaze. *Shit.*

"That's the other part of the equation, sir. Giada was with an upperclassman, so he was allowed off campus and he had a later weeknight curfew. And I know it's a sensitive issue with kids this age, but if my teenage daughter snuck off with a boy, I certainly would want to know."

My parents both nodded like freaking lemmings.

"Who was the boy?" my dad demanded.

Mr. Andrews paused, and for a brief moment, I thought maybe he wouldn't say due to confidentiality rules and I'd be spared further mortification. But no, apparently God was still mad that I lied about going to church.

"Luca Marino. He's a Junior here, and…"

My mother's eyes widened but my dad's mouth ticked upwards into a Cheshire cat grin.

"We know Luca," my dad said. "I don't think we have any problem with Giada spending time with him, do we?" He turned to my mother, who still looked appalled, but didn't wait for her to comment. "We trust the boy. He's a close family friend. Like a brother to Giada, really," he said.

I didn't think it was possible for my face to turn even redder, but Mr. Andrews was now starting to blush. He cleared his throat, then reached for the glass of water on his desk behind him.

"That has not been the nature of the relationship we have observed between your daughter and Mr. Marino."

"Luca?" my dad clarified, apparently now worried I was dating old Salvatore Marino.

Mr. Andrews nodded.

"What do you mean?"

Mr. Andrews turned to me, as though I was going to jump in to save him. No way was that happening.

"I, um, I believe they are, uh, dating?" he said, again turning to me as though I'd eagerly chime in with the detailed saga of our romance.

My mother's hand drifted to her eyes, and my dad slowly turned to me. His expression was harder to decipher now, but he definitely wasn't angry. More like inquisitive, I supposed.

"We're friends," I said.

Mr. Andrews made a face right as my dad turned to him.

"What makes you think it's not just a friendship?" he asked Mr. Andrews.

Now, the headmaster looked downright pained. "Well, they, um, they've been observed on campus holding hands, and kissing, and—"

"When did this happen?" my dad interrupted, asking me.

I shrugged.

"Giada…" his tone sharpened.

"Right before Thanksgiving," I said. It wasn't exactly the truth, but if my parents knew Luca and I had become a couple at our family home, they may never let him come visit again.

My mother massaged her temples with both hands.

"You've been dating Luca Marino since Thanksgiving and no one bothered to tell me?" My dad's annoyance was tangible.

I lifted my shoulders again. It actually was a little surprising he didn't know, with how often he had people watch me.

He turned to my mother, as if to ask if she had any idea, but she shook her head.

"You can't honestly be surprised though, Marco," she said. "You practically forced them together."

"Does Luca's father know about this?" my dad asked me.

"I have no idea."

"What were you doing off campus with him?" my mother asked.

"We went to dinner. There's an Italian restaurant in town. And then we were just talking."

She stared at me in that way moms do where they're clearly trying to read minds. "Are you having sex with him?"

"Oh my God, Mom!" I wished the floor could swallow me up whole. "We went to dinner, not a brothel. Is that what you think of me? That I would… And why would you ask me that in front of the headmaster? Is this seriously a discussion we need to have now?"

"I could step out and give you a few minutes," Mr. Andrews offered, his relief palpable.

"It's fine. We won't kick you out of your own office, Mr. Andrews," my dad said lightly, ignoring that my mom and I were shooting daggers at each other. "We trust our daughter and, just as importantly, we trust Luca. We appreciate you filling us in on the situation, but I don't think we have any objection to those two continuing to spend time together on campus or off, do we?" he turned to my mother, but she didn't answer.

"Well," Mr. Andrews began, still looking shell-shocked. "As it's Giada's first infraction, she'll just have to remain on campus for the next week, including the weekend. Any future violations will carry steeper penalties, but…" his voice trailed off as my dad had already begun to stand.

"Sounds good. Thanks again. Giada," he nodded to me. "A word?"

I groaned inwardly and gazed to Mr. Andrews, almost hoping he'd insist I stay, but instead he nodded.

"I wish you would have told me you were dating Salvatore Marino's only son," my dad said the moment we were outside the Dean's office.

"I think you missed the point of that meeting, Dad. The issue is just that I missed curfew by a couple of minutes, not who I was with."

My mom bit back a smile.

"Am I supposed to tell you every time I go on a date with a boy?" I continued.

"If that boy is the son of one of my closest business associates, then yes," he said, much to my surprise.

"Was it just one date?" my mother asked, seemingly hopeful.

"No."

"Is it serious?" she continued.

I flung my hands up in time with my eye roll. "I'm fifteen. Nothing in my life is serious."

"Are you dating other boys, Giada?"

I hesitated. "Not right now."

"Is Luca dating other girls?"

I sighed and stormed ahead of them.

"I think we should invite him to lunch," my dad suggested.

"I can't leave campus for a week, so that won't work," I said, suddenly grateful to be grounded.

"We could just take Luca."

"Oh my God. No. Just no," I said, turning to face my parents. They exchanged a quizzical look and then both laughed. Geez parents were weird. "Do you guys want to see anything else on campus or are you leaving now?"

My dad opted for a walking tour of campus, despite the fact that the temperature felt about thirty below zero. I wondered if he was just hoping we'd run into Luca so he could mortify us both. It occurred to me that the Dean didn't include anything about Luca in my punishment. So, I couldn't leave campus for a week, but I could still see Luca.

Not such a terrible fate.

- Luca -

Giada and I met up in an empty corner of the Student Union building after her parents left. Ever since I learned she'd gotten caught missing curfew, I'd felt terrible. But as she caught me up on the entire meeting with the Dean, I decided it wasn't actually so bad after all. And the parts about the Dean ratting us out to her parents, well that was downright amusing.

"It's not funny, Luca," she insisted, but I couldn't stop grinning.

"It's kind of funny."

"My mom actually asked—in front of Mr. Andrews—if we were having sex," she continued. Even just mentioning it, her cheeks flushed red.

"I bet Mr. Andrews was even more embarrassed than you."

Giada pursed her lips together as she thought. "Maybe. He did offer to leave his own office."

"Poor guy, I bet he'll never try to out another teenage girl again."

Giada shook her head, but at least she was smiling now. I felt bad that she had gotten in trouble, but she hadn't actually gotten into that much trouble. And now her parents knew and we knew that they knew. Better yet, we knew that they approved.

"I can't believe your father didn't already know we were dating. I thought he knew everything."

"That surprised me too. Especially because of that time Enzo picked me up from campus and saw us together."

"Nothing was going on then. You were just checking my teeth. With your tongue. Totally innocent."

Giada rolled her eyes, but giggled. "I thought he told my dad everything."

"Did you ask him not to?" I didn't know much about Lorenzo, but he seemed awfully young for how much Mr. Conti trusted him to handle. And I got the impression he had a little crush on Giada. Granted, I thought that about most men between the ages of twelve and twenty-five, but he practically lived in Giada's home. If Lorenzo was keeping secrets for her, that seemed even more suspicious.

"No, we never spoke about it again." She paused. "I'm going to text him and ask about it."

I wrinkled my nose, not wanting her attention on anyone but me while we were together. But then, it occurred to me it could be helpful to overhear their discussion. At least then I could get a better sense of whether I needed to be wary of Lorenzo. "Why don't you call him and ask now? I'm curious too."

Giada quirked an eyebrow while she considered it, then dialed. He was saved in her phone, which I supposed shouldn't have been surprising, but that detail annoyed me nonetheless. She kept the call on speaker, and Lorenzo answered on the second ring.

"Everything okay?" he asked. There was some indiscernible background noise on his end, but it sounded like he was speed-walking away from the chaos as it was quiet within a moment.

"Yeah, do you have a minute?" she asked.

"Of course," he replied.

I rolled my eyes and Giada shot me a look.

"The headmaster told my parents about Luca and I today. They both looked really surprised to hear we were dating." She paused. "Had you not told them?"

Her driver took his time answering. "Why would I?"

"I don't know. I thought that was part of your job, babysitting me and reporting back to my dad."

"I am not a babysitter."

"Well, I'm just surprised you hadn't told him."

"He didn't ask. If he had, I would have told him."

Giada turned to me and shrugged. I mirrored her gesture, having no more questions for the man.

"Alright, well, thanks. Sorry for being such a bother."

"You're never a bother, Giada," he replied, eliciting another eye roll from me.

Giada was about to disconnect the call when Lorenzo spoke up again.

"Giada? Be careful with Luca. His life is a lot more compli-cated than you might think," Lorenzo said.

"Umm, okay. Thanks," she said, eying me awkwardly.

She shoved her phone back into her purse.

"I told you he wants you," I said.

Giada winced. "First off, you've never told me that, and second off, ewww. He's like the same age as Angelo."

"Lots of college guys like high school girls, and you look a lot older than you are anyway."

She cocked her head to the side. "Don't worry. I'm not going to dump you for the house staff. You're cute when you're jealous though. So what are these complications I need to know about?"

Giada traced her finger along my jaw line as she spoke, making me shiver.

"I'm positive I've never claimed *not* to be complicated," I reminded her. "And you've met my papà. Nothing involving him is ever simple or pleasant. That's why I need you around to constantly lighten me up."

She smiled, satisfied by that response. "I can do that, but only until curfew." She leaned in and kissed me.

CHAPTER 11

DOOMSDAY

- Luca -

I didn't think anything more of the whole curfew incident until my papà called a couple days later. I expected him to order me to accompany Lodovico and Iacopo on some dumb errands again, but instead he launched into a lecture about loyalty and honesty and all that crap.

"I don't even know what I did that you're mad about this time," I said when he finally paused for a breath.

"Really?" He didn't wait for my answer. "That must be frustrating, to have a phone call where you do not know what the other person is talking about. Just imagine how embarrassing it would be if that person were Marco Conti."

Dread filled my chest. I tried to quickly think of a way to explain, but my papà continued his rant.

"How does it look that I am about to entrust you with our family business and you don't even trust me enough to be honest?"

"I'm sorry," I said, though I still wouldn't tell him about Giada even if I could somehow go back in time and redo it all.

"So it's true then? You are dating Marco's only daughter?"

I briefly considered whether I could dodge a full admission with a tweak of semantics, then gave up. "Yes."

My papà was quiet for an uncharacteristically long time before continuing his interrogation. "Is this because of me? Are you trying to get to me or my business somehow by dating the daughter of—"

"No," I interrupted. "It's coincidence. She just happens to be the girl I'm dating."

"Nothing is coincidence."

"Well, she didn't know anyone else when she came to school. We have a lot in common, and we get along. But I wasn't trying to do anything by dating her."

"You like her?"

"Yes."

Papà sighed, and I couldn't tell over the phone if it was a sigh of relief or disappointment.

"How long has this been going on?" he asked.

I opted for full disclosure in case that helped my case. "She says she had a crush on me from the start of school, but our first date was around Thanksgiving."

"You know, if you hurt Marco's girl, it will be very bad for business."

"I don't plan to hurt her. I like her." I cringed already knowing that, no matter the circumstances of the future breakup, Giada probably would not take it well. And even if she was the one to end our relationship, I would end up dead at the hands of my own papà. Or possibly hers.

"Do you remember when I asked you if you were dating anyone special?"

I did. It was the day before the New Year. We'd been eating dinner, just the three of us, and the conversation had been disturbingly normal.

"What did you tell me?"

"I said no."

"So you lied?"

"Yes."

He sighed again, and this time, it was clearly his disappointed sigh. "Lodovico will pick you up around two pm tomorrow. Don't make him wait."

"Papà," I said quickly, desperate to get him to stay on the line until he at least softened a little. "At the start of the year, remember when I got in trouble for being in a girl's dorm and wouldn't tell anyone the name of the girl I was with? That was Giada. I was protecting your business even then by protecting Marco's daughter."

"So you've been dating her since September?" he asked, clearly misinterpreting my point.

"No. We were just friends then. I was helping her out."

"Well, that was a noble thing to do, Son, but when you keep someone's name a secret to protect them, you take that secret to the grave. You don't save it and then offer it up on a rainy day when you're hoping for a get-out-of-jail-free pass. Two o'clock."

He disconnected before I could say anything else.

I met up with Giada for breakfast at the dining hall the next morning, needing to see her and touch her before enduring whatever shit my papà had planned for me. She picked up on my uneasy mood, but didn't press for details when I said I didn't want to share. Already she'd learned that anytime I had to go home, I was cranky.

It wasn't Lodovico who picked me up, but rather some new guy. Well, new to me, anyway. He said Lodovico and Iacopo had been detained at one of their earlier stops and that he was driving me to meet my papà. Great. The moment the car slowed to a stop by the side entrance to the warehouse, my chest filled with dread. There was only one reason my papà would have someone bring me there, and it wasn't good.

I took a deep breath, held it in, then exhaled slowly. This

would be the last time he'd hurt me. No matter how it went down, it all ended now.

"Out," the driver said, pointing at the door on the passenger side.

"No," I replied.

He turned to face me, as if certain he couldn't have heard me correctly. When he repeated myself, I shook my head.

Then, for good measure, I added, "Make me."

I kept my eyes on him as he climbed out of the car, slammed his door and walked around. What I hadn't noticed was the man who must have walked up from behind the car.

He joined the driver at the passenger door. They opened the door as I lunged for the other side, thrusting my feet towards them to kick the face of whomever came at me first. I made contact with something, but before I could get the other door open, someone tugged on my ankles. I flew out of the car so fast that my head knocked onto the floor of the car and then the curb. The smack of the concrete reverberated all the way down to my neck, even hurting my teeth despite the fact that it was the back of my head that made contact.

The impact stunned me long enough that two of them were able to get me to the entrance of the warehouse, dragging me by my armpits. Just as they reached the door, I went limp, hoping to convince them I was out of it long enough to get my arm free. One of the guys released his hold on me to open the door. I took the opportunity and pulled Alessio's knife out of my pocket, flipping it open with a flick of my wrist and slicing the first thing I could reach—the hand still holding me.

The guy I'd cut released me and yelped. I lunged forward and slit through the shoulder on the suit of the other guy. Then I inched back, wielding the knife as a threat. I thought it was working too, until a sudden thunk on the back of my head knocked me onto my face. I watched as the knife skittered across the room. A boot slammed down on my bicep, hard enough to make me groan, and then another guy grabbed my other arm. Two guys dragged me to my feet, while the original two still glared at me.

I was outnumbered, four to one, and I no longer had my weapon. It was over.

"What the fuck?" the driver said, seemingly talking to one of the guys holding me.

"Call the boss," a guy behind me said. The voice sounded familiar, but I couldn't place it without seeing his face.

"Yeah, call the fucking boss," I said. "Tell him he'd better fucking kill me this time or I'll stab him in his sleep. Do you hear me? I mean it. I'm done with this shit."

"Shut up, Luca," the man said, smacking me on the back of the head.

If that was what they wanted, I'd be as loud as I could. Certain nothing helpful would come from screaming, I launched into my loudest rendition of Ninety-Nine Bottles of Beer On the Wall. I sang while they handcuffed me to a concrete support post in the middle of the room. When one of the guys came close, I swung out my leg to kick him. His irritation was apparent, and he lunged for me.

"Hey!" the same familiar voice called from across the warehouse. "Don't touch him. Don't even go near him until his father arrives. You understand?" The man stepped out of the shadows just long enough for me to recognize him. It was Tomasso, the guy who'd pretended to be my friend when he'd taken me shooting.

"Are you kidding me, Tomasso?" I shouted. "I see you. I fucking see you! Is this some good-cop, bad-cop bullshit? Because I'm done playing your games."

He gazed at me for a moment, his expression unreadable, then walked out of the warehouse.

I waited a minute, then returned to my song. I made it all the way down to zero bottles of beer, then started back over and worked my way from ninety-nine back down to seventy-six before a group of three men entered the warehouse. Behind them was my papà.

"Papà!" I shouted, sounding like a drunk sailor by this point. "Have you come to rescue me or to help your friends break my fingers?" I turned and glanced at the guy I'd tried to kick. "That is what you guys do, right? Or is it kneecaps?"

"It could be both," he snarled.

My papà pointed at three of the men. "Out," he commanded. They obeyed. *Not surprising.*

He approached me. His favorite security guard, Maximo, and his friend Tomasso flanked him on both sides.

"My men say you pulled a knife on them. Is this true?" he asked.

"Sì, signore," I said. Then, feeling emboldened, I spit at my papà.

Maximo's hand shot out to slap me but my papà moved faster, catching the guy's fist seconds before it made contact.

He glared at me with such disdain that I wondered how I ever saw our relationship turning out.

"Like I told your goons, I'm done with this shit. You want to fight me yourself? Fine, let's go. Otherwise, you might as well pay someone to kill me. I'm not letting you pass me around for your buddies to beat up from now on."

"Oh? What is your plan to stop me? The last I checked, you were but a boy," Papà taunted. "I have the money. I have the power. I have the fleet of men willing to carry out my every command."

"We read this book at school, about this old Greek dude who killed his father," I said. "Seems that's always an option."

My papà smiled. "I'm pleased that you're finally learning something in school. And I value your newfound self-respect, but I assure you, mio figlio, you do not wish to take my place before you are ready. And the moment I am gone, you stand to inherit the empire, for better or for worse."

"No thanks. I'll pass."

"It doesn't work like that."

"Seems to me it works however I say it does, since you'd be dead in that scenario."

Now my papà chuckled. "You have so much to learn, Son. And just to ensure you don't screw yourself over before you know any better, I've put some safeguards in place." He stepped closer, apparently confident I wouldn't spit at him again. "If you ever harm me, my men have been instructed to help themselves to whatever your little girlfriend has to offer, and then to kill her."

The implication of his words nauseated me. I knew it was just talk, but the thought of any of these monsters even touching Giada rolled my stomach.

"You wouldn't," I said, quickly rephrasing. "You couldn't. Her father would kill you instantly."

He shrugged. "You forget—I'm already dead in that scenario."

Papà was toying with me now and I knew it, but I couldn't figure out anything else to say to make him understand how serious I was. I was not going to continue to live like this. I could always run away.

"You have so much anger in you, Luca. I wish we could channel that into some useful endeavor."

"I'll go to the cops!" I said suddenly.

"Tell them I say hello," he replied calmly. "When you come to work with me full time, I'll introduce you to the ones who work for me. I'll teach you how to find your own friends to help you succeed without fear of being caught."

"You have nothing to teach me. You're just a bully."

He shook his head, seemingly annoyed. "What do you want, Luca? You just want an easy life, want me to ship you back over-seas where you'll be unable to defend yourself and probably be murdered before you're twenty? Or do you want to earn your place in our world, to prove yourself as the leader you're destined to be?"

I didn't like either of his options, but I suddenly realized what I did feel like doing. "I want to fight. You and me, no weapons, no extra guys. Mano a mano."

My papà chuckled, and I actually had to look away at the sight of his smile. His stupid lopsided grin, the dumb dimple that popped out only when he was truly happy, it all nauseated me.

"Xavier!" he called. After a moment, the guy who'd tied me up returned. Papà turned back to me. "I don't fight, Luca. The point of being the boss is that I no longer have to do such things myself. But Xavier will be more than happy to fight you in my stead, won't you Xavier?"

He turned to Xavier and the man nodded, but looked a bit confused.

"Untie my son," he said to his bodyguard. "Let's see, we need some ground rules. How about, first one unconscious loses?"

I nodded, although that didn't exactly sound like a rule. "And if I win, I'm free. You never touch me again."

My papà chuckled again. "You, my son, are never free. But win or lose, we'll call it a day."

The metal hinge of the handcuffs slid open and my arms fell loose at my side. I rubbed my wrists, then rotated them both in circles.

My papà and his bodyguard both backed away. "Have at it, gentlemen," he said.

I stared at Xavier, who seemed just as unclear about it all as I was. I figured I had about ten seconds before my papà ordered someone else to tie me up and kick me till I was unconscious anyway, so I went for it.

I ran at Xavier, ducked my head, and slammed into his midsection, tackling him. He got a few good punches in as he went down, but so did I. And I didn't stop. I wailed on him like he was a leather punching bag, a safe place to take out all my aggressions of the past year.

I kept hitting him, long after my fists became slippery with his blood and mine, ignoring the searing pain in my own knuckles and taking pride in the crack when my hand met his face.

It wasn't until two men lifted me off of Xavier that I realized I had won the fight. Xavier was unconscious. Or possibly worse.

My papà surveyed the scene as though it bored him, then turned to his men. "Daniele, clean this up," he said, gesturing to Xavier's bloodied body before smiling at me. "And Luca, we should go have a drink to celebrate your victory."

"I'll pass," I said. I started to the door, not caring what punishment came to me for walking out on my papà. All I knew was that I needed to get out of there.

I winced as the sunlight hit my face, stinging like salt in my wounds. I spit in the dirt, further disheartened by the amount of blood that came out.

"Come on, let's get you cleaned up," a soft voice said behind me.

There stood Tomasso. He at least had the decency to look ashamed of his role in this debacle of a day. He gestured to his car, so I followed. He unlocked it so I could get in, then told me to wait. I watched as he walked over to the SUV I'd ridden in, grabbed my coat and bag, then tossed it in the seat behind me.

"Do you want to go to your dad's club, your friend's house, school?"

I snorted at the last option. "Where are we?"

"New Haven."

I paused to consider the possibility that my papà was using one of Marco Conti's warehouses to beat me up for lying about dating Marco's daughter. It seemed to be the type of irony he'd appreciate.

"Alessio's house," I said.

Tomasso dipped his head in acknowledgement, then took off.

We drove for less than a half hour before he stopped at some random gas station. He pointed to the bathroom. "Go get cleaned up. I'll get you some ice."

I trudged into the bathroom and delicately washed the blood off my hands before starting on my face. It wasn't so bad, actually. My lip was bleeding and my gums felt like something had sliced through them, but that was the only blood on my face. My cheekbone throbbed and my eye already looked a little swollen, so I'd have some swelling for sure, but nothing terrible. My hands though… some of the blood had already dried and I couldn't distinguish between the caked on globs of blood and the raw scabs. My knuckles were all swollen and already I could barely straighten my fingers.

I returned to the car and Tomasso handed me two bags of ice. I pressed one against my face and clutched the other in my free hand, then switched after a few minutes. My hands were painfully cold, but I figured once they went numb, everything would be better. I felt Tomasso's eyes on me as we drove.

"Shouldn't you keep your attention on the road?" I snapped.

He didn't reply.

"You were the one who told me to do that. Do you remember? You said he'd like it if I stopped following blindly." I snorted at the ridiculous notion.

"You made him proud today, Luca. You may not see that, but I did."

"Yeah, well, I'm not sure what that says about me, if a sociopath is proud."

Tomasso didn't speak again for several minutes. "He is right, you know. If you tried to run away, you would be in danger the rest of your life."

"Because I'm so safe now?"

"He wouldn't have let Xavier truly hurt you. He may seem cold, but he has given very explicit instructions that no one is to ever cause you any permanent harm or break any bone in your body. Under his protection, you are safer than you think."

"I guess the way I see it, I wouldn't have been beat up by a bunch of grown ass men…let's see, three times now, if I were on my own."

"If you try to leave the family, men from other families will come after you. They will see you aren't protected and they will take you out to try to end your family line." He paused. "The type of business your family has—"

"The mafia," I interrupted.

He didn't comment on my interjection. "They generally follow the family tree. Power runs from father to son, and continues in that linear pattern. If your father had a brother—"

"He did."

"If he had a living brother who could take over, that would be one thing," Tomasso continued, clarifying. "No one would stand to benefit by killing you. Or if *you* had a brother, then it might be different. But as it stands, it isn't just outside families that pose a risk to you. Even people within your own family might seek to kill you if you're no longer under Salvatore's protection."

"And why would they do that if they're so loyal?"

"Some might because they'd view you as a traitor. Others might hope to take over for Sal themselves and think that getting you out of the way is the best option."

I sighed. "So you're saying I'm fucked no matter what I do."

He didn't answer right away, but sorrow filled his eyes when I gazed at him.

"I'm saying your best option is to play the game. Show everyone that you are tough, loyal, and that you will do what needs to be done. If you earn Sal's respect, you have earned everyone's respect. And with the respect comes power. I'm not going to sit here and tell you the next few years will be easy." He paused and stared at me again. "But what I can say is that you have been raised as the prince. And someday, you will be King."

- Giada -

I treated Elise to a spa day Saturday afternoon for an early birthday present. We both got facials, massages, and a mani/pedi. Then we stayed up too late eating popcorn, singing karaoke, and playing Truth or Dare with the rest of the girls on our floor.

I expected a fun night, but what I got was vindication, when Aubree, a girl from a few doors down, chose me at her turn.

"Truth or dare, Giada," she said, her fiercely blue eyes focused on me.

I didn't know her well enough to risk a dare, so I went with Truth. Judging from her subtle grin, that had been what she'd wanted.

"Did you fool around with Liam on your date?"

All eyes in the room turned to me. For once, I was glad Blair was nearby. I sought her out in the room, smiled my sweetest smile, then answered. "Nope. I'm sure he's a nice guy, but we didn't click on our date. We didn't even kiss, let alone do anything else. Funny thing is, he doesn't even know where that rumor started."

Elise began fake-coughing. "Blair," she croaked.

A couple of the other girls laughed and turned to Blair, but I wasn't done.

"It doesn't even matter, really. I know the truth, Liam knows the truth, and only a total loser with nothing going on in her own life would even care what *I'm* doing on my dates. I'm just glad that most girls here aren't into tearing each other down for sport."

Blair rolled her eyes, stood, and stomped out of the room while everyone else nodded and mumbled in agreement. It wasn't true, of course. Destroying each other's reputation was one of the most popular hobbies of the girls at my school. But we also liked to pretend it wasn't.

Regardless, it was an awesome night.

On Sunday, I spent the morning at church, which relaxed me even more. I didn't see Luca there, but I hadn't expected to. I'd learned by now that when he said he had to help his dad with something Saturday, he rarely returned before Monday.

I was surprised then when I was walking back from the dining hall after Sunday dinner and saw Luca climbing out of a beat-up car.

"Hey, I'll catch up with you guys later," I said to my friends, scurrying off towards the parking lot to greet Luca.

I finger-combed my hair as I approached, my smile widening the closer I got. He was talking to some friend I didn't recognize and didn't see me coming, so I scurried up behind him and wrapped my arms around his waist.

"Guess who!" I sang.

His fingers tickled my hand against his stomach, and then he turned to face me.

My breath caught in my throat when I saw him. Luca's lip was split open, a bluish hue adorned his swollen left eye, and a big bruise covered most of his cheek. He looked like Frankenstein.

"Oh my God!" I lifted my hand to inspect his injuries, but he winced, so I stopped. "What happened?"

Luca shook his head. "Small misunderstanding."

"Small?" I rolled my eyes. "You were fighting?"

He didn't deny it.

"Luca, you could get expelled for fighting. How are you explaining this to your teachers?"

"Bike accident," he said lamely.

"No one will believe that!" I shook my head. "What will your dad say?"

Beside Luca, his friend snorted. I shot him an annoyed look. Clearly, he didn't know how Luca's dad could be.

"My papà doesn't care," Luca said.

"He doesn't care that you were fighting?" That was hard to believe. "Who were you fighting anyway? And why?"

"No one. I wasn't fighting."

I blew out a sigh. It was one thing for him to lie to the school and his parents, but why lie to me? "If we're really friends, you wouldn't lie to me. Especially if we're more, you should trust me."

"I'm telling you the truth."

I reached for his hands. A slew of bruises and cuts decorated the knuckles on his right hand. "Sure." I dropped his hand.

"I didn't…" Luca stopped, sighed, then shook his head. "Look, I don't know how to explain it, okay? It just happened. I couldn't help it."

"Like, you just ran into someone with your fist?"

He took his time answering. "I didn't start it," he finally said.

"I want to believe you, Luca. I just…" I sighed. I'd always felt like there was a part of Luca's life he was keeping from me, but now he was lying to my face. I wouldn't put up with that from a friend, let alone a boyfriend. "I need some time to think, okay?"

Luca nodded slowly, not seeming the slightest bit surprised or bothered by that. I started off, but his friend jogged after me.

"Why are you following me? Do you even go here?"

He ignored my questions. "He's hurt, you know? You could try being nice."

"I'll be nice when he tells me the truth."

"He is. He was attacked."

I swiveled to face him. "Attacked? Like what, a wild bear?"

"No. People, obviously."

"Why would random people attack him?"

"I didn't say they were random."

"He knows who it is?"

His friend nodded.

"So why doesn't he say something?"

The guy frowned. "He can't. Just…I don't know. Maybe just give him the benefit of the doubt."

I gazed back at Luca, who was still leaning against his friend's car, scrolling through something on his phone like he didn't have a care in the world.

"He doesn't want that," I finally said. "He doesn't want me around him now at all." I stormed back to my dorm before he could disagree.

The next day, I saw Luca at lunch. He was sitting with his usual group, and the seats on both sides of him were taken. In the past, I knew that he would make room for me beside him or move to a new spot with me if I approached. Now, I wasn't so sure. I didn't bother to test my luck. Our eyes met, but his were completely expressionless, so I just kept walking and sat at my old table.

I'd assumed Harper would sit next to me, but Colton swooped in before she could, scooting so close that our legs were touching. I glanced over at Luca just in time to see him roll his eyes, then turn towards Gavin.

In World Religions, Luca didn't talk to me at all.

The next day, it was the same. Except this time, at lunch, Blair and Emily were both at his table. I grimaced watching him smile and laugh with them. Well, if he wanted to make me jealous, fine. Two could play at that game. I squeezed in between Delaney and Barret, a boy from my math class. I immediately turned to Barrett.

"That's a cool shirt," I said, stroking the collar. "Where's it from?"

He looked totally flummoxed. "Uh, probably Gap? I don't know. My mom bought it."

I smiled in lieu of rolling my eyes but managed to keep talking to him for a few more minutes. But every time I glanced over at Luca, he was still talking to Emily.

I sighed. I had officially lost my appetite. I left the table, dumped my food in the trash, then walked out of the cafeteria.

I barely made it to the doors when I felt a hand on my shoulder. I didn't have to turn to know it was Luca.

"So are you just moving on to Barrett now?"

I rolled my eyes the second I was facing him. "Please. You're the one over there flirting with the two girls who hate me most in the world."

"You're ignoring me. Am I not allowed to talk to anyone while I wait for you to stop ignoring me?"

"First off, you were not talking to *just anyone* and you know it. Second of all, I am not ignoring you. You are the one ignoring me."

"I don't know what you want me to say. You told me you wouldn't talk to me until I told you what happened. I fucking told you the truth and you didn't believe me."

"You did not tell me the truth, Luca."

He stared at me, his expression unreadable. "Giada, I'm sorry. I had a really shitty weekend, and—"

"That's not an excuse, Luca. You can't treat me like crap every time you have a bad weekend."

He opened his mouth, then closed it. "You're right," he finally said.

I waited for him to say more, but he didn't.

"I should get to class," I said.

- Luca -

I felt like a dick after talking to Giada. I didn't know what was wrong with me. It hadn't been my idea to sit with Emily and Blair. When they came over, my first thought had been that they were hoping to piss off Giada. But I wasn't any better. I hadn't sent them away.

I couldn't tell Giada everything that was going on with my papà. The knowledge would put her at risk, it would put her relationship with her own father at risk, and it could definitely cause more problems for me with my own family. But she was right that it wasn't fair for me to keep avoiding her and being an asshole for days every time my papà hurt me.

I just didn't know what else to do. Giada was the best thing in my life. She was what made me smile, what kept me going when there wasn't any point. And what was I for her? Probably the opposite. Giada had been happy before I barged into her life. That was what had attracted me to her—how damn happy she looked all the time. I wanted a part of that. Except right now, Giada wasn't happy and it was my fault. She deserved better.

I pulled out my phone and stared at it for several minutes, trying to decide what to say to her. Ultimately, I went with the truth. "You don't need me in your life. I'm no good for you." I clicked send before I could convince myself it was too pathetic.

I half expected her to text back with a stream of expletives. Giada had a temper, and she wasn't one to go down without a fight.

Instead, she replied with a simple question mark.

Hmm. Guess I needed to be clearer.

"We should go back to being friends. If that." I wrote.

"If that?" she replied. "Wtf? Can we talk in person?"

It was nearly curfew and I looked like crap. "What's the point?" I texted.

"If you're trying to break up with me via text, that's a shitty move."

She had me there.

"I'm a shitty guy."

"You owe me a face to face conversation."

She was right again.

"Tomorrow after last period?" I wrote.

"Fine."

I returned to my moping by chugging some booze I had stashed in my sock drawer, then joined my roommates for some video games before bed.

The next day, Alessio texted at lunch. His sister was going to pick up her stuff from her boyfriend's apartment that afternoon. He'd told me a little about her boyfriend before, or at least enough for me to know the guy was a dick. Like, the guy was even worse than me. Alessio was worried he'd try to hurt Ginevra or stop her from leaving him, but she wouldn't let him go with her to help.

I owed Alessio more favors than I could repay in a lifetime, so the least I could do was help out his sister. I quickly agreed to accompany her and asked him to text me the address. He did, then replied later that she thought it would be better if we rode together. I asked Ginevra to pick me up behind the admin building right at 4:30. I couldn't miss more class, not after missing a couple days the last time my papà's guys used me as a punching bag. But that should give us time to get Ginevra's stuff cleared out before her boyfriend returned.

It did mean I'd have to bail on Giada though.

I waited until after World Religions, then approached Giada. She looked surprised to see me actually talking to her in person, but I could barely make eye contact with her. She looked gorgeous, which I assumed was intentional, to make me see what I was giving up if I broke up with her.

"I'm really sorry, but I screwed up on my physics lab and I have to work on it this afternoon. Can we meet later tonight?"

"Sure. Anything I could help with?" The sympathy in her voice actually made me feel even worse for lying.

"No. Thanks. I'll um text when I'm done."

Two hours later, Ginny and I were driving off campus.

"Thanks again for tagging along," Ginevra said as she steered through of the school's main gate. "I don't expect any trouble, but Chris is just..." She shook her head. "He's an asshole and I'm an idiot."

"An idiot wouldn't be leaving the guy," I pointed out. She glanced at me, then kept driving.

"Alessio says your parents are still together," she said after a long pause, quickly adding, "I mean, not saying your mom is an idiot. Or anything about—"

"It's fine. She is. Or maybe, I don't know. I don't think it's not so much that she's stupid as that she's made her choice and she wants that money. That lifestyle."

Ginny shrugged. "I could see that. We all make sacrifices."

I didn't think Ginny knew about my papà, but if Alessio had told her about my parents, I supposed it was possible. I needed to be certain though. I couldn't risk having people know about my family business without me realizing it.

"It's not a problem for me to help you out today," I began, cringing at how awkward I sounded. "I mean, I owe Alessio big time, and I really don't mind, but um, I was curious why you wanted me to come along." I paused, but she didn't immediately answer so I kept talking. "It seems like Chris might be more intimidated by an older guy or something."

I gazed at Ginny and realized her eyes were glossing over and turning red. *Shit.* That had not been my intention, and now I was thinking about Giada. How many girls could I seriously make cry in one day?

"I'm sorry..." I began, trying to figure out how to finish that sentence.

She waved her hand dismissively. "No, it's fine. Fair question. Umm, so I don't really know any guys my age. I mean, I have friends, but they're all Chris's friends too. So I'm not sure who I can trust. And like I said, I don't think we will even run into Chris, but if we do, I don't think he'll realize you're any younger.

I mean, you could probably pass for twenty-one, and it's not like he'd be looking closely anyway."

I would've loved to test out that theory sometime, but I decided not to think about that just yet.

"And to be completely honest, you're a little scary. Every time I've seen you, you've been hurt and you don't even seem to notice. So, I assumed you're tough and that you know how to fight. Not that I think it'll come to that," she said, cringing and casting me a conciliatory smile.

I laughed. Every time I'd gone crawling to Alessio's, it was after getting my ass handed to me in a fight and I was feeling like an absolute weak, helpless, loser. How Ginevra could see a tough guy who knew how to fight was beyond me.

"Like right now, I'm terrified and that's why I'm rambling like a moron, but you're just sitting there cool as a cucumber like people ask you self-defense favors all the time."

I reached over and patted her thigh. I meant it as a comforting gesture, but she stiffened. I pulled my hand back quickly and turned out the window.

When we reached the apartment, Ginny started into a spot.

"Hang on," I said. "Drive around first, make sure you don't see his car. Then park someplace he won't see your car if he gets back while you're here."

It seemed like basic advice to me, but she looked impressed. When we reached the apartment, I used her key and went in first. After confirming the unit was empty, I asked her to show me pictures of Chris. Once I was confident I'd recognize the jerk if I saw him, I left her alone in the apartment to pack up her stuff. I parked myself on the top step of the only staircase leading to her floor. My plan was to sit there and pretend to be waiting on someone, and if I saw Chris, I'd text her a warning and start up a conversation with him to delay his arrival.

That way, if he did come back early, she could confront him in the hall, in front of a "stranger," *i.e.* me. Hopefully he wouldn't be dumb enough to try anything with an audience and if he was that stupid, well, like she said, I knew my way around a fight. But also I figured it wouldn't help anything if he came back and found her alone with another guy in the apartment.

Without my help, she warned me the packing would take longer, so I quickly texted Giada and said I'd be later.

She replied immediately. "You poor thing. Still in the physics lab on campus?"

Something about her question rubbed me the wrong way, but I was too distracted to figure it out, so I simply replied that I was still in the lab. "Raincheck for tomorrow afternoon?" I wrote, figuring that would buy me another day to figure out what I was doing and what to say to her anyway.

This time, Giada's response took a few minutes, and it included an image. I read the message while I waited for the picture to download. It said, "No need. Tell your new GF I said hi." Panicked, I was about to insist I didn't have another girlfriend, and then the image filled my screen. It was a fuzzy image clearly taken from a distance, but it was from that very afternoon. Ginevra, in typical Italian fashion, had greeted me with a friendly kiss on each cheek. Somehow, Giada had captured that precise moment in a photo and from that angle, I could definitely see how it looked like a real kiss.

"Fuck," I said aloud.

Shortly after, Ginny emerged from the apartment, her arms overflowing with stuff. I helped her carry a couple trash bags of stuff and we shoved it in her trunk and took off without any sign of Chris.

"Thank you so much," she said. "If you hadn't agreed to go with me, I probably would've left it all there and I really don't have the money to buy a whole new wardrobe now."

"It's no problem," I said, chewing on the inside of my lip.

"Is everything okay? You seem...off."

I considered telling her about Giada, decided against it. She offered to treat me and Alessio to pizza, and no longer having any reason to get back to campus, I accepted. Alessio met us there, and then he and I stayed long after Ginny left.

"Are you gonna tell me what's going on with you?" Alessio asked as soon as we were alone.

"I'm fine," I lied. "You think your sister will be okay?"

He shrugged. "Probably not."

"What do you mean? Do you think she'll go back to that guy?"

"Or another just like him. It's genetically predetermined, isn't it? No matter what we do, I'll grow up to abuse women and children and she'll end up with man that beats her and the kids. Isn't that how it goes?"

Now it was my turn to shrug. "If that's the case, we're both fucked. But then it's probably for the best." I hadn't meant to say the last part aloud, and of course Alessio latched on to it immediately.

"What is for the best? What did you do, man?"

I sighed, then told him everything with Giada. He listened without interrupting, aside from asking a few pointed questions. When I finished talking, it was nearing curfew so we started to his car.

"Maybe we could go out this weekend," I suggested. "I could use a wingman to help me find some new girls to take my mind off her."

"I'd love to go party this weekend, but your school is filled with hot chicks who seem interested in you. Why shop offsite?"

"I can't date anyone else at school, not yet." *Not ever*, I thought. "It would hurt Giada."

Alessio laughed. "Yeah, so if you want my take on all of this…" he began.

"I don't."

He continued undeterred. "You're being an idiot. Giada makes you happy. You literally just told me she's like this light in the darkness for you. Why the fuck would you give this up?"

"Because I'm not good for her. And it isn't fair to her."

"Well, if we're right about this destiny crap and if her father is who we think he is, she's doomed regardless. And you can't tell me you don't care about her. If she's with you, at least you know she's with someone who loves her and isn't going to intentionally hurt her. You'll protect her and keep her out of all her dad's shit, and she can keep you nice and happy and make sure you don't go off the deep end."

I listened to his speech, then considered it all. When Alessio started asking me how I was going to feel watching every douchebag at school try to date her or listening to guys talk about taking advantage of her, I realized he had a point.

By the time he'd dropped me off at campus, I decided Alessio was right. Calling it quits with Giada and then tromping around miserable the rest of the year was stupid. We could both keep having fun together and then I could reevaluate things this summer.

The problem now would be getting her to forgive me.

CHAPTER 12

HEARTACHE

- Giada -

Fighting with Luca had been hard enough, but I never actually thought we'd break up over him lying about a stupid fight. I figured we'd both stay mad for a couple days and then I expected him to text me an apology and we'd make up. I truly had not anticipated Luca trying to dump me via text. And if there was something worse than that, it had to be realizing he'd lied and cheated on me during the time he'd planned to dump me in person.

I felt like an idiot. I was completely humiliated and nothing could make me set foot into class with Luca.

The bigger problem, though, was that I was also heartbroken. I'd always hated that cliché saying, but now, I understood it. I wasn't just sad and lonely; there was a physical pain in my chest. My whole body ached the same as when I had the flu. Knowing Luca didn't care about me anymore, maybe even that he never had cared, left me with a barely tolerable throbbing deep in my bones.

I immediately blocked his number on my phone, but that wasn't enough. I needed distance. Lots of it.

After Art the next day, I walked to the nurse's office and said I was sick and needed to come home immediately. She let me stay there during the entirety of sixth period, when I would have seen Luca, but then she sent me back to class since I had no fever and no verifiable symptoms.

That wouldn't do. I needed to get away from the school altogether. I couldn't handle Friday, let alone the whole weekend, knowing Luca was nearby.

I called home. I had debated telling my mom the truth, but instead went for an old classic—cramps. I insisted they were the worst I'd ever had and that I couldn't possibly survive the next several days and that I needed a hot bath and heating pad and all the comforts of home to make me feel better. When she still resisted, I reminded her of my perfect attendance and how cooperative I'd been thus far about being banished.

Mom told me Enzo would pick me up later that evening. I packed quickly, then hid in my room until he texted that he'd arrived. I didn't want to risk running into Luca or Emily or anyone else.

I handed Enzo my bags then climbed into the car. He eyed me warily.

"Are you okay? Your mom said you weren't feeling well but that I wasn't supposed to ask questions," he said.

"And yet here you are, asking questions," I snapped.

His eyes widened and he turned to the road.

Great. Apparently, Luca had also turned me into a bitch. Maybe I actually was getting my period.

"I'm sorry. I'm fine. Nothing contagious, just…drama. I need a break from school and all the people in it."

Enzo's expression softened. "Do you want to talk about it?"

I nearly laughed at the thought of this cute college-aged boy listening to my high school problems. "No." I said.

He nodded and turned on the radio.

True to my word, I spent my entire first night home soaking in a hot bath in my childhood bedroom.

The next day, I self-medicated with ice cream and stupid movies. In the evening, we ordered pizza and then Matteo invited me out with him and his friends, but I didn't feel up to it. Saturday morning, I went shopping with my mom and then to church. When we got home, my dad's office door was closed.

"He better not have forgotten we have plans in the city tonight," my mom said, knocking on the door. I was about to head back up to my room, when his office door swung open.

There stood Luca.

As I gazed at Luca, every muscle in my body tightened uncomfortably. I hated that I still endured such a strong physical reaction to him, hated that I still wanted to touch him, still ached to hear his laughter. But I was equally upset at myself for even staring at him as long as I now had.

"What are you doing here?" I asked, my voice sounding more annoyed than anything.

"Honey, why don't you two go talk in the kitchen," my mother said, shooing us along.

I headed in that direction, but then kept going until I was outside. I did not need to have this conversation within earshot of my parents or brother. Luca followed me, his head hung sheepishly.

"You weren't returning my calls or texts," he said, his tone filled with accusation.

"I blocked your number."

His eyebrows rose as though that was surprising.

"Whatever you have to say, it's really unnecessary. I don't need excuses, apologies, or whatever. And I don't want to be your friend. Not yet anyway. Maybe someday, but…" My voice trailed off as he had stepped closer, closing the gap between us.

"I don't want to be your friend either, Giada. I want to be your boyfriend."

I opened my mouth to speak, but no words came out. He reached for my hands, and goosebumps spread across my skin.

"I'm sorry about the way I handled things when I came back to campus. I don't get along with some of the other guys in my neighborhood. Sometimes I get in fights when I go home. I don't want to be that guy though, especially not with you. I don't want you to see me that way. And I'm sorry about Emily and Blair. I wish they hadn't sat by me, and I should've just moved. I could happily go the rest of my life without ever talking to either of them."

I wanted to believe all that, but he still hadn't explained the biggest deception of all. "I need to be able to trust you if we're going to be friends."

"I know, and I'll do better."

"Who was the girl, Luca?"

He dropped my hand and reached into his inside coat pocket. He pulled out a Christmas card and handed it to me. "You know my friend Alessio? The one who doesn't go to the school? That's his sister, Ginevra. She needed a favor that day, and I owe them big time, so I had to go."

"You didn't have to kiss her."

"It wasn't a real kiss. She's Italian, and it was just that cheek thing. Her lips didn't even touch my cheek. She's older and I have zero interest in her and she has zero interest in me."

"If that was all it was, why not tell me the truth? Why make up a lie about physics?"

"Because she wanted me to help her move her stuff out of her boyfriend's apartment, and the reason she wanted me for that was because she knows I can fight. And I didn't want you to know that's the reputation I have off campus."

I believed what Luca was saying, but wasn't sure what it all meant. And I didn't even start to process the significance of him telling me people came to him to help with fights. He was staring at me expectantly, though, so I quickly came up with something to say.

"Alright, well, thanks, I guess. It was nice of you to clarify all that. Sorry you had to come all this way."

"I'm not," he said.

"You're not what?"

"I'm not sorry I came here." Luca cupped my chin in his hand. "I missed you. I missed your eyes and your smile and your laugh. I miss the way you smell, the way you taste…"

As his voice trailed off, I found myself gazing back at his eyes. It was easy to get lost in those deep pools of melted chocolate.

I blinked and snapped out of the trance. "Luca, stop. You don't even like me. I can't do this. I'm not going to fall for you again just so you can humiliate me and break my heart all over again."

"I do like you, Giada. I like you more than I've ever liked another person. I actually… I love you."

I stopped breathing, but felt my heart pounding harder than ever in my chest. I couldn't have spoken if I wanted to, but luckily, he continued.

"I love that you're always thinking of other people, and I love the noises you make when you eat and your ridiculous sense of humor. I love spending time with you and when I'm not with you, I'm thinking about you."

Luca snapped his lips shut as if he hadn't meant to say all of that. Then, he simply gazed at me expectantly.

"I…thought you wanted to break up with me," I finally said, my voice breathless.

He shook his head, charming me with his lopsided smile and that pesky dimple. "I don't. I only said that stuff because I thought you'd be better off without me. I still do think you probably deserve someone else, someone better than me."

That was a lot for my already-flustered mind to process. "So you don't want to break up with me?"

"No. I would like to kiss you though."

I opened my mouth to reply, but he was already leaning in. He moved slowly, pausing with his lips mere centimeters from mine. I could feel his breath on my face and his eyelashes tickled me. When our lips finally made contact, my eyes fluttered shut.

We were in the exact spot where we'd shared our first kiss, and this one was every bit as powerful. My knees wobbled and my head felt woozy, but something about Luca's hand steadying my face, holding my lips against his, centered me. My senses were overwhelmed with him. I could smell his cologne, taste the minty gum he'd been chewing on his way over, and I could feel him everywhere our bodies touched.

He didn't deepen the kiss for an eternity, and it finally occurred to me that he was waiting for me. He'd said how he felt, and now it was up to me to show him that I felt the same. My hands found his sides, pulling him closer then squeezing his hips. Our tongues crashed together, dancing across each other's teeth then tangling around each other. We hadn't been apart that long, hadn't even gone a full week without kissing, and yet something about that kiss…it felt like coming home.

I ended the kiss, suddenly remembering we were at my house, with my parents or brother easily within view of a window, but Luca didn't release my chin. He tilted his forehead down till it pressed against mine.

"Tesoro mio. What you do to me…" he whispered.

Pulling back abruptly, Luca grinned. He reached into his pocket, retrieved a switchblade, and flipped out the knife. Walking around me, he stabbed the knife into the wood on the back side of the support beam for the pergola. He grinned while his hand worked back and forth.

"What are you doing?" I asked.

He didn't answer, and after a minute, I decided to attempt to walk. Luckily, my legs brought me right beside him. He folded the knife back into his pocket and grinned.

"LM + GC," he'd written.

"On our wedding day, I'm going to remind you that's here," he said.

I felt my lips part, but no words came out. Ten minutes ago, I was certain he was just breaking up with me and now, he was talking about marriage?

- Luca -

Giada barely said a word, but she also didn't hit me or ask Lorenzo to shoot me, so I figured we were on the same page. I had taken Alessio's advice. I had been completely honest. Well, I supposed I had not told her everything about my situation with my papà, but I had told her how I felt, and I hadn't held back at all. I had hoped when I told her I loved her, she'd say it back.

After a moment, I convinced myself it was for the best that she had not. Now, when she said it to me, I would know she meant it, and not that she simply felt compelled to parrot the words back to me.

Besides, the way she'd looked at me… It wasn't the way Emily had looked at me, or any of the girls I'd dated before Giada. Giada gazed at me like she was both trying to see inside my soul and like she was desperate to memorize every detail. Giada seemed to see me beneath the surface. I was flattered, but also terrified.

"You're freezing," I said, pressing my hands over her rosy ears. I still had my coat on; she did not.

I nodded for her to follow me back into her house, but she hesitated. "Why do my parents think you're here?" she asked. "I never told them we…were fighting."

"Your dad assumed I was here to check on you, so I went with that."

"Oh."

"He doesn't buy that you're sick though. He definitely thinks you're faking."

"Are you going home tonight or back to school or…?"

Truthfully, I didn't know. Any of those were options. I'd rather drive back to campus than head home where my papà was, even though it was a much longer drive. "I don't have any plans till class Monday morning, so I can do whatever."

"Stay here tonight," she said, her eyes still searching mine.

"Pretty sure your parents won't go for that. I can give you a ride back to campus tonight though if you want."

"You've stayed here before."

My lips tugged upward, but I tried to conceal the grin, not wanting to look smug. "Things have changed since then."

Giada's expression changed to the determined look I knew so well. "What the princess wants, the princess gets," she said, smirking playfully and traipsing towards the door. I followed her inside, then waited in the kitchen as she walked towards her dad's office. She rapped on the door with her knuckles before swinging it open.

"Daddy, can Luca take one of the guest rooms tonight? Or he could drive me back to campus now but it'll be dark before we get halfway back."

I couldn't hear his response, but a moment later, Giada skipped back to the kitchen, smiling. "Can I get you a drink?" she offered.

We hung out in her sunroom for a while, keeping a respectful distance from each other since her parents were nearby. It couldn't have been more than an hour when I saw Lorenzo lugging a bag downstairs. I gazed over at Giada, whose grin widened.

"My parents are staying downtown tonight," she explained.

The impact of her words went straight to my groin. I gritted my teeth, pulled a decorative pillow over my lap and pretended to focus on my phone. Her parents left a little while later, without any other cautions to us. Giada and I decided to order subs for dinner, and I went to take my bag up to the guestroom.

I tossed my bag on the bed in the room across from hers, then turned sharply, hearing a noise behind me.

Lorenzo, Giada's driver and Marco' Conti's errand boy, stood behind me, leaning against the side of the door jam. His arms were crossed over his chest.

"Hi," I said, uncertain why he was standing there. He sure didn't look like he had any intention of moving. "Lorenzo, right?"

He raised and lowered his head slowly, his eyes squarely on me.

"Did you need something?"

Lorenzo waited a moment, then pushed off of the door. "I was debating whether I should give you a heads up."

Well that sounded ominous. My mind immediately flitted to my papà. God I hoped he wasn't coming here. "About?"

"Marco said if you went anywhere near Giada's room while he's gone, or if you left your room in the night for any reason, I was to shoot you."

"He asked you to shoot me?"

"In the foot," he clarified, shrugging like it changed everything.

"Right. Um, okay."

"So you understand?"

I supposed I did, but it would be more fun to mess with him. "What happens if Giada comes to my room in the night?"

"You get shot in the foot," he replied, deadpan.

"How do I keep her out?"

He reached around to the door and twisted the lock on the knob. "You have a lock. Use it. And as my mom would say, make good choices. Capisci?"

"Si."

He nodded and started out.

"Wait, Lorenzo!" I called after him. "Any other behavior that will get me shot? I'd really like to avoid that."

"That's all Marco said. But he does grant me a lot of discretion, so…" he held his hands up as if anything were possible, and then he left.

Great.

- Giada -

I wasn't sure what to make of Luca's entire spiel, but I decided not to overanalyze it. He had apologized. He told me the truth. And he told me he loved me. I could dwell on all of that later, but for now, I planned to just enjoy a parent-free night with my boyfriend.

We ate takeout, laughing and joking, then snuggled on the couch and watched a movie. When Matteo left to go out with friends, I thought of a better plan for the evening.

"I don't suppose you have swim trunks in your bag, do you?" I asked.

Luca's brows narrowed but he was clearly struggling not to smile. "No, I don't suppose I do."

"Hmm. Well, that's okay. You can borrow some of Matteo's. Be right back!" I scampered away, grabbed two different swimsuits from my brother's room, and handed them to Luca. "You can change in a bathroom if you don't want to go up to the guest room. I'll be back once my suit is on."

"Uh Giada," he interrupted. "It's freezing outside."

"We are going to the hot tub, not the pool."

He still looked skeptical.

"Trust me. It's even better when it's cold out," I promised.

"Your parents won't mind, us being in the hot tub together while they're gone?"

I giggled at the irony that Luca was the one reminding *me* of the rules. He still seemed hesitant, but by the time I scampered back downstairs in my bikini, a towel wrapped around my waist, he had changed into the swim trunks.

I handed Luca a giant fluffy towel, then watched as he reluctantly slipped off his two shirts. When he gazed up at me, his eyes widened. He licked his lips, then swallowed loudly.

"God, Giada, you are…stunning."

I beamed, then motioned for him to follow me outside. I dropped the towel before we reached the hot tub, leading the way in. Luca was still watching me, his eyes wide as saucers.

"This is a bad idea," he said. He followed me to the hot tub, stepping in and slowly lowering himself down to the bench at the exact furthest point from me. "Cavolo! This is scalding!"

I giggled, having no clue what the expression in Italian meant but finding it adorable. "You'll get used to it in a minute. But why are you way over there?"

"I don't trust myself to sit closer. Your papà will kill me if I touch you, and if you're within my reach, looking like that…I can't help it."

Part of me was tempted to respect his boundaries, but a larger, more persuasive part of me felt cheated out of a week of kisses from Luca. I stood and delicately made my way across the spa, careful not to stub my toe on the drain. Then I sat beside him.

"Sorry," I said, in my least apologetic voice. "But it's really hard to hear over the jets. And I thought we should talk."

"Talk, hmm?" His eyes wandered from my face to my chest.

"Umm hmm. That stuff you said earlier, was it just to get me to forgive you?"

"Yep, totally."

"So you didn't mean any of it?"

"Not a word," he said.

I thought he was just distracted by my cleavage, but then I noticed the dimple at the side of my mouth, betraying his effort to keep a straight face. I splashed him. "Jerk."

He grinned.

"So that stuff you said about loving me."

"Yeah, all lies. You are definitely not lovable."

I splashed him again, but then he reached for my hand under the water.

"You are funny though," he began. "You're always doing nice things for other people. And you're smart. Also," he leaned closer so his lips brushed against my ear, "You look amazing in a bikini."

I smiled shyly as he pulled back.

"So if I was going to fall in love with someone, I'd probably pick you."

I swallowed the lump in my throat. "I love you too, Luca."

His face blanched. "You don't have to say that."

"I know, but I want to. It's the truth. I wish I could make you see yourself the way I see you." My fingers found his beneath the water again, and he smiled.

"I would like that too," he finally said.

I leaned in slowly, kissing him tentatively. I didn't think he'd reject me, but after he tried to sit so far away, I couldn't be sure.

The moment my lips met Luca's, everything was perfect. The steam from the hot tub was relaxing and the rumbling of the jets masked any sounds we were making. The contrast of the frigid night air and the sweltering water soothed every muscle in my body. Luca tasted like a familiar mixture of cocoa and peppermint, and as his tongue clashed with mine, I figured I was as happy as I'd ever be.

It was awkward sitting side by side though, so when his hand nudged my side, I shifted. Luca lifted me off the bench then guided me to him. Perched over his knees, I had much better access to kiss him, without the undue strain on my neck. As I gradually settled against him, closing the gap between our chests by roping my arms around his neck, I became aware of another sensation. Something was pressing against me. Something large and firm and oh so inappropriate.

My breath caught in my throat, but I didn't stop kissing him. Kissing was fine. Nothing else was going to happen. But *oh God*, I was definitely thinking about it now. Luca's hands remained firmly on my lower back, and for that, I was thankful. Whenever his hands started to roam, I was nervous. I knew he was more experienced than me, and I was certain he knew that, too. But I was less sure what he made of that information.

I lost all sense of time as we kissed. My body tuned in with every delicious sensation, but my mind registered nothing beyond Luca—Luca's hands, Luca's lips, Luca's breath as hot as the water bubbling around us. It was exquisite. Nothing could top this.

I vaguely registered some sound in the background, almost like a growl, but I didn't care. Not until Luca's hands tensed at my hips a moment before he pulled his lips away from mine. I began to lean forward, eager to get back to the kissing, but Luca held me at a distance, nodding to the side.

Beyond annoyed at the interruption, I followed Luca's stare, eager to see what could possibly justify this tragic disturbance.

What I hadn't expected was to see a man, standing just off to the side. His arms were crossed, but his head was to the side, like he was averting his eyes. Steam partially obscured my view too, so it took me a moment to identify him.

As he cleared his throat a second time, I figured it out. Lorenzo was standing by the pool.

I jumped, trying to propel myself off Luca's lap and across the hot tub as fast as I could, but something tightened near my ear and yanked me back, painfully.

"Ouch! Shit!" I reached my hand to my ear right as Luca did the same.

"Here, it's twisted," he said, fumbling with his metal chain that had somehow looped itself around my earring.

I pulled back repeatedly, making no marked progress, until finally Luca lifted his chain up over his head, freeing me.

I pushed back to the opposite side of the water and sunk lower, submerging my chest. I suddenly felt very naked, even though I was wearing my perfectly decent bright Christmas bikini. The top was bright red and shaped to resemble a bow, and the bottoms were dark green with red stripes. It was festive and cute, and totally appropriate, except when my driver was glaring at me.

"Lorenzo, what are you doing?" I snapped at him.

"I could ask you the same question, except that's pretty obvious," he said, turning back to face us. Luca had located his necklace loose in the water and was placing it back around his neck, avoiding eye contact with both me and Lorenzo.

I crossed my arms over my chest and glared. "Well?" I prompted.

"Your father asked me to keep an eye on you," he finally said.

"I don't think this is what he meant."

"This is *exactly* what he meant," Lorenzo replied, now eying Luca like he was a shark.

"My father loves Luca."

"He wouldn't if he'd walked out and seen that."

"We were just kissing."

Lorenzo's sigh was loud enough for me to hear it over the voracious bubbling of the hot tub. He leaned back against the wall, as if to signal that he wasn't going anywhere.

"We should head inside anyway," Luca said, his voice soft. "Your skin will start to prune."

The moment had been lost for sure, but I still wasn't about to get out with a babysitter glaring at me.

"Fine, I'll be inside in five minutes. I need to dry off first," I said to Lorenzo.

He grabbed my towel off the back of the pool chair near him and walked it closer.

"Go!" I snapped.

Enzo dropped the towel on the ground and made his way inside.

I shook my head, covering my face with my hands. "That was mortifying."

When I dared to look at Luca again, he was grinning. "You're cute when you're embarrassed," he said.

I splashed him then slowly rose from the water, wrapping the towel around myself even though the way Luca was watching me made me feel like the most gorgeous woman alive. I wrung out my hair then went to get his towel, holding it out to him.

"I was afraid you were going to rip off your ear," he said. "I've never seen anyone try to get away from me so fast."

I let my eyes wander down his body as he dried off. I didn't notice anything protruding from his swim trunks, so I figured the interruption from Lorenzo resolved that anyway.

"That's why men shouldn't wear jewelry," I finally said.

Luca bit back a smile but couldn't keep his dimples down. "I'm Italian, baby. Get used to it," he replied, stepping closer. "Besides, you know you like it." He pressed his hand against my cheek, cupping my face as he kissed me one last time, then walked past me and into the house.

I followed him inside, glaring at Lorenzo as I skulked past him.

CHAPTER 13

WAITING TILL MARRIAGE

- Giada -

Back at school, life was good. Everything between Luca and I was better than ever. I hadn't thought it would be possible to feel more connected to Luca than I had before, but hearing him say he loved me—and believing it to be true—was powerful. Every time I heard those three words in his sexy accent, my stomach did flipflops and goosebumps trickled down my arms. I found myself smiling incessantly, and if I wasn't with Luca, I was thinking about him.

We went to the winter formal together, obviously, and every moment was pure bliss. I'd enjoyed school dances before, but this time, I didn't have any of the jitters from dating someone new, and I still enjoyed all the romance. Together, Luca and I were unstoppable. We laughed, sharing more inside jokes than I'd ever had with a girlfriend, and I felt more comfortable talking to Luca than anyone else. And slow dances with Luca? To die for. Just being close to him made my heart thump erratically.

I began shopping for my prom dress before we even reached spring break.

The only hiccup in our paradise was the future. The semester was flying by in a blissful blur of kisses and secrets and laughter. I needed time to slow down. Summer was approaching way too fast.

Normally, I adored summer. But Luca planned to spend the entire summer in Italy, and my parents told me we'd visit for two to three weeks, max. Thus, this summer would be torture.

I couldn't imagine surviving an entire summer without Luca. I'd grown spoiled by talking to him every day, touching him whenever I wanted, and kissing him until my lips went numb.

Usually, we'd hide someplace on campus to make out. But if it was cold or rainy, that plan sucked. The rebel that he was, Luca would sneak into my dorm on those days. Elise and Jason had broken up, but she still respected our privacy when I told her Luca and I would be in the room.

On a rainy Sunday, we'd gone to a movie together, then snuck into my room to kiss. We started in a seated position at the end of my bed, but somehow we'd ended up stretched out lengthwise along my bed. We were on our sides, but Luca's leg hooked around mine, effectively pinning my legs in place. Honestly, I could've kissed him all day. Everything about his touch brought my senses to life. But as his hands slowly moved up my torso, I realized we were edging towards dangerous territory.

"Luca," I said, so breathless that my voice came out more like a whimper.

"Giada," he breathed against my cheek, before leaning closer and delving his tongue into my mouth.

"Luca, stop. We need to talk."

"Mmm hmm. Later baby. Right now I think we need to finish what we're doing," he said playfully, shifting so he was more fully on top of me.

The feeling of his full body weight on me was indescribably exquisite, and at least from this position, he couldn't exactly grope my breasts anymore.

Except the more we kissed, the more I realized there was something else pressing against me. Something large and firm and definitely relevant to the discussion we needed to have.

I grappled around for his shoulder and then nudged him backwards. "Luca," I whined.

He pulled back and gazed at me, his sparkling eyes filled with mischief and promise. "Tesoro," he said. *Treasure.*

"I'm not having sex," I said, struggling to stay focused.

"Right. This is called kissing. Sex involves a couple of body parts that can't really connect with all these clothes in the way."

"Luca, I'm serious. I know you've...done things. And I know you're going to be disappointed, but I'm not that girl. I will never have sex in a limo."

Luca sighed and rolled off of me and onto his back. "We didn't have sex in the limo. It was just..."

"I know, I know," I said, pressing my hands over my ears. I couldn't handle hearing him say it. "And honestly, to me, that is sex. I'm not going to suck...that...in a limo."

Luca bit back a grin, but his face turned ashen as I continued.

"Or anywhere."

"Anywhere?" he repeated.

I shrugged. That couldn't possibly be that uncommon of a stance. It did not seem like the sort of thing that belonged in a mouth. Sanitary concerns aside, it still just sounded ridiculous. Silly, honestly.

"Okaaaaaay," he finally said. "I guess that's good to know. Were you wanting to try other stuff?"

I almost asked what other stuff there was, but then I realized I was not at a buffet where everything was included. I was having an important discussion to inform my boyfriend of some basic moral limits.

"I'm not having sex before marriage. Any kind of sex," I finally said.

Luca didn't say anything, and at first, I figured he was just processing it. But after a full minute of silence, I started to get worried.

"Luca? Did you hear me? Is that, like a dealbreaker for you?" I winced in anticipation of him storming out of my room.

"Baby, no. It's…" he sighed. "It's disappointing, yeah. But if you don't want to do that, we don't have to do it."

I couldn't believe Luca actually said that. Hearing those words made me fall even more in love with him and made me super regret my resolve not to sleep with him. "It's not that I don't want to. It's that…I believe it's wrong. The Church forbids it, and my body is a temple."

Luca rolled onto his side facing me. "Baby, I want nothing more than to worship that temple. I want to touch you and kiss you and make every part of you feel good."

A heaviness settled deep in my core. "I just…no. Not until I'm married."

He stared at me, as though searching for some caveat, then nodded. "Okay then. So is it cool if I still go to other girls for that stuff, or…"

I felt my eyes widen, and he must have noticed because he quickly pressed his palm against my cheek.

"Tesoro, I'm kidding. I don't want to do that with anyone else. Only you. So if you say no, then I guess it's a no for us both."

"That doesn't seem fair to you," I admitted.

Luca mustered a smile. "I think we are both missing out, but that's fine. I'm patient."

"No, you're not."

Now he laughed. "Okay, true. Well, maybe this will teach me patience."

He might've been right.

"So…is everything but sex still okay?"

I considered that. "Well, I mean, I think with the mouth, it's still technically sex, so…"

"Can I still touch you?" he asked, his hand poised above my shoulder.

I nodded, and he gently stroked the side of my face, then my hair, then my shoulder.

"Can I touch you here?" he asked, stroking the length of my arm.

I nodded again.

He shifted to reach my legs. "What about here?"

I shivered, but nodded as his hand roamed my calf to my mid-thigh then stopped.

"Here?" He rest his hand on my abdomen then pressed his lips against mine.

"Yes," I said between kisses.

"What if I move this direction?" he asked, sliding his hand along my shirt towards my groin.

I stiffened and his hand returned to my stomach.

"That's a no, then," he said, resuming the kissing.

We both focused on our lips and tongues for a few minutes, and then his hand shifted higher, barely grazing the underside of my breast. I ached for him to touch me there, but it seemed wrong somehow, almost like a gateway drug. Except it wasn't sex, and frankly, I was allowed to touch his chest, so why should mine be any different?

"Is this okay?" he asked, pulling away and gazing at me.

I made no attempt to stop him as his hand shifted to fully cover my breast, pausing before lightly stroking the soft curve. My eyes fluttered shut and I thought my heart actually skipped a beat.

"I...I...I don't know. Maybe?"

He moved his hand and resumed kissing. "I can work with maybe," he mumbled against my lips.

- Luca -

I could've kept kissing Giada for hours, even with her depressing revelation about waiting till marriage. Normally I would've ignored my phone during such a critical moment, but something made me check it.

And thank God I did.

It was a text from Alessio, but no words. Just an image.

An image that clearly could not have been sent to me by Alessio, since the picture showed him lying on the pavement, battered and bruised.

"What the…" I mumbled, pulling away from Giada. I clicked to enlarge the photo, trying to understand what I was seeing.

The image couldn't be real. It just couldn't. It looked like a picture of Alessio, beaten to death.

"What's wrong?" Giada asked.

"I…" I didn't know myself, let alone know how to explain it.

She leaned over to try to see the picture, and I angled the phone away. Just then, I observed a critical detail. He was laying at the base of my car.

"Fuck!" I said. I flew off of Giada's bed, slipped into my shoes, then sprinted out of the dorm without any concern for who might see me. I made it to the parking lot in record time, praying the photo was only a sick joke.

I slowed as I neared my car, but noticed nothing out of the ordinary. As I started to walk around it to the other side, I heard a moan. My chest dropped into my stomach.

"Alessio," I whispered, diving onto the ground beside him.

His eyes were so swollen that I doubted they were even capable of opening. Blood dribbled out of the side of his mouth and congealed in his hair. His clothes were ripped and stained with blood, and he was curled up. Alessio's cell phone lay by his feet, where he couldn't possibly have left it himself.

"Alessio," I said. "Are you…" then I stopped. I didn't need to ask if he was okay. He wasn't. Clearly. "Are you conscious?" I finally asked.

A slight whimper escaped his lips. I felt for my car keys, then opened the back door. Lifting my friend as carefully as I could, I hoisted him into my car, struggling to scoot him in far enough to enable me to shut the door.

Then I jumped into the front seat. I drove to the nearest hospital, realizing as I was almost there, that I should've called an ambulance.

There'd be so many questions to answer now, and that was bad. I shouldn't be seen bringing someone to the hospital. I supposed I could try to dump him at the emergency room doors then take off unseen.

Except, why?

I had done nothing wrong. Running would make me look guilty, when I had an alibi and I had simply found him. And running might also delay Alessio getting help.

I pulled up to the ER entrance and, without even killing the ignition, I hopped out and began trying to slide my friend out of the car without exacerbating his injuries. After a moment, I decided that was useless. I walked through the automatic sliding doors into the brightly lit waiting room, turned to the triage station, and yelled.

"I need help. My friend is in bad shape. I can't get him out of my car."

A petite nurse rushed over, but thankfully, before I could explain that she wasn't going to be able to help much, two more people came along. They strapped Alessio onto a stretcher, and then even more people rushed out. There was a flurry of activity and I just kept backing up, not wanting to get in their way. As I bumped into the side of my car, I realized no one was paying attention to me. I could just leave and no one would know, except me.

But I couldn't abandon Alessio.

I stared at my friend as they began to wheel him away, and then the first nurse came over to me.

"Sir, why don't you park your car and then come inside? We need some medical history on your friend."

"I don't know anything," I said. "I just found him like that. Is he going to be okay?"

"We need you to park the car and come inside, okay?"

I nodded lamely, fully cognizant that she hadn't answered my question.

By the time I returned, she was waiting for me just inside the door with a thin towel. She offered it to me and I just stared blankly at it, not understanding what it was for until she gestured to my hands.

They were covered in blood.

She offered me a cup of water and then sat me in the corner of the waiting room.

"Can you tell us your friend's name and age?"

"Alessio Rizzo. He's 17."

"Is he on any drugs that you know of?"

"No."

"Do you know if he takes any medication?"

I tried to think straight, but I couldn't. "I don't think so, but…" His mom would know. *Shit*. His mom should be here.

"I need to call his mom," I said. "Oh God. Is he going to be okay?"

"Your friend was badly beaten. We'll have to do a lot of tests before we know what kind of internal injuries he sustained. Do you have a number for his mom?"

I reached for my phone, but pulled out Alessio's instead. I stared at it for a moment. "I don't know his passcode," I said lamely.

"Okay, do you know his mom's first name?"

I shook my head.

"May I?" she gestured to the phone, then looked at it. "We can have him unlock it. He doesn't have an emergency contact saved that we can access elsewhere."

"I know where he lives," I said.

"That's okay," she glanced nervously behind her. "I'm going to go try to reach his mom, but the police here have a few questions for you."

I flew to my feet at the mention of cops. "I don't know anything. I didn't see anything. I didn't do anything. I just found him!"

The kind nurse backed away anxiously as two uniformed police moved closer. They both were eying me like I was a venomous snake.

"Kid, we'll need you to calm down and take a seat. If we can't talk here, we can head back to the station."

"I'm not leaving my friend," I said.

They cornered me into my chair, then went back over the basics. They wanted to see my ID and then went into all sorts of questions. Where I'd found him, when, how I knew he was there. They seemed suspicious when I mentioned the text, then asked to see it.

I reached for my phone, then paused. "Am I like a suspect or something? Because I didn't do anything. And I have an alibi." I didn't know a lot about American laws, but I was sure I didn't have to give them evidence they could use against me. What I didn't know was if this was even something they could use against me.

"We're just trying to piece together what happened. Clearly someone attacked your friend. We want to find out who and catch them before they can hurt another kid."

That seemed reasonable enough. I showed them the text on my phone, and the younger one jotted down the time and then they handed it back to me, asking me not to delete the message or change anything. They asked if Alessio had any enemies, which of course he didn't, at least not that I knew of. Then they asked how we met.

I hesitated. I didn't want to out him to the cops, but maybe that was why he got beat up. "He's friends with one of my suitemates."

They asked for Marcus's contact information, then wanted to know if Alessio ever got in fights.

"No," I said. I figured that was true enough. He was a scrappy guy, and I was sure he'd been in fights, but nothing of note. Not lately anyway.

"What about you? You ever been in a fight?" the older one asked.

"What does that have to do with anything? I sure wasn't fighting with him. He's my best friend."

"Maybe whoever hurt him knew you two were friends. Maybe they wanted to send a message to you. We've got to explore everything, and since he sure didn't take that photo of himself, we've got to ask ourselves why whoever did this chose you to send the photo to."

"I was probably the last person he called."

The older cop shrugged, then asked when we'd last spoke. It had been the night before according to my phone log, so probably I wasn't Alessio's last call after all.

"I don't know why me," I finally admitted. "But they didn't just text me, they stuck him by my car."

"It almost seems like they wanted him to get help quickly," the younger cop said to his partner.

My own phone rang for the billionth time. It was Giada. Just like all the previous ones.

"Someone's trying to reach you," the older cop said.

"My girlfriend," I said. "I was with her when I got the text. Hang on." I rejected her call then typed out a quick text apologizing for running out and telling her that a friend had an emergency and I'd driven him to the hospital. She replied almost instantly saying she was so sorry and would pray for him. For once, I was so grateful for that.

"So she could vouch for your whereabouts when you received the text?"

"Yeah."

He leaned forward. "If there's anything else you want to tell us, it's best if you say if now. If we find out later that—"

"What could you possibly find out to make me look guilty? Obviously I didn't do this. I couldn't have just sent the text to myself," I said.

As they both stared blankly at me, I realized the truth. *Yes*, I could have.

I swore under my breath in Italian then shook my head. "I'm calling my father. I feel like, being a minor and all, that I should at least have a parent here when you're questioning me. Or maybe a lawyer."

"That's fine," he replied.

I stood, wanting some privacy for the call to my papà. He was sure to yell at me regardless, but combine that with the fact that it was the middle of the night in Italy. I really didn't want to call him. I hesitated. Maybe Lodovico could help.

"Something wrong?" one of the cops asked.

"My father is in Italy. It's the middle of the night there. He's gonna be mad."

As I considered my options, something occurred to me. The cameras.

"No, you know what? This is dumb. There are cameras in the dorms. You can watch the fucking footage of me leaving the dorm when I got the text. And you can watch the parking lot footage of me rushing to my car and finding him there. Hell, you can even probably see the video of whoever did this. Did that even occur to you morons, or was your plan just to taunt me until I confessed to something I obviously didn't do?"

I should've just shut up, but now, I was mad. My friend was

suffering. I'd done the right thing and the cops had no interest in finding the actual guilty parties.

"God, is this because I'm Italian? You assume I'm guilty just because I'm not a stupid WASP?" I shook my head, then thrust my hands out at them. Now that I'd wiped the blood off, my hands looked nearly pristine. "Do I look like I just beat the crap out of someone? Did you notice we're about the same size? How would I have done that to him and not gotten a scratch on me?"

I brushed past them. "God, you guys suck at your job. If you want to arrest me, fucking arrest me. But my father will sue your asses for discrimination and everything else he can."

I stormed over to the area of the hospital where Alessio was being treated. I wanted an update. The cops left me alone for a minute, and then the annoying younger one came over and handed me a business card.

"Don't delete anything off your phone. We'll likely have more follow up questions for you, but no one planned to arrest you. Like we said, we just needed information. Sorry about your friend," he said. And then he sauntered off.

Pig.

CHAPTER 14

VISITING HOURS

- Luca -

That first night Alessio was injured, I stayed until the nurses kicked me out, claiming visiting hours were over. Mrs. Rizzo arrived as I was leaving, but I didn't stop to say hi, not wanting to delay her or subject myself to any more questions I couldn't answer. I texted Giada another apology on my way home, then crashed the moment I reached my comfy dorm bed.

I couldn't focus on anything the next day at school. I called the hospital for updates, but they wouldn't tell me anything since I wasn't family. I'd filled Giada in generally on what had happened, and she was surprisingly supportive. Immediately after my last class, I drove back to the hospital to check on Alessio.

The nurse who'd been there when I brought Alessio in the night before told me he'd been moved to a regular room. She gave me the number and smiled. "You're a good friend to visit," she said. "I'm sure it'll perk him up."

"Wait, he's awake?" I asked.

"He regained consciousness before we transferred him to a private room last night."

Relief flooded me. I followed the maze of corridors through the hospital until I reached the correct hallway. I located his room and turned the knob without knocking. I nearly left when I saw Alessio's mom hunched over the bed, but she heard the door and turned.

"Oh Luca!" she said, rushing to me and roping her arms around me.

Not a big hugger, I wasn't sure how to respond.

"Thank you so much for getting him here in time. We owe you his life!" she gushed.

"Ma!" Alessio snapped from behind her.

Thankfully, she released me then.

"I heard you were awake!" I said, unable to contain my grin even though Alessio looked nightmarish.

"I'll let you two catch up. I have some errands to run and I'll be back first thing in the morning Alessio, okay?"

She bent over her son and kissed his cheek, making him cringe, then she left, closing the door behind her.

"You look like shit," I said, taking the chair his mom had scooted next to the bed.

"Thanks, dick."

"Your spirits seem raised."

He shrugged. "I'm on a lot of good drugs right now. I can't even feel my face."

I gazed at his face, swollen and bloody and more purplish red than white. "That's probably a good thing. Can you see?"

A bandage covered his left eye, but his right one was open, just cut and swollen.

"Yeah. The doctor said I should keep my vision in both eyes." He paused. "But I can't eat solid foods yet because this is as far as I can open my mouth until my jaw heals. Luckily, I'm okay with soup and milkshakes."

"God, I'm so sorry. That sucks. Have the police come to talk to you? They asked me a ton of questions and I told them what I could, but it wasn't much. I want them to catch whoever did this to you"

His eye closed for a moment and I almost thought he'd fallen asleep, but then he spoke. "Yeah, you actually don't."

"What?"

"You really don't know who did this?" Alessio asked, his tone unreadable.

"No. They texted me a picture of you from your own phone. When I found you, you were alone."

Alessio pointed to his cup and I handed it to him, holding it while he angled the straw towards his lips. He turned his head away when he'd had enough, reminding me of a child. "I brought this on myself, but it's over now. The cops aren't going to solve anything."

"If they don't find the guys, we will. *I* will. They won't get away with this." I shook my head, trying to forget the horrific image of his body crumpled against my car. Unfortunately, that picture was likely burned into my brain forever. "Jesus, Alessio, you could've died. This is bad."

"Yeah. It doesn't feel so great." He paused. "Apparently, the doctors told the cops I was lucky."

"You are. You could've died."

"No, that's the thing. They said the guys who beat me knew what they were doing. The doctors said there was no way it was coincidental that they inflicted this many injuries without causing any permanent damage. No trauma to my internal organs, no blindness. I didn't even lose a tooth. I will be good as new. Eventually."

"I don't understand. Why is that significant to the police?"

"They said someone was trying to send a message by beating me. They didn't want to kill me, they just wanted to prove a point."

"That's sick."

"Yeah." He reached for a button connected to his IV bag and pressed it until it beeped. "Anyway, I told the cops some guys jumped me after I hit on them. I said it was a hate crime."

My stomach churned at the thought of it. People were sick. Just truly awful. "I'm so sorry, man. That's bullshit."

"Jesus Luca, that's not what actually happened. That's just what I told the cops." Alessio yawned and then his eyes closed.

I waited several minutes, then when he didn't seem to wake, I left. I wanted to bring him a milkshake or something, but the nurse said he probably wouldn't wake until the middle of the night since his pain meds made him drowsy. I'd have to come back the next day.

As I walked across the parking lot, a black sedan rolled slowly in front of me. My instincts were to run, after seeing my friend's battered and bruised body, but before I could convey that message to my feet, the window rolled down.

"Papà?" I asked, not believing my eyes.

"Get in," he said.

"No thanks, I'll walk."

His expression firmed and he nodded to the large man beside him.

They would make me get in one way or another, so I reached for the doorknob. "Fine."

"How is he?" my papà asked.

"Who?"

"Alessio. That is who you were visiting, right?"

"How did you know that?" I asked. "Actually, when did you get in town? I thought you were in Italy."

"I came back for some business. I've been here since Sunday."

Sunday was the day Alessio had been attacked. My throat ran dry and my vision blurred as rage took over my body. "Was this you? Did you do this to my friend?"

"Mr. Rizzo did this to himself. I didn't lay a hand on him."

"He didn't beat himself," I said.

My papà shrugged.

"He could have died!"

"He will make a full recovery."

"How would you…" I began to ask, but then it all fell into place. My papà had done this to him. *Of course he had.*

Papà frowned. "Is he not awake yet?"

"He is awake, no thanks to you. He sounds miserable."

"So you spoke to him? And he really didn't tell you?"

I was going to murder my papà if I spent another minute with him. I reached for the doorknob and pulled, but I was locked in. "Stop the car and let me out. I'm done. I'm so fucking done with you, with this whole family."

My papà chuckled. "We're on the highway."

"My car was back at the hospital."

"I'm having it cleaned. There was some blood on the seat. We'll return it to your dorm later this evening."

"What did you do?" I asked, staring straight at my papà.

"Your friend has courage and integrity. The fact that he is a person you've chosen to spend your time with reflects well on you."

"So, logically, you hurt him?"

"He contacted me. Seems you'd complained to him about some of our private family matters, specifically pertaining to my disciplinary methods." He paused, but continued before I could speak. "He wanted me to stop. I agreed, on the condition that he meet with me in person."

I swallowed the bile rising in my throat. Was my papà telling the truth? Did Alessio really stand up to my papà for me?"

"He came ready for a fight. But, of course, I didn't lay a hand on him."

"Of course," I said with an eye roll.

"We had a civilized discussion and he was perfectly fine when we concluded our meeting. If something happened to him later, when he was leaving the warehouse, well, that's unfortunate. It's not the best neighborhood."

"If you ever touch Alessio again," I began.

"No one will hurt Mr. Rizzo again," he interrupted. "I'll see to that personally, provided of course that neither he nor you disobey or cross me again." He paused before adding, "No one will ever hurt you again either, Son. Your friend's sacrifice ensured your safety. You should thank him sometime."

I shook my head. "I didn't ask him to do that for me."

"That's what makes it so impressive. He is truly loyal to you. And as long as you both remain loyal to me, you will both go far in this world."

"I don't want to be in this world. Neither does Alessio."

My papà patted my bicep. "My son, you *are* this world. There's no choice to be made. But when we make things official next spring, you should bring him on board as well. In fact, I'm sure Lodovico would enjoy training you both now."

"I'm going to be sick," I said, nausea hitting me like a tidal wave. I half expected my papà to slap me, but instead he motioned for the driver to pull over. I flew out of the car and threw up all over the side of the road. After a moment, someone handed me a handkerchief. To my surprise, it was my papà.

He tugged his suit jacket tighter, apparently determined to stay professional while watching me hurl on the side of the road.

"Luca, this family is your destiny. The sooner you embrace it, the sooner a world of privilege and pleasure is yours."

I wiped my mouth then inhaled several deep breaths of the cool night air.

"You have much to learn about the family business, but you will succeed. You are smart and cunning, and you will continue to be trained by the best until you are ready. But you need someone like Alessio by your side, someone who will take a hit for you without being asked. And I know you don't trust me, but a man is nothing without his word. I give you my word that your friend and you will be safe and well cared for as long as you remain loyal."

I rubbed at my eyes, terrified a tear would slip out in front of my papà. "I need to get back to the dorm before curfew," I said.

He held the car door open, waiting for me to climb in.

Silence filled the car for several minutes, then finally we pulled into the long private drive leading to the school's campus.

"I've taken the liberty of making some advance payments to Mr. Rizzo's hospital bill," my papà said. "When they receive notice of the remainder of the balance, please let me know and I'll take care of that as well. And if there's anything else he needs in the meantime—"

"Yeah, thanks," I interrupted, flying out of the car before it even came to a complete stop in front of the dorm.

I trudged to my room slowly. I felt sick. Really sick. My stomach was now empty, yet I was still nauseas. My muscles ached and my head throbbed. I wished I had some of whatever magic drug they'd given to Alessio to let him survive all the pain he had to be feeling. I'd down those pills in a heartbeat and never wake up again.

Except then, my friend would've suffered for nothing.

I unlocked my door and picked up the first thing I spotted. I threw the book against the wall, growling as it smacked into the already dingy paint before falling to the ground. I was completely and totally trapped, and my papà fucking knew it.

My papà was a monster, and apparently, it was my destiny to follow in his footsteps.

I was doomed.

- Giada -

"Guess who," I challenged, lowering my voice to make the task harder.

Luca about flew off the bench when I snuck up behind him and wrapped my hands over his eyes. I dropped my hands and stepped back just as he swiveled to face me.

"Shit. I'm sorry. I didn't…" he shook his head and reached for my hand. I accepted and let him tug me onto the bench beside him.

"You're jumpy," I observed.

"Si," he agreed. He dragged one hand through his hair, squeezing my fingers with his other hand. "I haven't slept much the past few days."

"How is your friend doing?" Ever since Luca sprinted out of my dorm room over the weekend, I'd gotten the feeling he didn't want to talk about his friend. He told me the guy had been in a fight and had gotten badly hurt, but he'd been vague with all the other details. I couldn't help but wonder if Luca had somehow been involved in whatever situation led to the fight.

Even without the details, I was sure I didn't like Luca's friend. He was obviously the bad influence on Luca, the one who'd gotten him into trouble before. But I still wanted to be supportive of Luca, since he was stressed out about it.

"He's still in the hospital but he'll make a full recovery."

"That's good. He's lucky to have a friend who visits him so often."

"Giada, I'm sorry I've been busy…"

"No, I didn't mean it like that. I love that you're the type of person who visits a friend in the hospital. You're a good guy, Luca Marino."

A pained expression crossed his face as he shook his head, but he didn't explain.

"Do you need any help studying for your midterms?" The

tests were the following week, and then we would head out for spring break.

He tried not to smile, but his dimple betrayed his efforts. "A, you'd just distract me. And B, you're a year behind me, so not sure you'd be helpful anyway."

I shrugged. He wasn't wrong on either account. "Well, don't say I didn't offer."

We were both quiet for a moment.

"I wish there were something I could do to relax you. You just seem so…tense."

Luca gazed sideways at me, a mischievous twinkle in his eyes. "I mean, I can think of something that would relax me…" he teased.

I punched his bicep, but he caught my fist with his free hand before I could retract it. He leaned in for a kiss, pressing his lips against mine until the world around us melted away and Luca was the only thought on my brain.

After a few minutes, we both jumped apart as a teacher walked by and loudly cleared his throat.

Heat flooded my cheeks as I dropped my eyes to the pavement. I licked my lips, pleased that a sweet flavor had replaced the boring cherry Chapstick I'd been wearing. "You taste like chocolate," I said, a little surprised. Luca wasn't the biggest fan of desserts.

"Ice cream," he said, inching his hand close to mine again. "Well, milkshake. Chocolate though. It's um, well, Alessio is on a liquid only diet so I've been bringing him shakes. And he doesn't like to eat alone."

"You're a good friend." I rubbed my thumb beneath his lip, wiping off a hint of red from my mouth. "I've been praying for your friend. Maybe I'll add in a request for your grades, too."

Luca smiled at that, and I felt my mood lighten. Luca wasn't overly generous with his smiles, not the authentic ones, anyway.

And seeing I'd actually brought him joy, particularly when he was so worried, was the most amazing feeling.

"Are you excited about your trip?" he asked, abruptly changing subjects.

My brothers had a different spring break than I did, so my mom and I were flying down to Florida to spend the week with my aunt "Yes, but…"

"But what?" A pointed frown had replaced his carefree smile from a moment before.

"I'll miss you."

Luca rolled his eyes. "I am not that fun to be around. You'll probably find a dozen guys to entertain you every day you're in Sarasota."

His assessment made me giggle, even if we both knew it was patently false.

"Besides, I can't plan your birthday party if you're here distracting me."

My eyes widened at the magic word. "How did you know about my birthday?"

Luca laughed. "Tesoro, you've been counting down for months. You're not exactly secretive about the date."

He had a point. "Well, it's a big one," I said.

"It is."

"I'll be almost as old as you."

"For three months. Baby."

I stuck out my tongue and his eyes widened, his nostrils flaring.

"Don't tease me with that mouth of yours or I'll start kissing you again and then we'll both flunk midterms."

"Yeah, yeah. Let's go get dinner." I stood and offered him my hand. He rejected it, instead roping his arm around my waist and walking me into the dining hall.

- Luca -

I brought a cookies and cream milkshake to Alessio when I visited the next day. He perked up when he saw it, but quickly frowned.

"What's wrong with you?" he asked.

I hesitated, casting a look towards the nurse reviewing something on his chart. Just in case, I switched to Italian. "Were you ever going to tell me?"

"About what?" he asked, catching on and using our native language, too.

"Mio papà."

"Oh," he switched back to English, looked away for a minute, then shook his head. "No. I mean, now that you know, sure. But it doesn't change anything."

I considered that and decided Alessio was right. I already hated my papà, already thought he was a violent thug. This did nothing but affirm that belief.

"Why would you do such a thing?" I asked him.

He reverted to Italian. "I understood the dynamic you had with your dad. I saw how he was making you feel, and I thought this would work. I know how people like him work."

"We need to change your bandages one last time at the end of my shift, but page me if you need anything before then," the nurse said cheerfully, awaiting his nod before letting herself out.

"She's my favorite," Alessio said. "She's hot."

I chuckled. She was, and I probably would've made some joke about a sponge bath if I hadn't been so distraught over my friend.

"Look, Alessio, you didn't have to do that, but you did. And I want you to know it really means a lot to me. No one has ever sacrificed…anything for me, and you risked everything."

"Yeah, yeah, I'd say I love you too, man, but you're not my type," he teased.

"Could you be serious for one minute? You could've died."

Alessio shook his head. "No. They had no reason to kill me and every reason to keep me alive. Your dad is grooming you to take over. He wants you to be strong and he wants you to have allies. He made a lesson of me because he had to maintain his stupid reputation. But deep down, you know he respected what I did."

"He told me he did. He said you were a man of honor. He called you loyal and brave."

"That's me, alright." Alessio smiled, but I caught him wincing as he tried to purse his lips to suck the shake through the straw. He was still in so much pain, and it was all my fault.

"How can I repay you?" I asked. "Should I pay a visit to your father?"

"No."

I was quiet for once. I really didn't have any other ideas on how I could make it up to Alessio, or even how I could ever express my gratitude or make him understand the magnitude of what he had done. "My papà said he'll abide by the terms of your agreement," I finally said. "He won't have anyone hurt me—or you—again."

"Good. I figured he would. Those types tend to value their word."

I wanted to ask how he knew so much about men like my papà, but I didn't have to. Alessio was from a working class family with ties to Sicily. This wasn't his first run in with the mafia.

"He also said he'd protect me, as long as I did what he asked." I paused before adding the rest. "He said the same for you. He wants you to...I don't know, work for him maybe. He talked about wanting to train us both. He said I needed someone like you by my side."

Alessio mustered a half grin. "I'd be honored."

I shook my head and pushed to my feet, dragging my hand through my hair. "No. This is insane. Do you understand what he's asking? He wants you to join the mafia. Like the actual Italian mob. You're doped up on painkillers. You can't just agree to something like this."

Alessio laughed. "I might not be getting straight As at a fancy private school like you are, but I'm no idiot. I've got street smarts. I knew exactly what I was getting myself into when I asked your father for a meeting."

"I never thought you were dumb. But trust me…you don't want this life. You have a choice, and—"

"And it's my choice to make," Alessio interrupted. He struggled to sit a bit higher on his pillow. "My whole life, my mother has worked two jobs to make ends meet and she can still barely afford to buy me clothes at Target. Your father owns houses on two separate continents and has money left over to buy you whatever designer shit you want. I'd kill for a fucking Gucci tee shirt and you never even wear yours."

I wasn't even sure which tee shirt he meant, but I made a mental note to buy him the entire spring line from Gucci. That was the least I could do.

"Being poor didn't stop me from having an asshole father to disappoint. It didn't stop me from getting the shit kicked out of me by my own dad. This life your dad is promising might not be perfect, but we'll have money. And money means power."

I didn't know how to explain to my friend the cost of all the morally questionable shit he'd have to tolerate, all the shady sins he'd have to commit, just to roll with my papà. I was no saint, but even I struggled with my conscience over some of the things I knew went on.

"It might be different if he were just making you one of the other guys, someone who might someday hope to be second-in-command to a captain or something. But he's not. He's training you to replace him. Someday, you will be the boss. And I could be your second-in-command. When you and I are in charge, we will make the rules. We will rule the world."

I blew out the breath I'd been holding. When Alessio said it like that, it didn't sound half bad.

"Hand me that shake," he said. I did, and he started to sip it, then paused. "If I spill this on myself, do you think the hot nurse will come clean me up?"

I laughed. "I think it's time for you to up your morphine drip man." Thinking about his meds reminded me of the other thing my papà said. "My papà said he paid upfront for some of your medical bills but to let him know when the rest come in and he'll cover them all."

Alessio grinned at the news, then pressed the nurse call button.

"You should go, man. Things are about to get messy," he said, peeling the lid off the shake and dumping the contents directly onto his lap.

"Jesus," I mumbled. "You're insane, but I owe you. Enjoy your sponge bath."

I passed the nurse on the way out.

CHAPTER 15

A FAREWELL TO CHILDHOOD

- Giada -

World Religions was my second to last midterm. As I finished the final essay, I glanced in Luca's direction, careful not to let my eyes pause long enough for Mr. Cobb to accuse me of cheating. Luca's head was still down, his hand thrust into his hair. He wrinkled his nose as he scribbled something, and his adorable expression brought a smile to my face. I checked over my answers, then closed my test booklet and nudged it to the corner of my desk. A few minutes later, Luca did the same.

He caught my eye and winked.

When the instructor called time, Luca flew out of his seat and grabbed my hand. I barely had time to pick up my backpack as he dragged me into the hall.

"Did you pass?" he asked, his eyes twinkling.

"A plus," I teased, closing my eyes in anticipation of the kiss I knew was coming.

Luca kept the kiss brief, but lingered with his lips near mine. His hand pressed against my cheek, shielding my face from most passersby. Of course, anyone who saw him would know it was me with him. We hadn't made any attempt to hide the fact that we were together. Everyone on campus knew we were a couple.

"I wish I could kiss you all afternoon," he said.

"Umm, you could. Well, not here, but..." I ducked out from under his arm but reached for his hand, leading him down the hall.

"I can't. I have to meet my papà."

"Seriously?" I groaned. "When?"

He wrinkled his nose. "He said right after my test. He's sending a car for me."

"Why? That's dumb. You need to study."

He bit his lip, but his grin still widened. "Study, huh? That's what you have planned for me?"

I shrugged. "We could study something."

Luca's nostrils flared as he reached forward with his free hand, tickling me. "I know what I want to study."

I shrieked in response to his tickling, then stilled and observed him for a moment. This was the first I'd seen him smile in days. He'd been stressed out and depressed ever since his friend's accident. As much as I wanted to spend time with him and celebrate finishing my finals, I also recognized that he needed this. He needed a chance to relax and just breathe.

"Just text your dad and cancel," I urged.

"Mio papà is not the type to take a cancellation well."

"Give me your phone. I'll do it."

Luca laughed but handed me his phone.

"Can't make lunch. Have 2 study," I typed, angling it to show him. "There. What's his number?"

Luca quirked an eyebrow but grabbed his phone.

"Oh come on, don't delete it," I begged.

"I didn't. I sent it. See?" He held his phone out for me to see right as a response popped up on the screen. It was in Italian.

"Uh oh. That was fast. What did he say?"

"He said the car is already on the way to pick me up at my dorm." Luca winced, then typed a response as I watched over his shoulder.

"What did you say?"

"Raincheck. Sorry. Already at the library. It's a study group I can't skip," he translated.

"Wow, that's good. So are we headed to the library?"

"No. It's a nice day. Let's go for a walk."

We walked around campus then finally stopped on the rocks overlooking the beach. On warmer days, this spot was sure to be filled with people, but today, we had it to ourselves. We sat and talked for nearly an hour, then spent about that long making out. Loud growls emanating from my stomach finally separated us.

"Come on. Let's get you fed."

"I'm sure the dining hall is closed by now."

"I'll take you out."

"Italian food?"

"Mmm, you got it," he replied.

- Luca -

Spending the day with Giada reframed my focus. Well, or at least it calmed me. The world no longer seemed quite so black and white. I didn't have to choose between betraying my papà or joining his evil empire. Well, maybe I did, but I now at least felt like nothing would really have to change after I made the choice.

As I walked out of Giada's dorm after dropping her off, though, I couldn't help but wonder...did I really even have a choice at all?

Thirty seconds later, I had my answer.

I spotted the cop car as I approached my dorm. It was a

clearly marked on-duty car, so it would've been hard to miss, even though the lights and siren weren't actively disrupting the peaceful campus. A uniformed officer leaned against the side of the sedan, partially blocking the word POLICE printed boldly against the body. I assumed it was a cop visiting a relative, although, how someone on a law enforcement salary could afford a private boarding school was beyond me.

As I neared the car though, the cop pushed off of the car and stared at me. "Luca Marino?"

He said it like a question, except he was already adjusting his belt in a way that suggested he meant business.

"Maybe. Who's asking?"

Another officer climbed out of the driver's seat then, opening the back door and gesturing to it. "Get in," he said.

I cocked my head to the side. "Yeah, um, my parents taught me not to get in the car with strangers. Thanks though."

I started to jog up the steps of my dorm, nearly slamming into Mr. Peters, the dorm parent.

"Ah, Luca. These officers had a few questions for you. You're not in any trouble, but I hear you were a witness to some incident," he said.

"I already told them everything."

"We, uh, spoke with your dad and he said he'll meet you at the police station."

Behind his back, one of the officers chuckled. I gnawed the side of my cheek, debating my options. There was clearly something fishy about this all, but avoiding them didn't seem plausible.

"Fine," I said. "But I can't do my homework if I'm with the police, so I better get a note for my teachers."

"Sure," Mr. Peters agreed, walking me to the police car.

I waited until we had driven off school property to begin the interrogation. "Which station are we headed to? And what case is this about? What time will I get back to my dorm?"

The two cops exchanged a glance, and then the passenger answered me. "We are going to meet your father. He can answer your questions."

Great. "How long of a drive?"

The driver switched on the siren. "Shorter now," he said with a grin.

I rolled my eyes at the noncommittal answer and pulled my earbuds out of my pocket. I texted Alessio what had happened so far, then switched on some music and leaned back in the seat.

I wasn't surprised when the cruiser came to a stop in front of a nondescript building rather than a police station, but I did have more questions.

"This is not a police station," I said as the driver killed the engine. The other cop opened my door and smirked.

"You're observant. Let's go." He gripped my arm and walked me up to the door.

"Geez, watch the jacket," I said, shrugging free of his grip. "That's Italian leather."

"Of course it is," the driver replied, knocking three times on the dingy door.

The second the door swung open, I recognized where we were. "My papà owns this club."

The two cops walked me down the back hallway and straight to a closed door at the end of the hall. I assumed my papà was inside, waiting with some of his goons to beat the crap out of me for blowing him off earlier.

"Are you guys even real cops?" I asked, even warier as Massimo moved aside to let them into the office.

They didn't answer. My papà stood in front of his desk, ready to greet us. He wasn't smiling, but he lacked the menacing glare that usually occupied his face too.

"You promised no one would hurt me again," I reminded him.

"You promised to obey me."

He had me there. "I assumed you meant in the professional

capacity. But I'm also your son, and it really wouldn't be normal if I did everything you said. You can't beat me up for that though, that would just be child abuse. And you don't want these guys to think you're involved with that, right?"

My papà chuckled and gazed at the cops. "Would it bother you if I beat my son?"

They both shook their heads. "Happy to help," one offered.

"That won't be necessary. Thank you for your service to the fine State of New York. Your food should be up by the bar." My papà said, dismissing them.

Then, he turned to me. "Luca, sit," he instructed.

I did, and he sat in the chair beside me, angling it so he was facing me.

"I'm disappointed that you chose not to follow up with me this morning as I had requested."

"I needed longer to think."

The crease between his brow deepened. "Luca, I asked my friends to bring you here today in case you were under the misguided notion that you had options. Let me be clear. You don't." He paused for effect. "Your friend Alessio has the right attitude about this situation, so it perplexes me why you don't see your lot in life as a gift."

I opened my mouth to protest, but he raised his hand to shush me.

"You are privileged with money and power. If you follow in my footsteps…no, *when* you follow in my footsteps, you will have men on multiple continents lining up to serve you. Women will want you, and their men will fear you."

"What if I'd rather just grow up like every other trust fund kid on campus?"

"That life would bore you, and you know it. Luca, I see myself in you. You are ambitious and cunning. You have what it takes to succeed in this world."

"And that is a good thing?"

"Si. If you were weak or stupid, people would take advantage of you. If you were unlikeable, they wouldn't trust you."

He missed my point, but I didn't bother saying so.

"Do you understand why I asked police officers to bring you to me?"

It was a dumb question. He already said I was smart, so of course I'd figured out his point. He wanted me to know that he had men everywhere. There was no one I could call for help, no one who wasn't on his payroll.

I nodded.

"Good. And let me assure you, as wide as my reach is here, it is incomparable to the power I hold back home. I think it would be good for you and your friend to experience that firsthand."

"You want us to go to Italy?"

"Yes. You will both join me this summer. You will shadow me or my men and start to familiarize yourselves with the business."

That had been the plan for me all along, even before I had explicit confirmation about the type of work my papà performed.

As my papà spoke, I realized I had questions about the plan.

"Can we speak openly?" I asked.

My papà nodded once.

"Will I have to kill people?"

He quirked an eyebrow. "I am not in the business of killing people, Luca. I am an entrepreneur. In addition to our many businesses with which you're familiar, we also trade in favors. We help other businessmen, you see. We'll keep them safe, protect their assets, whatever they need. To do that job effectively, people need to know that you can and will enforce the rules, by whatever means necessary. That is something you will learn this summer, but mostly I just want you to familiarize yourself with the notion of respect. You see, you may not agree with everything I say or do, but you will respect me. You will not openly question me or my decisions, ever. When I tell you to do something, you do it."

"Got it. You say jump, I ask 'how high'?" I teased.

I didn't expect a chuckle, but I was surprised when he frowned and shook his head.

"If I tell you to jump, you jump. You don't question me. You don't question anyone higher ranking than you which, at this point, is everyone." He paused. "As my son, people will expect more of you, but they also won't be able to shoot you if you screw up. It is a double-edged sword."

My papà gazed at me for a moment before standing. He punched in a lengthy combination to the safe behind his desk, revealing multiple stacks of money and several handguns. He retrieved a small envelope, then swung shut the safe's metal door. He pulled a small ring from the envelope.

"I had this made for you a while back, but I wanted to wait to give it to you until you fully understood the weight of your commitment to this family."

I took the ring and turned it over in my fingers. I recognized the ring instantly. It was identical to the signet ring my papà wore, except that this one bore my own initials.

"My father and his father wore identical rings as well," he said, smiling.

"Cool. So, um, just so we're clear, if I follow you around this summer and do all this stuff you're talking about…"

He nodded encouragingly for me to continue.

"Well, what if after that I decide it's not for me? Like, if I just don't want to join the family business?"

The smile on my papà's face didn't falter for a moment. "Then I will have your friend Alessio killed. We'll make it look like a suicide. Or maybe we'll pin it on someone else you love."

He shrugged casually before continuing. "Who knows how we'll do it? There's options, but regardless, your friend would be dead."

I swallowed the lump in my throat. Given the option of

Alessio's blood on my hands, or the stupid signet ring and everything it symbolized, I knew what I had to do.

"Alrighty then," I said, glancing at my papà to note he wore his ring on the middle finger of his right hand. I pinched the ring, determined not to let him see that my hand was shaking as I slid it down my middle finger. Instantly, the weight of it felt uncomfortable.

"Welcome to the family, son. Let's go get you a drink."

As my papà stood and patted me on the back, I recognized his expression as one I rarely saw—pride.

I rubbed my thumb along the thick band choking my middle finger as we walked, wondering what the fuck had I gotten myself into.

The End

ACKNOWLEDGMENTS

This book emerged out of necessity. When I realized Mafiosa Princess was destined to become a full-fledged series rather than a standalone novel, I knew I needed to develop the backstory of the main characters as much as possible. The more I contemplated the possible details of Giada and Luca's history, the more obsessed I became. I decided to start writing the story and see what happened. The end result was not one, but two, full-length prequel stories.

Thank you to everyone who has joined "the family" on this Mafiosa Princess adventure. Stay tuned for the final book of the prequel and the conclusion of the Mafiosa Princess series.

ABOUT THE AUTHOR

Liza Malloy writes contemporary romance and women's fiction. She's a sucker for alpha males, bad boys, dimples, and muscles, and she can't resist a man in uniform. Liza loves creating worlds where her heroine discovers her own strength and finds her Happily Ever After. When Liza isn't reading or writing torrid love stories, she's a practicing attorney. Her other passions include gummy bears, jelly beans, and the occasional marathon. She lives in the Midwest with her four daughters and her own Prince Charming.

Visit her website at https://authorlizamalloy.wixsite.com/lizamalloy

Join her email list at http://eepurl.com/gnuROD